JEWISH TALES *from* EASTERN EUROPE

JEWISH TALES *from* EASTERN EUROPE

selected and retold by
NADIA GROSSER NAGARAJAN

foreword by
HOWARD SCHWARTZ

JASON ARONSON INC.
NORTHVALE, NEW JERSEY
JERUSALEM

This book was set in 11 pt. Hiroshige by Alpha Graphics of Pittsfield, NH and printed and bound by Book-mart Press, Inc. of North Bergen, NJ.

10 9 8 7 6 5 4 3 2 1

Library of Congress Cataloging-in-Publication Data

Nagarajan, Nadia Grosser.
Jewish tales from Eastern Europe / by Nadia Grosser Nagarajan.
p. cm.
Includes bibliographical references.
ISBN 0-7657-6086-X
1. Legends, Jewish. 2. Jewish folk literature—Europe, Eastern.
I. Title.
BM530.N25 1999
296.1'9—dc21 99-18833

Printed in the United States of America on acid-free paper. For information and catalog write to Jason Aronson Inc., 230 Livingston Street, Northvale, NJ 07647-1726, or visit our website: www.aronson.com

To the memory of
Gisela Steiner Silberring
BABIČKA

my grandmother who is always with me

Contents

Foreword

The folktales of Eastern Europe have come down to us in several different ways. The vast majority of tales were included in rabbinic and popular anthologies such as the *Maaseh Book*, compiled by Jacob ben Abraham of Mezhirech, and first published in Basel in 1601. The stories in the *Maaseh Book* were written in Yiddish and were drawn from talmudic and midrashic sources, and from the abundant Jewish folklore of the Middle Ages.

Then, starting with S. Ansky, the first Jewish ethnologist, tales were collected orally throughout Eastern Europe. Important collections of these oral tales were published by Y. L. Cahan and Immanuel Olsvanger, and these tales formed the early basis of the YIVO archives, which still exists, now located in New York. A great many additional oral tales of Eastern Europe have been collected in Israel by the Israel Folktale Archives, established forty years ago by Professor Dov Noy of Hebrew University.

In addition to rabbinic anthologies and orally collected tales, there is a third source for the folktales of Eastern Europe, and it is this source that Nadia Grosser Nagarajan has largely drawn upon in this landmark collection, *Jewish Tales from Eastern Europe*. We might call this source "Literary Folktales." These are Jewish folktales which have been retold as polished tales by known Jewish authors. Sometimes we can trace the sources for these retold tales to earlier collections, and sometimes they are simply drawn from the existing folklore which flourished orally among the Jewish people.

Of course, the master of the literary folktale was I. L. Peretz. Peretz was a close friend of S. Ansky, and when Ansky would return from his ethnological travels, Peretz would debrief him and then begin immediately to write down, in his own unique style, some of the tales that Ansky had collected. In one case Ansky recounted how he told Peretz a newly collected story that he considered raw and unfinished. A month later, when he came for a visit, Peretz read him an exceptionally polished tale based on the one Ansky had told him, which overwhelmed Ansky with its beauty.

However, the process of the self-conscious literary retelling of Jewish folktales did not begin with Peretz. It can be traced to the publication in 1846 of a multi-volumed collection of Czech folktales entitled *Sippurim*. Despite the Hebrew title (meaning "stories"), the collection, edited by the Prague bookseller Wolf Pascheles, consisted of polished German retellings of Czech folktales drawn from a multitude of Czech Jewish authors. Among the stories included were some of the earliest published stories about Rabbi Judah Loew, known as the Maharal, and the Golem, the man made out of clay and brought to life by Rabbi Loew to protect the Jews of the Prague ghetto. It seems safe to say that most, if not all, of the stories included in *Sippurim* had their basis in Czech folklore, and were drawn from a rich oral tradition, which especially flourished in the city of Prague.

Sippurim had a very great success, and served as the basis for many subsequent volumes of Czech folklore, including collections by Heinz Politzer, František Kafka, and Eduard Petiška. The stories of Rabbi Loew probably also inspired Rabbi Yudel Rosenberg in the writing of *Niflaot Maharal*, published in 1909, the famous cycle of tales about the adventures of the Golem. Rosenberg claimed the stories had been compiled in the 16th century by a relative of Rabbi Loew, and this claim proved sufficient to establish his Golem cycle as authentic in the eyes of his readers. But recent scholars, such as Dov Sadan, Gershom Scholem, and Eli Yassif, have demonstrated that Rosenberg was almost certainly the author of the book, although there is no doubt that there was a rich oral tradition about the Golem, especially in Prague.

A well-educated Jew growing up in Prague over the past one hundred years would be intimately familiar with the stories Nadia Grosser Nagarajan has collected here. They make up the core of the best known tales both told and read in Jewish circles. But in addition to the stories from Prague, Ms. Nagarajan has included a wealth of tales drawn from Central and Eastern Europe. Here her primary source has been the orally collected tales of the Israel Folktale Archives, many of which are previously unpublished before their appearance in this book.

Jewish Tales from Eastern Europe gives the contemporary reader the opportunity to experience the imaginative realm of the Jews of Eastern Europe, a rich heritage that was inevitably lost because of the upheavals that have plagued the Jews in this century. Here are not only remarkable tales about Rabbi Loew, the indisputable giant of Czech Jewish folklore, but tales about such great figures as Rabbi Elimelech, the Hungarian Tzaddik, and even tales about Rashi, the great commentator. All of these stories are exceptionally polished and filled with rich detail, as is characteristic of the finest literary folktales.

Just as children today know by heart the most famous of the folktales collected by the Brothers Grimm, so Nadia Grosser Nagarajan has gathered the most beloved folktales of the Jews of Eastern Europe, tales such as "The Gilded Slippers" or "The Golden Street." To delve into this book is to journey to a lost Jewish world that was once alive with Jewish stories and still flourishes in these pages.

Howard Schwartz
St. Louis

Preface and Acknowledgments

Martin Buber retold hasidic stories in his own unique way. He stated: "I stand in the chain of narrators, a link between links. . . ." He believed that if he told once again the old tales, and if they sounded new, it was because the new already lay dormant in them when they were told for the first time. My grandmother never read Martin Buber nor was she aware of his philosophy, yet she too was a link that passed the wisdom and spirit of the past into the present and, by enriching the narratives with her own experience and insight, paved the way for another link that led into the future.

Babička—"little grandmother"—as I called her in Czech and as she was addressed by most people who knew her, was a small, vivacious person who continued to be active, passionate, and positive till the day she died. She passed away a long time ago, yet I still remember her very vividly, particularly her face and her dark, twinkling eyes that never lost their spark despite the many hardships that she had to endure in life. She was interested in everything that surrounded her—people, animals, plants, objects, sights, scents, and sounds. Her keen gift of observation, as well as her sensitivity and affection for others, left an impact on anybody who knew her. Ever since I was a small child, she revealed to me what she perceived as beautiful or plain, what to her was outstanding and remarkable, pitiful and heartbreaking, and even what she thought was unworthy of attention, degrading, and sinful but still human. Without realizing it, she was a true storyteller and I owe to her more than anyone else my lifelong interest and abiding love for tales.

I am deeply indebted to my husband for his loyal support and help, for listening to the stories many times, and for giving me his honest input; to my son Ravi who is always there for me, for his comments and valuable insights; and to my son Amith for his interest and constant encouragement.

I would like to express my sincere gratitude to Howard Schwartz for his regard, support, and for writing the foreword; to Peninnah Schram, Cherie Karo Schwartz, and Corrine Stavish for encouraging me to pursue this work. All four of these very special people have been my inspiration for many years and I consider myself privileged to have them as friends. Special thanks are due to Arthur Kurzweil for his enthusiasm and guidance in this project; to Hope Breeman for her conscientious and friendly liaison throughout the production process; and to Donna Hall for her meticulous copyediting.

To my dear friend Michele Anish, I owe many thanks for sharing with me her personal and heartwarming experiences and memories, and to Yakov Talmi from Moshav Nechalim in Israel, who is not just a musician and teacher but also a wonderful storyteller. I am obliged to Edna Heichal for providing me with the stories recorded and stored in the invaluable Israel Folklore Archives in Haifa, as well as to my good friend Zipora Saad who was of great assistance to me.

Acknowledgments are also due to friends and relatives scattered around the world who have supported my ideas from near and far and who have had confidence in my work.

Introduction

Come and listen to legends from ancient times. Listen to tales about our forefathers who came to our country from faraway lands and settled down along the rivers Vltava and Labe. Come and listen to what has been preserved from the tenebrous past and cherished for centuries, come and listen to our wondrous tales of old. . . .

This is how Alois Jirásek, a prominent Czech folklorist and historian, starts his famous book of old legends. It is of particular interest to the Jewish reader since Jirásek faithfully recorded the legends that had been passed on for centuries and did not omit those tales that had a foreign flavor and that indicated influences that were beyond the Slavic experience.

And thus we marvel when we read a somewhat familiar story. . . .

Thousands of years ago, two brothers by the names of Čech and Lech dwelled in the western Carpathian Mountain region of Europe. Both were rulers of their tribes and came from a mighty and noble line of leaders. One day they decided to leave their native place which was devastated by endless wars among the many incompatible Slavic clans that had settled in the area. They yearned for a land of their own, where their people could live in peace, work the earth, and multiply without being forced to fight continually for their livelihood. They believed that there was a beautiful country waiting for them somewhere and thus, after praying to their gods asking for their support and guidance, they all began the exodus in search of the promised land.

The multitude followed the brothers into unknown regions where many challenges and dangers awaited them. Their wanderings took them along parched plains, high mountain ridges, valleys, and across lakes and streams. After drifting and roaming for a long time, the tribes were getting tired and disillusioned, doubting that their exile would ever end. Then one evening, after having crossed the mighty river Vltava, they saw from afar a high mountain, bluish in color, that suddenly and sharply rose from the plain. Čech ordered them to camp there for the night.

The next day before dawn, Čech ascended the mountain Řip all by himself. When he reached the summit, he saw before him a wondrous sight. There, spreading far into the horizon, he saw dense forests and green pastures. He saw lofty peaks, winding rivers, and emerald lakes, and the beauty of the fertile land he beheld took his breath away. When he descended from the mountain, he summoned his brother Lech and the elders of the tribes. He told them that their wanderings were over, they had found their promised land, the land of milk and honey, where they would prosper and live in peace for generations to come. They offered their thanks to their gods, swore unending devotion and loyalty to their new country, and named it after their leader Čech—the Czech land.

Many generations later there ruled in the Czech land a wise queen by the name of Libuše. She was blessed by the gift of prophesy and predicted the founding of the marvelous city of Prague, as well as other events that would take place in the future after she had joined her forefathers in the afterworld. One day she had a vision in which she saw a group of strangers approaching the Czech land from a faraway country in the east. She summoned her son and told him to convey her prophesy to his grandson who would be the one whom this group of people would ask for asylum. She wanted them to be welcome and given permission to settle down in Prague. She was positive that they were bearers of good tidings and would bring blessings and prosperity to her land. And indeed, so it happened. . . .

According to this legend, the Jews found a refuge in the Czech land and considered it their home many centuries before the historical data that place their arrival in the middle of the tenth century. Based on records from Jewish cemeteries, Ibrahim Ibn Jacub, a Jewish merchant from an Arab country, settled in Bohemia around that time. From the very beginning, the Czech Jews were different from other East European Jews. They did not live in isolation, spoke the language of the land, and were secular in their way of life. Most of them kept the traditions of their forefathers and many were religious but few were truly fanatic. They nurtured a strong emotional tie to the land of their birth and that was many times more dominant than their religious inclination and practices. As time went by the Jews contributed considerably to the economy and culture, but for a long time were not given much credit in history books.

The city of Prague has served over the centuries as an inspiration to many creative minds, be they writers, poets, painters, or musicians. It has also been the cradle of various legends inspired by its colorful history, the beauty of its buildings, the mystery of its surroundings, the people that call it home, and the many influences it was exposed to over the centuries. Prague served as a center for Jewish commerce and culture since the fourteenth century. It had been the crossroads, an important business center for Jews coming from the east and the west—the Ashkenasim from Germany and Holland and the Sepharadim from Spain, Portugal, Italy, and as far away as the island of Crete. Many important events in the life of the Jews of Prague happened during the rule of Rudolf the Second, when Jews fled the religious persecution in Spain initiated by Philip the Second.

Several legends come from the Old Town of Prague. It has the oldest synagogue in Europe, the famous ancient cemetery, and the museum which used to be a cleansing house for the dead. A hundred years ago, there was a Jewish quarter, named Josefov, where only Jews lived. Today most of them are gone but the tales live on. A large number of stories have roots planted in the Middle Ages and describe in detail the persecutions and pogroms that the Jews were fated to endure for generations. Some stories are based on rabbinical studies and kabbalistic works. Some deal with specific kings and members of the royal households, as well as other friendly and hostile Christians. They all paint a canvas of the kind of life Jews lived in those days. The most famous and popular are the tales about Rabbi Loew and the important and not so important people that shared his way of life in sixteenth century Prague. These legends have been told and retold many times over the years, yet their magic has not subsided.

Jewish legends sprang like spring flowers all over the Czech land, whether it was Bohemia, Moravia, or Slovakia, in cities, outskirts of towns as well as small villages. Colorful tales also blossomed along the borders of the Carpathian Mountains and spread into all of Hungary and Poland. After they were gathered and made into bouquets and wreaths, they did not necessarily lose their original beauty but rather were enhanced by the different elements that were added to them. At times they were not just embellished but also changed to a certain extent and emerged in a somewhat different garb. Some of the legends carry non-Jewish themes that were mostly infiltrated into the authentic tales by Christians who wanted to spread their influence as much as possible. Anti-Semitic undertones do exist as well and it is up to the story-reteller and the reader to decide whether, or if at all, they affect the core of the story. These tales were created not just because of the people's desire to tell stories and fantasize, it was an attempt to explain the fates of the Jewish people within the communities in those days.

Religious themes that were almost always the subject of the tales often gave way, particularly in the Czech land and to a lesser extent in Hungary and Poland, to topics that were Jewish in substance but had also been affected by the outside world. Thus, for instance, nineteenth century Romanticism had a strong effect on the legendary past of the Jews. So, for example, the figure of the ever-suffering wandering Jew, who initially had an evil image, was elevated and put on a pedestal. Like Faust, the Jew became the symbol of the man whose quest was for the wisdom and understanding of the human condition.

There exists a very large amount of material regarding Jewish life and culture in Central and Eastern Europe, yet there are very few Jews that live there nowadays. History has recorded the events and happenings of past times but the image of the Jewish population and the way they lived and functioned has become a vague memory in the eyes of the new generations, an old legend rather than a modern tale. Yet legends have a marvelous way of surviving and as such they will never dissipate or fade away. They will continue to thrive in different forms and renewed shapes despite all the obstacles that the Jewish people might encounter in the future.

The stories in the book are a sample of a multitude of tales that have been transmitted orally and in written form all over Central and

Eastern Europe. Many of them I have selected from the hundreds of abstracts collected and safeguarded by the Israel Folktale Archives (IFA) at the University of Haifa in Israel, numerous ones from other sources such as old manuscripts, books, as well as individual narratives, remembrances, and anecdotes that I have had the privilege to record personally. All the sources and origins of the narratives, as well as comments and miscellaneous remarks, are given in a separate section, Annotations, toward the end of the book.

The tales I have chosen—Czech, Slovak, Polish, and Hungarian—cover a wide range of topics and span several centuries. Some are tales of fantasy and imagination while others lean on reality and fact rather than legend. A few are based on contemporary personal events and reminiscences. We encounter different kinds of love stories, romantic and innocent as well as obsessive and misguided. Joy, euphoria, fear, and guilt, the sense of the sweet and bitter that comes with it all, are either obvious within the context of the tale or hidden between the lines. Multiple narratives describe a copious array of feelings people have for themselves and others such as children, parents, and friends. Various tales convey a deep belief and trust in God. Some are tragic and morbid, some radiate with the pulse of life, some are mysterious and puzzling, and others bring us laughter and amusement although, at times, they convey serious lessons. All the stories, nevertheless, provide entertainment in the broad sense of the word and more than that, regardless of whether one needs to suspend disbelief, they lift a curtain and reveal the past.

I

Love and Trepidation

Love is sweet as well as bitter, yet interlaced at times with fear.
—Slovak proverb

1

The Golden Street

On the right bank of the river Vltava, where centuries ago the people of Israel built their homestead, there stood the house of the wealthy Rabbi Kalman. On a beautiful spring day, the Rabbi's lovely daughter Hanina was sitting on the porch. She was the Rabbi's only child and her beauty and virtues, which well exceeded those of other daughters of Israel, were known far and wide. On that day she was in a pensive mood. She cupped her head in the small palm of her white hand and her face had a doleful expression. She was in love, apprehensive, and uneasy. Suddenly she heard the sound of speedy oars hitting the surface of the water and she ran to the river. It was him! A young man in a green hunting coat and white hat was hastily rowing to the shore. With a few powerful strokes he reached the bank and the lovers fell into each others arms, holding on to each other tightly as if they had no intention to ever let go.

Finally, Hanina released herself from the embrace and with a deep sigh asked: "Why did you come again? You know that father. . . ." The young man looked deeply into Hanina's eyes and tried to persuade the maiden to step into the boat and leave with him. He said that he was more to her than a mother or a father and prayed to the same God she did. "The God of all worlds is also my Lord," he insisted.

Kalman's exquisite daughter urged her lover to go and see her father and request the blessing of their union. She lovingly embraced the reticent man and asked him: "What is the matter with you? Your hands are cold and your breath is as icy as the northern wind." The young man broke his silence and called out in pain: "I am lost. There is no true love on earth! The quest for personal success, greed, and vanity are the moving forces of earthly love! I am leaving and will never come back. Even you are no better than the other daughters of Adam. In a moment my body will be swallowed by the waves!"

With those words he headed toward the river. Desperate, Hanina ran after him, begging him not to harm himself. She promised to follow him wherever he wanted. At that moment her father's strong hands caught her from behind and held her tight.

"You won't go with him, you fallen daughter, the seed of Lilith and Satan! Woe to me that I have to experience this ordeal in my lifetime! While I pray in the synagogue to the God of my forefathers, my daughter is sweet to the son of Edom!" the Rabbi lamented despondently.

"Please, do not be angry father," begged the frightened daughter, "he is not the descendent of Edom. He is a son of Israel, a son of the Law!"

"A son of the Torah? And on this sacred day did he go to the temple?" gloomily commented the father. "He is a swindler who wants to seduce you but this wicked emissary of Azazel will not succeed. In a few days you will wed Nachum, the son of the butcher, and he will keep an eye on you. Let's go!" With those words he grabbed his daughter's arm and forcefully dragged her away.

The young man did not utter a word. He jumped into the boat and rowed to the middle of the river where the current was very swift. The unhappy Hanina glanced back and with horror saw how the small boat stalled in the center of the stream and how the young man threw himself into the water with the cry: "Follow me soon, my beloved!"

Hanina sat silently in the corner of the festively decorated living room. She was devastated. Her father paced the room back and forth praying quietly while his wife angrily and continually accused him and her daughter of permitting the nice young man to drown himself.

The expected holiday guests arrived shortly and, as was the case every year, enjoyed spending the evening with the Rabbi, reading the Torah, praying, and eating fresh stew and cooked fruit. When Hanina lifted her eyes, the first thing she saw was the ugly face of Nachum, her groom, her destined future husband. With disgust she turned her head away and looked out of the window at the shiny surface of the Vltava glittering in the moonlight. She thought she saw again her beloved in the boat, smiling and motioning to her . . . come, come. . . .

Quickly she left the room. Nobody noticed that she had disappeared except her worried father who followed her, rapidly sensing an upcoming disaster. But it was already too late. He had just crossed the threshold when he saw his beloved daughter throwing herself from the steep bank into the swift current. The ravenous waves closed upon her slim body forever. A desperate scream interrupted the guests' prayers. They rushed out and found Rabbi Kalman lying on the ground like a body without a soul. Only with great effort were they able to resuscitate him and he told them about the horrible events of that day.

As a true son of Israel, Rabbi Kalman accepted God's judgment and felt like Job that what God had given he had also taken. He was, nevertheless, wretched and could not find consolation. Even time, the mighty wizard, could not heal the wounds in his heart. He stopped tending his estate, neglected business, and distributed a lot of his wealth, remembering the words of forefather Abraham that a person does not need wealth if he is destined to die without children.

A year and a half passed. One Sabbath afternoon, a well-to-do and experienced midwife, Mrs. Shifres, the only sister of Rabbi Kalman, was looking out of her window, watching people pass by. She was hoping to digest quickly the heavy lunch she had just eaten which made her feel quite uncomfortable. Her devoted husband stood next to her and they discussed and compared the living conditions of their neighbors, the financial problems of some acquaintances, recent quarrels of some friends, as well as upcoming weddings and possible funerals. This is what happens today too behind many open windows, when people have nothing to do and indulge in hearty gossip. Suddenly they were interrupted by the heartbreaking moan of a big black cat meowing on the opposite roof as if asking for help and protection.

"Have a look at that cat, she has such a gigantic belly," said Mrs. Shifres.

"What do you care about a cat and her swollen abdomen! You are not thinking of helping her to have her litter?" playfully asked her husband.

"Why not? If I knew to whom she belongs I would calmly help her when the time comes."

The cat stopped moaning and disappeared among the roof tops.

Around midnight the bell that was attached to the door started ringing and woke up Mrs. Shifres from her sleep. She got up and dressed quickly, collected all the necessary equipment and followed the messenger who was waiting outside summoning help for a woman in labor. The conscientious and devoted midwife was scared to death when at the bank of the river the messenger asked her to step into a boat. She tried to resist but the man lifted her into the small vessel and at once she felt the motion of the waves carrying them downstream. Mrs. Shifres had closed her eyes out of fear but opened them when the boat suddenly stopped. She was in for the surprise of her life. They were deep under the river facing a most beautiful palace made out of crystal glass. Its pillars were decorated with precious stones and the road to it had been opened up by the waves that held on tight without closing.

"This is my dwelling," said the man. "Come with me and be not afraid. My wife, the queen, needs your help, do you understand?"

If the beauty of the palace had caused the woman to marvel, the glory of the inside made her ecstatic. Never in her life had she seen such wondrous glamour and riches. The fact that she was going to help a queen in labor, she thought, would make her neighbor Miryam, burst with envy. Carefully she pressed the golden handle of a door and at that point her surprise was so great that she almost turned into a pillar of salt.

"Hanina, is it really you? You did not drown last year in the Vltava?" called out Mrs. Shifres and ran into the open arms of her royal niece.

Hanina placed her finger on her lips and whispering asked her loud aunt to talk very quietly. Then she began telling her what had happened after the current of the river had closed upon her. She felt somebody holding on to her and carrying her somewhere. She regained consciousness only in the castle. Her beloved was kneeling at her feet and thanking her for having saved him from his fate. He had been cursed by the ruler of the watery domain, the mighty Dagon, because of a disagreement the later had had with his father. He had to suffer for his father's sin and wander endlessly on earth till he found one human being who would love him unconditionally and sacrifice everything for him. Only then the curse could be lifted and he would once again become the ruler of the rivers Vltava and Labe.

Having confessed to Hanina, her beloved said: "I have wandered for a thousand years in different disguises among many people, good and evil. Many times I started a relationship with an earthly daughter but none of them was loyal and constant till I found you, the noblest and most beautiful of all human maidens. Therefore be mine forever after and share with me my power and might!"

At that point, Hanina tried to calm down her agitated aunt, whose religious views were shaken considerably when she realized that her niece was living without a rabbi's blessing as the wife of a non-Jew. She told her distraught relative: "My dearest, sweet auntie, you do not understand this. These creatures are neither Jews nor Turks, they do not have churches or synagogues. Their creator is God, their shrine is the world, their religion is nature. Envy does not exist here, neither avarice, ambition, revenge, nor gossip. Nobody here knows what fraud, deception, or cover-up is. It is a good, a really good place to live. If only it were not so monotonous and I would not be so bored."

At that moment, the beautiful queen had to interrupt her tale since her labor pains took over. Mrs. Shifres, true to her calling, cleared her head from all the amazing things she had heard and concentrated on the preparations to help the new water prince emerge into the world. Out of her deep pockets came the necessary tools, and she lifted and positioned her noble niece to deliver the child. All this she accompanied with a torrent of niceties and affectionate words to calm down and ease the pain of labor. Shortly, she was able to place the newborn baby boy in the arms of the exhausted mother.

Hanina recovered quickly and was able to continue her story. After a short and happy period in the watery realm she began to miss home. Her husband allowed her to roam among her people, but only in the shape of a black cat.

When Hanina began to beg her aunt to stay with her a little bit longer, the perturbed Mrs. Shifres said firmly: "How can you even think of it? What would my husband say? That is out of the question. I have a lot of work, Mrs. Judith is going to give birth any time now and later all the others. No, no, I have to go back."

Disappointed, yet with great urgency, Hanina whispered to her aunt: "If you treasure your life, keep quiet. Silence . . . silence . . . my husband . . . you have to be careful and not let him even suspect that you know me. He is not favorably inclined to the human species since people with shrewdness and trickery devastate and pollute his realm. People think that they can recognize him because of the green coat and the fact that water drips continuously from his left pocket, but that is a complete delusion. He appears among people in different shapes depending whom he is investigating. To an usurer he will appear as a carefree gentleman, to a scholar as a librarian or writer. In front of ladies he becomes an officer or an actor, and a judge or lawyer will perceive him as a promising client. Therefore beware! As a reward for your services he will offer you precious stones, pearls, gold, and silver. Do not take any of those. In the last room before you exit, you will find a lot of coal. Take as much as you can. I am warning you again, do not be tempted by the glitter of the precious stones, they will disappear before you reach home. And do not tell anybody, but anybody what you have seen!"

No sooner had she uttered those words when the door opened and the handsome king walked into the chamber. He lifted the young, sleeping prince from his mother's arms and kissed him tenderly. He was deliriously happy and after returning the baby to his mother he turned to Mrs. Shifres and offered her to take anything she wanted from the treasure chest. The shrewd woman modestly refused the precious stones and gold. If the monarch was surprised to hear that he did not bat an eyelid. On the way out Mrs. Shifres asked only for the coal that was lying in the corner of a room. "My husband is a tinsmith, and it will be to his liking," she said.

The king gave his permission and she filled the huge pockets of her apron with so much coal that she could hardly straighten herself as she walked. He rowed her back to the river bank and once more warned her not to tell a soul where she had been. "One word and you will be lost. Do you understand?" he asked her with a menacing voice. Although Mrs. Shifres was a gutsy woman she, nevertheless, felt a weakness in the knees when she was left alone on the shore. She collected herself and rushed home in the darkness of the night. She was in such a hurry that she did not notice that one side of her apron was a little loose and that some of the coal dispersed on the street.

Her husband was delighted and relieved to see her after an absence of two nights. The exhausted midwife went to bed right away but it did not take long before she was awakened from her sleep by the ecstatic screams of Mr. Shifres. "Woman, for God's sake, wake up and look at this!" he yelled. "It is a miracle, gold, gold everywhere, real gold, pure gold!"

"Do not make a fuss, the neighbors will come running," said the clever woman. "I brought a lot, the apron is full of it. Quickly, let's hide it so that nobody finds out how rich we are!" And so, together they hid the gold in a trunk.

In the meantime there was a big commotion outside on the street. A big crowd gathered, fought, pushed, and even crawled on the ground to get the scattered pieces of gold that the midwife, in her haste and fear, had lost on her way home. People believed that gold had sprung out of the ground and many called out: "It is a miracle, this is a golden street!" But even though they dug up the surface of the road with hand-picks and shovels, they did not find any more gold. Nevertheless, since that day the street has been called the Golden one.

Mrs. Shifres never told anybody about her adventure. Her whole life she kept quiet out of fear that her treasure would disappear. Only on her deathbed did she summon her brother and disclose his daughter's fate.

What happened to Hanina, though, nobody knows. Is she still the watery queen of the Vltava? Till this very day, nobody knows.

2

Rabbi Loew's Betrothal

Since his birth in 1513, Rabbi Loew was destined to be the savior of the Jews. His father, the revered Rabbi Bezalel son of Chaim, came from the lineage of the famous Rabbi Hagaon who was a descendant of King David.

Years passed and the boy's reputation as a prodigy spread in his native Poland as well as other countries in Europe. As was the habit in those days to send young scholars to study under the tutelage of well-known teachers in other places, young Loew traveled to Prague which was at that time a center of Jewish learning. One of the most prominent members of the Jewish community there, Samuel Reich, a rich and powerful religious Jew, took an interest in Loew. He had a daughter called Pearl who was worthy of her name. She was not only beautiful but pious and good-hearted as only few maidens were. Samuel Reich, who was better known by his nickname Shmelke, was in search of a husband for his young daughter and his eye fell on Loew. And so, following the tradition of those days, Shmelke chose the fifteen-year-old lad to become the future husband of the delightful Pearl. As the prospective father-in-law, he followed the young man's career carefully. According to his wishes Loew left for the town Lublin in Poland soon after his engagement, to study in the famous rabbinic school of that city. It was headed by Rabbi Shlomo Luria, who at that time was the brightest star in the firmament of Jewish learning.

Some time after Loew's departure, Shmelke encountered bad luck that became worse as time went by. He had undertaken a series of bad business deals and lost almost all his fortune. Despondent yet aware of his duty, he notified Loew, who was eighteen at that time, of what had happened. Since he could not honor the dowry he had promised initially, he released Loew from the engagement and gave him back his freedom to look for another wife.

Loew wrote back: "I do believe in the help of God and will wait till He helps you regain what you have lost. I consider my engagement to your daughter binding and void only if you should decide to marry her to someone else."

Yet God's help was slow to come. Finally Pearl, who was not only intelligent but also a very decisive young girl, decided to do something on her own to pull her family back from the brink. She set up a small stand, stocked with different food items, mainly bread, salt, and other staples, and was able to support her parents and herself.

Ten years went by and Loew remained faithful, solid in his belief that he and Pearl were meant for each other and that God's help would not fail to come at the right time.

One day a group of soldiers was traveling through town and they passed by Pearl's little food stand. One of the officers, sitting high and mighty on his horse, noticed the golden loaves Pearl had spread out for display and, taking his sword, pierced through the fragrant bread ready to take it away. Pearl was truly scared but, pulling herself together, called out to the soldier not to take away the goods without paying since she had to support her aging parents with her work. The officer paused for a moment, then took the saddle off the horse and threw it on the counter saying: "I am hungry but have no money to give you, so take this in exchange!" Then he galloped away and disappeared in the blink of an eye.

Pearl's surprise was immense when she discovered a large number of golden coins hidden in the saddle. Excited and full of joy, she ran home and showed the treasure to her parents. Shmelke bowed his head and said that he realized it was a miracle and that the officer must have been Elijah the prophet himself. Pearl believed that good fortune had smiled on them thanks to Rabbi Loew's unending faith and that was the real miracle. Shmelke notified Rabbi Loew about his change of luck and their great relief and asked him to come to Prague without further delay to celebrate the wedding.

Rabbi Loew arrived in Prague soon after these turn of events and married the incomparable Pearl.

3

At the Banks of the Vistula

A small, lonely boat was sailing up the river that had escaped freezing that year. It had been a mild winter and spring had come early, particularly in the south where the Vistula emerges from the Carpathian Mountains before taking its meandering course up north. It was in the early hours of the evening, near the Royal Castle of the city of Krakow. A single tourist was standing near the gates watching the day come to an end. The dispersed clouds that had been floating around went from off-white to pink and their reddish hues were another indication that the sun was about to retire. The pensive visitor started walking towards the car that was parked in the almost empty lot. The small neatly dressed woman was in no hurry to go anywhere. Her sad eyes, that seemed to fill her whole face with a melancholy expression, swept once again over the whole landscape and unwillingly she opened the door of the car, sat down, and lingered for a moment before starting the engine.

She looked upward at the changing colors of the sky that was becoming azure blue and for a moment had to close her eyes since the color was so intense. When she opened them again and looked up, two small but very bright lights lit up in the firmament, nestling on a couple of pink, fluffy clouds that seemed to be unable to move. It was quite strange. The flickering lights were like candles in the sky and the clouds served as their holders. With surprise and delight she continued looking at them for a while until suddenly she hit her forehead with the palm of her hand in utter frustration and said aloud with anger in her voice: "Dear God, it is Friday evening, time to light the Sabbath candles, and here I am completely oblivious. My friends must have started without me and I deserve a scolding, no doubt about it!" Once again she looked up at the flickering candle lights and the translucent holders that were still there and, with a smile on her face, recited the Sabbath blessing over the candles the way her grandmother had done all her life and her mother as well. She started the engine and drove off, fighting the urge to look back and up again. She knew the stars would be there but the clouds must have dissipated into the darkness of the night.

Two days earlier she had arrived in Krakow with a group of friends and they had taken a tour of the city. It had been not only interesting but heartwarming particularly to her, since her maternal grandmother had lived in the old Jewish quarter a long time ago before she left for America. She remembered the special lady quite well despite the fact that her mother had given birth to her late in life and her grandmother, at that time, had already been old. She could recall the sound of the old woman's voice, her enthusiasm, and at the same time grief when she described the old country and especially the city of Krakow. Somehow she remembered well the contents of the stories she had been told and the musical sound of her grandma's simple English laced with the Polish accent which made it so unique to her. She felt drawn to the old city with its ancient Jewish heritage and wanted to savor it all as if she was compelled to do so by some unexplained force.

She had joined a group of friends on the trip to Europe and was just finishing her tour, ready to fly back to New York the very next day. That Friday, being their last day abroad, she decided to take advantage of the free afternoon and mild weather and roam around all by herself without any particular purpose. She ended up on the hill, once again at the Royal castle which she found both fascinating and enchanting. This was the place where the wise Krakus, in whose honor the city had been named, outwitted the ferocious dragon and saved his people from a cruel fate. It would have been fun to try to find the ancient cave where according to the old Polish legend the terrible beast had dwelled. She loved those old tales but it was too late to look for a cavern. She needed some time to be alone and reflect quietly without having to tell anybody about her worries. She felt almost forlorn but did not want to share her burden with others, partly not to spoil their vacation but mainly because she could not talk about it. Before leaving on her trip she had just taken her physical and the doctor had discovered a lump in her breast which, he said, was most probably benign. Nevertheless he did a biopsy and sent it to the lab for testing. It happened just before her departure. She could not wait for the results and had to leave with a heavy heart despite the doctor's kind words telling her not to worry and have a good time. How could she not be apprehensive? It was not just the horror of the thought that she could have cancer, the fear that maybe her life despite all the possible hideous treatments could be ending, but the image of her mother in the wheelchair, sitting all by herself in her small, modest apartment with no one to take care of her.

She and her mother had to rely on each other all those years after her father's death. She was an only child and as such received the most generous amounts of love and attention a person could get. Yet when her mother got older and health problems seemed to add on year after year, she began to feel the heavy burden of an only child's concern and responsibility for an almost helpless parent. Oh, how she wished she had a sibling, just one, only one to share her worry and trepidation! Sure, she had good friends but she could not share all her heartbreaking anxiety with them. Every year she went on a trip leaving her mother in the care of a competent professional and every year things worked out well, but then she had not had the additional worry of her own health, the nightmare of dying before her mother did.

She entered the hotel lobby and rushed into the dining room where her friends had almost finished dinner. She apologized and joined them for dessert. When the evening ended early since everybody retired to get ready for the flight home, she felt extremely restless. After attempting to sleep for a while, she got up quietly, dressed swiftly, and left the hotel for a short walk. She could see the river from her hotel window gleaming in the moonlight and felt she wanted to linger a little bit for the last time at its banks.

The hotel was located very close to the Vistula, and, while walking slowly towards the river, she wrapped her coat tightly around her body. It was not very cold, only a little windy, and there was some mist rising from the water. The street was almost deserted and she wondered what people did on weekends in Krakow. She saw a few coffeehouses. Some had a few tables and chairs positioned around trees on the sidewalk, but they were all closed, no soul around. "Probably when it gets warmer, in the summer," she thought to herself. When she reached the banks of the Vistula she looked at the gliding waves for a while, trying to imagine her grandmother in her youth standing at a similar place—most likely not at night—and hopefully in a better mood. She felt extremely desolate and tears started flowing down her cheeks. She did not try to wipe them off. The breeze seemed to pick up and the mist was getting thicker.

Suddenly she experienced a strange sensation as if somebody was standing next to her. She looked around, there was nobody there. Yet, no matter how hard she tried, the sensation would not go away. She had the most unusual feeling that it was her grandmother who was close by and although she could not see a thing she knew she was not mistaken.

"Grandma," she said quietly, "I am very unhappy and concerned about myself as well as my mother. You have to help me, you have to do something to help your daughter. When I am gone, if I have to leave soon, there is nobody who will cherish my mother the way I do, the way you did in the past." Her voice rose and she almost screamed through the mist, "You have to take care of your daughter, do you hear me, you have to!" Her voice broke, the sound of her sobbing scattered to the wind. She had never felt as inconsolable and heartsick as at that very moment. Yet at that very instant she felt a light pressure on her forehead which remained there for a split second. Then it happened again and for a third time, as if somebody was barely touching her but caressing her lovingly and softly. Suddenly she felt at peace, knowing that things would take care of themselves. It was not just her grandmother whose presence she sensed so strongly but there were others surrounding her, as if many of her departed relatives had come back, just for a while, to let her know that there was no reason to feel dispirited and discouraged. They would help, they would take care, they all would never forget her or her mother, never.

The next morning she still had the irrepressible feeling that all that had happened at the banks of the Vistula was not a figment of her imagination. It had not been a nefarious joke played by some evil Polish river imp hiding in the darkness. It was real, it had to be.

The sleepless night and long flight home left her tired but calm and clear-eyed. She rushed to her mother's apartment as soon as she got out of the airport and felt a great sense of relief and pleasure when she saw her standing with her walker at the door, greeting her, and smiling happily for having her back. She told her a little about her trip and promised to have breakfast with her the next day, bright and early, after a good night's sleep. In her own apartment she eyed the answering machine with some apprehension but pushed the button without panicking. The deep voice of her doctor informed her that the biopsy had been negative and expressed the hope that she had had a pleasant vacation despite her concern.

She pulled up a curtain and looked out at the park she could see from her window. It was dusk and two young women were trying to convince their toddlers, who were swinging happily, to go home before nightfall. She gazed at the sky that was getting darker by the moment and saw a few stars glittering up there. They were not as bright and shiny as the ones she saw in Krakow but they were there nevertheless and, although they seemed to be much higher up and remote, they were still there. She opened the window and a soft breeze caught her face. Looking up she whispered into the night, "Thank you Grandma, thank you all!"

4

The Jew in the Attic

In a small village at the foot of the Tatra mountains in Slovakia there lived together three generations of women. A curse seemed to have descended on the household. Each time one of the women married and begot a child, her husband passed away while she was still in labor. The men seemed to be in great pain as if having contractions while the women suffered no complications during the delivery. This had gone on for about a hundred years and there did not seem to be any cure. All the babies born were female and inherited the curse that had befallen their family. They accepted their fate but, being devout Christians, attended church regularly and continually prayed for God's mercy and salvation.

The youngest member of the family, a pretty, vivacious eighteen-year-old girl, was told by her mother that soon she would have to travel to Košice, the big town where nobody knew them, and find a husband. He could be poor and of humble origin yet would be expected to follow his bride to the small village and help out in the tiny farm they owned. Alica wondered many times why she could not choose one of the local young men whom she knew since childhood and felt comfortable with. She was afraid of the big city and did not know how to find a man on her own there. Nobody had told her about the family problem and she was puzzled that all the women in the village prevented their sons from courting her.

Yet the predicament was not just her own. A handsome lad by the name of Juraj, proud and stubborn with a mind of his own, fell in love with Alica and would not listen to his parents' warning that the girl was no good for him. He had heard all sorts of rumors about Alica and her family but nothing that would have clarified the mystery. Nobody wanted to talk about it, and finally he made up his mind to solve the riddle no matter what.

One day while Alica was busy in the field working with her mother, he sneaked into the house and approached the grandmother who was sick in bed that day, quite feverish and uncomfortable. The young man apologized for his bad manners but expressed his anxiety and desperation, telling the old woman how he felt about her granddaughter and the obstacles that lay in his way. The old woman looked at the young man with a lot of compassion, asked him to help her sit up and, fluffing up a few down pillows for support, turned her face towards him and said: "My dear Juraj, you are a good person and I guess the time has come to tell you the story of our family's curse. I do not want you to suffer and this way, knowing the truth, at least you will not die."

Juraj's expression was that of utter astonishment: "Die, what do you mean??" The grandmother, who was a spunky old woman, stopped him short from any further questions. "Listen," she said, "you will know it all soon."

"This is what my own mother told me, many years ago," she started her tale. In those days the village was really tiny and everybody knew one another, took care of each other, and lived in harmony, more out of necessity than any other reason. Being close to the Ukrainian border, they were used to strangers coming and going, and at times were quite compassionate and kind, helping them out particularly in the winter. The only ones they resented were the gypsies who had the reputation for stealing anything in sight, even kidnapping little children. Whenever dark people descended from the Podcarpathian Mountains the villagers were on guard.

"One day a stranger arrived in the village. At first the peasants thought he was a gypsy, since he was dark, with a long beard, shiny black eyes, and looked hungry and weak. They were surprised, nevertheless, that he was all by himself as gypsies always traveled in groups. It turned out that he was a Jew who was fleeing from some sort of persecution. They did not look at him kindly but handed him some bread and milk since it was late in the fall, cold and windy. They did not offer him a place for the night and expected him to leave as soon as he had his fill. My mother was standing nearby and saw how tired and exhausted the man looked, and when their eyes met for a moment she felt a real urge to help him. He thanked them for the food and turned toward the woods where he most probably would have spent the night. The villagers went to their own homes and forgot about him, but my mother followed him quietly from afar. It was dusk and the figure of the lean man almost disappeared in the mist that was coming down quickly. She ran and caught up with him. Flushed and uneasy, she made him an offer to spend the night in their attic. He looked at her with deep gratitude and followed her quietly to this house which, in those days, was very close to the dense woods. She made sure nobody saw them and fixed a simple bed for him in the attic with a few covers and an old down pillow. She left, pleased he would not be cold that night and that she had done a good deed, surely that was all it was.

"The next morning she concealed most of her breakfast under her apron and carefully went up to the attic to give the food to the pitiable fugitive. She found him feverish and weak, unable to even lift his head. She felt tremendously sorry for him and nursed him for a week till he was able to stand on his feet again. It was very hard for her to keep the secret from her family but nobody suspected anything. They were all very tired by the end of their hard days. Their sleep was sound and profound and early each morning they rose and rushed to work in the fields. There was a lot to be done before the winter came. My mother was in charge of the house and so it was not difficult for her to take care of the sick man and feed him. Nobody went up to the attic those days of late fall, they were busy in the basement storing potatoes and cabbage, as well as some apples for the harsh long winter.

"When the stranger recovered completely from his long illness the winter had arrived, the ground was covered with deep snow and the cold, freezing wind blew almost constantly. My mother did not have the heart to ask the man to leave since she knew he would be going out to his death. He had packed his few things shortly after the high fever subsided but it did not take much to convince him to stay and wait for the spring. Most of the time he spent reading some strange, old books which he had in his knapsack. He also prayed for long hours, covering his shoulders with a shawl and his head with a small round cap. My mother found him fascinating and very sweet. He was very grateful to her, kissed her hand often, and as they grew closer told her many unusual tales. His voice was deep and soothing, she felt many miles away from her home and country, and was utterly enchanted when he told her about the Holy Land and the city of God, Jerusalem.

"Their warm friendship never developed into love since the man was very conscientious and did not want to jeopardize the reputation of the kind Christian girl who had helped him and for whom he cared deeply. It was very hard at times for my mother since she was the one who loved the man more than he loved her. Yet, she was never too bold and, being a virgin and very innocent, accepted the fatherly affection the man showed her and was content and happy with the way things were. And then one day as spring arrived, the Jew was gone. One morning as my mother swiftly carried her food to the attic, she saw at once that he was gone and had left no trace of himself, as if he had never been there.

"For days she mourned as if he had died and at times she thought that maybe the whole incident was a creation of her own fertile imagination. For many weeks she walked around like a body without soul. She did not dare tell anybody her secret and could not ease her pain weeping during the day so as not to be noticed by others. But they did. The sleepless nights she spent crying took their toll on her looks and her family noticed her pale face and red swollen eyes. They came to the conclusion that it was time for her to wed and found her a handsome lad in a neighboring village.

"My mother married the man and within a few months was expecting their first child. When the time came for the baby to be born, her husband also, inexplicably, seemed to have labor pains. This caused her such trepidation that she even forgot her own overwhelming physical suffering, and could only watch in horror as he lost his struggle and died. People could not understand what had happened and consulted the local medicine woman who believed that he had been bewitched. Suspicion fell on my mother. Time went by and, although she was a well-to-do young and pretty widow, nobody would even think of marrying her. Years passed and I grew up and married a man I really cared for. I was not worried when I got pregnant and the time to give birth approached quickly. To our great distress and grief, my husband also died during my labor and later the same happened to my daughter who gave birth to Alica. So you see, dear Juraj, why you cannot marry our sweet girl. No matter what, she will carry your child and you will never see it since you too will die at the time of birth. This curse fell upon us because my mother, good soul that she was, helped a stranger, a Jew, and he paid her back by bringing disaster on our family."

Juraj had listened attentively. His face expressed at times amazement, sorrow but mostly disbelief. He asked the grandmother whether they had tried to seek help from the priest and the old woman, crying bitterly, told him that all their efforts had been in vain and that only God could help them from there on.

Juraj left Alica's house in a daze. He could hardly believe what he had just heard. Although the situation seemed hopeless, he decided not to give up and somehow find a solution. He knew that in Košice there was a Jewish community with a rabbi and thought that he might seek his advice. Without telling anybody about his plan, he left for the big city and sought out the house of the local rabbi who had the reputation for being a very wise man. The rabbi was surprised to see a young gentile man who wanted to talk to him but invited him into the house and treated him kindly. Juraj, who was a little apprehensive in the unusual surroundings, looked at the hundreds of books the rabbi had neatly arranged on the walls and thought to himself that surely, somewhere in those books, there must be an answer to his problem.

He began telling the old rabbi the story of Alica's family and the curse. The rabbi was listening attentively. His narrow eyes widened as the story went on and he kept caressing his long beard, not interrupting the young man even once. When all that had to be said was told, the rabbi sat for a moment with his eyes closed, not saying a word. Juraj waited patiently. He was a simple man but he knew that men of spirit needed time and silence to collect their thoughts and come to some conclusion.

When the rabbi finally opened his eyes, he looked keenly at Juraj and said: "My dear lad, I am not sure I can help you but I will try. This seems to be the doing of Lilith, although she usually attacks the child, not the husband. That puzzles me but then she is very devious and tricky." Seeing the blank look on Juraj's face, the rabbi told him the legend of Lilith, the vicious spirit, Adam's first wife, who had left her husband and had sworn to cast her curse on mankind. She specialized in killing little babies in their cribs and bringing as much unhappiness as she could to men in general. The rabbi then told Juraj that there were a few amulets that could prevent Lilith from her deadly acts, and he was willing to try one he thought would be the most effective.

When Juraj left the rabbi's house he had in his pocket a strange object. It was shaped in the form of a hand, made out of shiny silver and there where some odd inscriptions all over it. The rabbi had called it a hamsah and instructed him on what to do. He decided to follow the advice to the letter.

Juraj returned to the village, visited Alica's mother, and asked for the hand of her daughter, assuring her that he had found a way to get rid of the curse. When Alica became pregnant, the whole village went into a state of fear and desperation since they all thought Juraj was spending his last days on earth. The day of birth arrived and Juraj lay close to his moaning wife. He put the strange silver hand in between their reclining bodies. The labor was hard and painful. Juraj did not feel a thing, yet he thought he heard groans that came not only from his wife's mouth but from all over the room. The screams grew stronger and stronger until he heard the first cry of their child. It was a beautiful baby boy, strong and healthy, and the young parents were delighted and almost delirious with joy. They knew that the wise rabbi had been right, the curse was broken. Lilith was gone and they had their little baby and each other as well. They put the hamsah in a beautiful painted wooden box and hid it in a special place hoping it would protect their home in the future.

They lived happily for many long years, if not forever after as they say in fairy tales.

5

The Storyteller

She died many years ago but those who heard her stories still remember her: an old Hungarian lady, always neatly dressed, her long white tresses nicely gathered at the crown of her head. Those who loved her enjoyed giving her small presents and soon she had a large collection of lovely barrettes that she wore on her hair, a different one every single day.

Born in Budapest, Blanka had married a Slovak and moved to Bratislava where she lived happily for a number of years until the Nazis came and completely destroyed her life. She had been visiting with a friend of hers in the neighborhood and, when she reached home that fatal afternoon, her husband and both daughters had been taken away. She never saw them again. Years later she found out that they had been murdered in Treblinka. Her loyal friend, who was a gentile, hid her for many months in the cellar and thus saved her life. She had never been sure whether it was for the better or the worse. Her unhappiness was so great and her sadness so boundless that, had it not been for her good friend, she would have probably passed away out of sheer desperation. The two women were both lonely widows and operated a small grocery shop. In addition to a variety of foods, they had a collection of books that they sold or loaned to interested customers.

It was during that time of her life that Blanka discovered her hidden talent. Her customers used to bring their children with them and, while they were shopping, Blanka entertained the little ones with stories she remembered from her childhood in Budapest. Soon the word was out that she was a wonderful storyteller and grown-ups joined their offspring to listen to the tales she so colorfully described for them. Her reputation grew and she became known as Blanka the Storyteller in the immediate neighborhood as well as in other parts of the city. She found as much pleasure in her telling as her audience in listening, and over the years she began to believe that she had acquired a large, wonderful family that cherished and loved her. She was happy, as happy as she could ever be, carrying within her the wound that could not heal. But she never mentioned it and her sweet smile always greeted those who came to visit her.

"Why don't you write down the stories?" people asked her. They emphasized: "If you do not, they might be forgotten and lost in the future!"

Blanka did not tell them that she had tried to do so. At night in her small, narrow room above the store, she sat down more than once to write down the tales. Yet, as soon as she gazed at the white paper in front of her, she went blank. Nothing came to her mind, except for the vision. Engraved on the page she saw the faces of her husband and two little girls. Those were serious faces, nonsmiling, doleful, and in pain. She never told anybody that in order to tell stories she needed an audience, she had to see those animated faces in front of her to be able to perform. And when that happened, it was as if a secret fountain opened up within her and the stories came streaming from her soul; as if she were the vessel where the tales were stored, and they came to life and took their own course when she allowed them. And so the stories were never written down, but she continued telling them as long as she lived and she firmly believed that they would not die with her.

"Which are your favorites?" some friends asked her. She liked most of them but loved those that offered humor and were inane. She also liked those that showed the weaknesses in human nature, even among people who were considered impressive and revered. She delivered even the nonsensical and ridiculous in a candid and lucid way.

There was the story about the old Jew from Maad who, one day when he was sad, went to Tokay, the village famous for its fine wines. He wanted to compare the quality of their beverage to that of his native village of Maad, also well known for its wines, and hoping in the process to lift up his spirits. While walking he decided to light his pipe, but the wind was blowing quite harshly from the direction of Tokay and he was not successful. So he turned around, with his back to the wind and he did it! He began puffing and enjoying his favorite tobacco and started walking a little faster to reach his destination as soon as possible. And reach it he did much quicker than he thought, since he was walking back in the direction of Maad and everything looked tremendously familiar. He scratched his head and came to the conclusion that all places were alike after all and even the wine tasted the same.

And the one about the clever rabbi? "Tell it to us again," her friends used to ask, already giggling in anticipation.

Rabbi Meir Leibush, the son of Yechiel Michael Weizer, was a great sage, famous for his knowledge of the Torah. He fought the Reform Movement with all his might and hence had many enemies among the Maskilim. He was born in Russia in 1809 and had to leave his community because of the danger to his life. He lived in Bucharest as chief rabbi for six years but was chased away again by his enemies. While living in Hungary, he continued to fear for his life. One day in early spring, he received a gift package, a mishloah manot, as is the habit during the festival of Purim. When he opened it, he found a fancy cake that had been shaped in the form of a pig. There was no note added to the curious present but the rabbi knew who had sent it. He had a talk with his wife, who spent a few hours baking a delicious cake that resembled in its shape the rabbi's face. After the cake had cooled, the rabbi wrapped it nicely in silvery paper and sent it to his adversary with a simple note: "Thank you," it said. "You sent me your image and I am sending you mine."

And the one about the shopkeeper who saved the Sabbath?

There used to be a law in Hungary according to which a Jew who received a permit to sell cigarettes and liquor had to keep his shop open on the Sabbath. Yankl Polner needed the income for his family and although he was not an Orthodox Jew, he could not defame the Sabbath. He had to find a way out, and he did. When he came back from the synagogue one Saturday, he entered his shop and sat down to continue reading the book of prayers. A gentile came in and picked a package of cigarettes from the display and some liquor as well. He handed Yankl the money who could not handle it because of the Sabbath. Yankl started singing in Hungarian, using the tune of the Haftarah: "Put the money on the counter and come back on other days too!"

And what about the rest of Blanka's stories?

They are out there.

6

Irenka's Doll

Irenka and her family lived in the great city of Warsaw. She was the daughter of a fireman and very proud of it. Other children looked up to her and thought she was the luckiest girl in the world since her father was a hero and had saved many people's lives. Irenka loved only one thing more than her family and that was her favorite rag doll, whom she had had for years and never parted from. Unfortunately the doll was not in very good shape and despite the fact that Irenka's mother had patched her up many times, she was not the doll she used to be. All the care and love Irenka gave her could not hide her pitiful looks, the scars she had on her fixed up legs, the nose that looked pinched since the last time it was mended, and the dark buttons she had for eyes that did not match her yellow hair. Only her clothes were always nice and crisp since she inherited all of Irenka's dresses which her mother washed and ironed after she customized them to the doll's small frame. Despite all this, Irenka would not have traded her beloved companion for any other toy, except maybe for one that would look just the way her doll had when Irenka was a toddler. But that was not possible since that kind of doll had disappeared from the market a long time ago.

The king that ruled Poland in those days was a good monarch but very ill. When he died, his son, the very young Prince Matt became king and although he was considered a bright lad, everybody knew that it was not he who ruled the country but his ministers. The new king Matt was subjected to a heavy schedule of classes and rules and told to sit on the throne while his advisers would present him reports that he could not make heads or tails of. He also had to suffer bitter cold while this went on since the ministers did not allow the halls and vast rooms of the palace to be heated. They blindly followed old rules regardless of whether they were sound or not. The "no heat" rule went back many centuries to the days of one of Matt's ancestors, a very reasonable queen, who almost had a deadly accident due to a faulty stove and since then decided that it was better to be on the cold side than be asphyxiated. Matt also had to make his own bed, polish his shoes, and take cold showers since one of his predecessors, a militarily oriented king, had done so. The ministers were always complaining of something or the other; the Minister of War was concerned about damaged fortresses; the Minister of Finance was worried about the fact that he could not buy as many machines and cannons as the War Minister thought they needed since everything was so expensive. The Minister of Transportation needed new locomotives, the Minister of Foreign Affairs was worried about some neighbors who looked suspicious to him, and the Minister of Education was upset that children at school used foul language, would not study, got into fights, and refused to do their homework properly.

Matt tried to be a good king and learn as fast as he could. He knew that a king had to know a lot otherwise he would be no good as a ruler. He also learned to sign his name in a very fanciful way since all the documents that were important would be saved for posterity and so would his signature. He learned foreign languages willingly because he knew that he had to communicate with other kings when he went to see them or invited them to his kingdom. It just bothered him that he was not allowed to ask any questions and would not get any answers if he did. He was surprised how many things were forbidden to the king and how a ruler had to follow etiquette and definitely not try to change anything so as to keep his honor and respect in the eyes of the people. He realized that if a person did not know what he was talking about and did not want others to find out, Latin was a good language to use or write in. When a war broke out, diplomacy was used, meaning that they had to lie so that the enemy would have no idea of what they were doing. Proclamations, whether true or not, had to be issued to keep the soldiers in shape.

King Matt decided that enough was enough and that adults did not always know best. Despite the danger involved he felt he had to do something to reform the old ways for the better.

First, he had to find some children to keep him company. He did not like to play alone and used to watch longingly out of the window of the palace at how children enjoyed one another beyond the high walls of the royal garden. And that was how he met Irenka and her friends. One afternoon, when he was given half an hour for his walk, he sneaked out of the manicured grounds and joined the children that were, as was their habit, playing on the other side of the royal fence. He introduced himself to the youngsters and, although they were initially in awe that his majesty wanted to play with them, very soon they became good friends and helped out Matt with some very solid and logical solutions to problems that plagued his kingdom. One of the main things he learned from his friends was not to worry if somebody got angry at him since one could not make all the people happy all the time.

Irenka liked Matt a lot but would not show it to him since she did not want the others to know about it and make fun of her. For that very reason she used to challenge him and ask him to use his power as a king and do things he was not supposed to. The first thing he did for her to prove his might was that he had the paths of the palace garden sprinkled with eau de cologne and the dust wiped from the trees and leaves because Irenka had heard that it was unhealthy. He took a violin from the court musician and gave it to an old beggar who spent his days playing old Jewish songs outside the palace's ground and Irenka liked it very much. Matt actually did that also for himself since he did not like the scratchy sound of the old weather-worn instrument the old man had carried around all his life. He enjoyed listening to the melodies much more once the sound became crystalline and pure and the trembling fingers of the old man seemed to fly over the strings as his face lit up in delight. Matt also sent some candy and toys to the Jewish and Catholic orphanages in town since his mother the queen had done so when she was still alive. His father had followed the same tradition and Matt himself had authorized the entry in the royal budget so that the orphans could continue enjoying his gift of good will. He learned that to be popular and beloved, it is not enough to be the king, but one had to do things that people really liked. And the orphans liked Matt not just because of the candy but, because of having lost both parents at a very early age, he was one of them.

Matt won Irenka's heart completely when he did for her something that she thought would have been impossible. She had told him about her old doll and that if her father had been the king he would have bought her the same doll like the one she had but the new one would reach the ceiling. Matt responded that even kings could not do certain things and Irenka looked at him sadly and nodded her head. Soon that was all Matt could think off: Irenka wanted a doll that reached up to the ceiling! He thought that being the king he had the right to give orders and everybody had to obey them. Why be a king if he could not do what he wanted? At the next council of ministers he demanded from the Prime Minister that he should buy the particular doll he had in mind. The minister refused and talked a long time about all sort of reasons that did not mean anything at all and Matt knew that in the end nothing would happen. He recalled how his father, the king had handled a similar situation once and he did the same thing. He stamped his foot on the ground and said: "This is my absolute wish!"

That did it! After that the minister was busy for a long time trying to find a doll like the old one Irenka had and so much taller. In the end they had to call a doll manufacturer who agreed to make a doll according to specifications. When the doll was ready, the manufacturer displayed her in his window for everybody to see and admire. He boasted for many days and put a big sign in the window of his shop that he was the Purveyor to his Majesty, King Matt and that the doll was made especially for the king's friend Irenka, the fireman's daughter. People loved Matt for that special gift and hundreds of letters reached the palace. Very few of them were given to Matt, only those that expressed admiration for his deed. Those, from hundreds of little girls who requested dolls for themselves too, were destroyed by the order of the angry Prime Minister who resented the whole thing.

Matt was delighted with the outcome of events. He was pleased since he knew that even kings cannot always do what they wanted, but he had succeeded despite the odds to do such a wonderful thing for his friend Irenka and to make so many people pleased and proud of him. As he sat at his desk in the royal chamber he suddenly began feeling sad for himself. Despite his joy he realized how very hard it was to be a king. He had to work long hours trying to prevent wars, sign important papers and think how to improve the life of the children of his country, he could not play and sleep in late or even study, there was so much work to be done.

Matt went into his bedroom and pulled out a box from under his bed. There he kept his old toys, the ones he had liked to play with when he was smaller and his father was still alive. He looked at the toys that were covered with a heavy layer of dust. He sneezed twice before he bent and picked up a puppet that used to be his favorite. Harlequin the clown still had a smirk on his face as it had been painted when he was made but somehow it was more like an expression of sadness and Matt felt he had to apologize and explain to the neglected toy why he could not play with him anymore. He approached the window and suddenly heard the sad sounds of the old Jewish beggar's violin that were coming through the window. They lasted for a while and, when the music stopped, Matt the King sighed deeply and sat behind the desk to write some pending important letters.

7

A Simple Wife

Malka had a beautiful name but nothing much beyond that. She was a stocky, plain-looking girl and did not like herself very much. The only thing she considered pretty about herself was her hair. It was long and curly, the color of blackest coal and just as shiny as if somebody had taken the trouble to polish each hair on her head every single day. But even that she lost the day she married Motke. When it grew back, being a married woman, she had to keep it covered with a kerchief and nobody ever saw the one lovely thing God had granted her.

Malka's low self-esteem was partially the fault of her mother and father. She was born to the couple when they were already middle-aged and had lost hope of having a child. Maybe it would have been better if they had never had one. Malka grew up in extreme poverty and misery, and all she remembered from her unhappy childhood were the stories her mother used to tell her about grand kings and queens and how one day a handsome prince would come and take her to his palace as his wife. After all, her mother had had a premonition when she gave the baby the name Malka—Queen—and that was, so her mother believed, God's pledge to her that a great fortune was awaiting her daughter. Malka had listened to the tales hundreds of times and, being an intelligent girl, realized that her mother was living in a world of her own. Looking around her home she saw the bare walls, the dilapidated furniture, and the broken dishes they could not replace and was filled with bitterness. In time, looking at herself in the mirror, she began to resent her name and developed a strong dislike for it.

Malka's father worked as a helper in the butcher's shop and, every evening when he came home, she saw how bent and tired he was and how he ignored her mother's chattering and her as well. He withdrew into a corner of the room where he ate his supper all by himself. Malka felt sorry for him, a feeling she did not have for her mother, and hated the smelly bits and pieces of leftover meat he brought home which her mother cooked for dinner. All days were about the same. They never went to the synagogue and people did not come to visit except to bring some offering on the holidays. The only young person she knew lived at the other end of town and Malka saw her once in a while when she accompanied her mother to the market. The young girl belonged to a well-to-do family and Malka admired her from afar, her looks, the clothes she wore, and the way her laughter rang and lingered in the air as if somebody was playing musical bells. She did not envy her, she just wanted to be her friend but could not. She was doomed to live with a mother who was dimwitted and a father who had sunk into lethal depression years ago.

Malka was happy to leave her home when the matchmaker came to see her parents even though they agreed to marry her to Motke without consulting her. Motke owned a small shack at the outskirts of town which his folks had left him and had been a loner all his life. He was nevertheless proud of being independent; the community did not support him, and he made his living growing some vegetables and grain in the lot behind his cabin. Nobody ever saw him praying at the synagogue, and all he did when he came to the village was to sell his produce and go back to his tiny farm. For Malka it was almost as if she was back home. The scenery was similar, yet she cleaned the small shack as best as she could and kept it neat. She cooked vegetables for dinner and meat only very seldom when her mother came to visit her and brought her some. Her mother believed that Motke was the long promised prince she had told Malka about. Once Malka could not take it anymore and angrily pointed to his weather-worn clothes and to the poor surroundings, hoping her mother would finally wake up and leave her alone with her fantasies. Yet her mother only smiled and, embracing Malka, whispered in her ear that it was just a disguise to test her. After that Malka gave up and accepted the fact that her mother would never change.

One day Malka was surprised when Motke approached her and said: "Passover is around the corner. I do not know much about it but remember that my parents used to like it and thought it was the most important Jewish holiday. Now that we are married, I want you to prepare it the way it should be done."

Malka's face turned crimson and she had to admit to her husband that she had no idea how since they never celebrated it at her home or even told her about it. Motke was quiet for a while and then suggested she ask the neighbors. Those people lived nearby and owned a small farm, yet Malka had never talked to them nor did they show any signs of interest in them. When Malka refused to consult them, Motke told her that if that was the case she had to sneak behind their house and watch the preparations from a window without their knowledge. Malka did not like the idea but had no choice. When Motke was busy in the lot she slowly crept towards the neighbors' house and peaked through the window. She saw the wife spreading a white cloth on a table and talking to her husband. The window was closed and Malka could not hear a word. She could see, nevertheless, that the man was arguing about something, the wife seemed to be impatient and both of them began shouting at each other. Finally, the man grabbed the woman by her waist, and beat her up. Malka could not hear her screams very well but she saw the pain in her face. Frightened, she ran home as fast as she could.

She did not know what to do. She could not tell Motke what she had seen. She had known poverty and misery all her life but nobody ever hit her and she was not about to be abused by her husband, Passover or otherwise. Motke came in all muddy and sweaty and sat down for a while to rest. He was breathing heavily, his work was not easy and that day he was tired in particular. When he asked Malka what she had seen, she kept quiet. No matter what, she would not tell him. Motke was getting more and more frustrated by the minute and finally when Malka's stubbornness was too much to take, he got up and slapped her face. She withdrew into a corner of the cabin and, crying bitterly, addressed her husband:

"If you already knew how the preparations for Passover are done, why in the world did you force me to spy on the neighbors?"

Motke was sincerely puzzled. When the misunderstanding was cleared they both had a good laugh and since then their relationship improved a lot. They became friends and shared their concerns as well as cheerful moments.

Malka felt happy for the first time in her life. She gathered some courage and decided to go and speak to the rabbi about their situation, and was pleasantly surprised when the old man took her under his wing and asked his wife to be her mentor. Malka learned quickly and started to run a basic Jewish household, something she had had no idea about just a short time earlier. It was not easy though, and she made mistakes, some of them worse than others. Since she was a novice, many times she cut corners when she did not want to put too much effort into it. Yet, after an incident at the well, she decided to become more meticulous.

One Friday evening while getting ready for the Sabbath, Malka had been somewhat slow and had not gone to the well to fetch water. Motke would be coming home soon and she had not prepared the soup yet. She looked at the sky which was turning pink and, not seeing even a glimmer of a star, quickly took the bucket that was sitting in the corner and ran to the well. The well was in the back of their lot and she reached it in a few minutes. She attached the pail to the cord and slowly let it sink into the well. When she tried to pull it up she could not. There must have been some obstruction somewhere, and she bent down and looked into the well to see where the problem was. It was getting a little dark, dusk was descending, and Malka could not see much. Suddenly she lost her balance and fell into the well head first. She started screaming and calling for help, fearing the worst.

Nothing happened for a while but then she heard a voice and somebody looked into the well. It was not Motke, as she had hoped, but a peasant who had been on his way to the village and had heard her screams. He pulled her out with some difficulty but she was unharmed and very grateful. The peasant smiled politely, yet did not leave. He kept staring at her and she wondered what was wrong. She was sitting on a log trying to catch her breath and calm down and had not realized that her scarf had fallen off and that her hair was cascading down her shoulders. The peasant looked at her again admiringly and then said in Hungarian:

"Milyen szep asszony, ojan fenyes haj!" ("What a beautiful lady, such brilliant hair!")

Malka's face flushed a deep, bright red. She removed her wet, dripping apron from her waist and quickly covered her hair since her kerchief must have been lost in the well. She thanked the peasant again and, lifting the pail, ran home quickly as lightning. She knew she had desecrated the Sabbath and that it was wrong for a married woman to let another man, Jewish or not, see her uncovered head. Deep down though, she felt very flattered and pleased and that evening brushed her hair with more care than ever.

From that day on though, she kept the rules very carefully. She was afraid of being punished again and truly wanted to be a good Jew. And that was what she became: Malka, not a queen but Motke's woman, a simple Jewish wife.

8

They Covered Him with Clothes but He Could Not Keep Warm

At the age of eighty, Rabbi Loew was very frail and his tall frame was bending down closer, much closer to the ground. He was aware of his weakening condition but, being always more concerned about others rather than himself, did not fret about it. Yet he was not feeble, his mind was as sharp as ever and, although his eyesight was wavering at times, he "saw" better than he had before and had a very clear insight even into matters that had been somewhat blurred in the past. His body was not able to support him the way it had in days gone by but his mind was alert, and he still fulfilled his obligations full heartedly despite the physical discomfort. He participated in the services of the AltNeu Synagogue as well as other places of worship in the Jewish ghetto. He greeted visitors from many cities and provided advice to a countless number of people who traveled to Prague from distant locations to seek his help.

One Friday evening while praying at the AltNeu Shul, Rabbi Loew felt weak in particular. He made a great effort to recite the psalm a second time as had been the habit of the congregation since the day he had forgotten to take out the shem from under the Golem's tongue. At that time, he had had to interrupt the service and rush to stop the Golem from his destructive acts. Upon returning to the Shul he had sung the psalm a second time to ask God to forgive him for his forgetfulness. Now he recited it again with great passion asking God to forgive him once again, this time for his weakness. Two of his faithful disciples had to convince him to leave the synagogue before the end of the service. They led the pale, shivering rabbi home and made sure he laid down to rest.

The devoted pupils did not know that this was what the rabbi dreaded most. He was afraid of the long nights since he always felt cold and could not warm up. In the past it had been enough for him to sit next to the brick stove, and inhale the wonderful scent of the fir and pine wood, to feel warm and comfortable and be able to spend the whole night studying. The wood was brought from the forests of Křivoklad, provided by friends continuously over the years. The rabbi loved the broad stove that had the emblem of the lion carved on its mantle. His bed was placed nearby so that he enjoyed the warmth at all times, whether he was sitting or lying down. But that was quite a while ago and now he was not able to warm his aching bones even when using the heavy down cover he had had for years.

When winter came to an end, Rabbi Loew hoped that the warmth of spring and the heat of summer would help him. He spent hours outside in solitude, sitting on a bench near the Vltava river, watching the stream flow by, and letting the sun kindle his old bones. As the day drew to an end, he got up with difficulty and leaning on his heavy cane slowly walked down Široka street to his home. His hope vanished with the sun's last rays since his nights became even worse after spending the few hours in the warm sunshine. It seemed to him that his blood stopped flowing in his veins and froze in place. The most important element in a man's body, fire, was slowly but steadily being extinguished and only water and earth, the other primary components of a human being, seemed to be left. Yet, he would not allow the furnace to be lit in his room, he was too proud to admit his weakness and suffering and lay under the cover with his teeth chattering and his whole body shaking in freezing agony.

The rabbi's granddaughter Yara was staying with him at that time. Her parents, her mother Dvora, the rabbi's daughter, and her father Izaak, had left for Poland where they intended to spend a few years while Izaak served as a rabbi at the local congregation. Yara was a very loving girl and it upset her to see her grandfather's decline. She knew he did not want to talk about it but she noticed how uncomfortable he was and how much he suffered in silence. She wished her grandmother were still alive since she was the only one who always knew what was wrong with Rabbi Loew without him even uttering a word. One night Yara heard him moaning and rushed to his room to find him white as a sheet and shaking as a leaf in the wind.

"What is the matter, grandfather?" she asked quietly, trying not to sound alarmed. She picked up his hand and was horrified at how icy it felt. "I am cold, my dear child," whispered the rabbi and smiled with difficulty. "I do not seem able to warm up." It was the first time he had admitted how frozen he felt, as if with the heat escaping from his body he had also lost some of his pride.

Yara quickly ran out to bring some of the wood that had been already stored away for next winter. She lit the stove and in a while the room was filled with the scent of wood the rabbi liked so much. Yara covered the old man with some additional blankets and sat at his side till he felt comfortable. When Rabbi Loew noticed how flushed and hot his dear granddaughter seemed to be, he asked her to go to her own room and open the window to the gentle spring breeze to cool off. That night he slept better and Yara continued to light the stove each night despite the warm weather outside. She made sure that the fire would not die during the night and was relaxed as long as she could hear the crackling sound of the burning logs. Yet, this did not help for long. The rabbi did not complain but Yara could see how tired he looked, how deep his wrinkles had become, and how stiff and bent he was in the morning, almost unable to get up. Despite the respect she felt for his knowledge and wisdom, and her desire not to go against his wishes, she saw him almost as a child that needed help. Since her parents were far away, she decided to seek the advice of two good friends.

David Gans, a physician and scientist, was a student of Rabbi Loew. The old man had instructed him for years and appreciated his opinion and advice in many matters, especially astronomy. The rabbi had introduced Gans to the astronomers at the court of the Emperor Rudolf and, thanks to the rabbi, Gans had access to the famous Tycho Brache and John Kepler. The second friend was Isaiah Horowitz whose well-known grandfather Shabtai Scheftel Horowitz had been Rabbi Loew's teacher during his youth. Both

David and Isaiah were devoted and loyal to Rabbi Loew and were very concerned to learn of his problems. They promised Yara to keep it secret and to try to help the best they could.

Some days passed and the two men were still unable to come up with a solution. They knew that the rabbi was coming to the end of his life, but wanted to make whatever was remaining of it a time to enjoy rather than suffer. They were at their wits' end. Herbs and different kinds of potions were out of the question since the rabbi was not suffering from a disease but just old age. The hot beverages he consumed did not seem to aid him much and they dismissed the idea of providing him with alcoholic beverages. Even if drinking could help him somewhat, he would have refused unless it was kosher wine on holidays. Doctors would be quite useless in a situation like this and Yara was already doing all she could to help him. Yet something had to be done, something had to be thought of to ease the rabbi's suffering and soon. Both men decided to include one more person in their plan and hoped that the three of them would find a way out. They approached Mordechai Maizl who was the mayor of Prague in those days and had the reputation of an honorable and wise man. They knew they could trust him. He was also very wealthy which, of course, would be of help if it was money that they needed for the rabbi. Even the Emperor valued Maizl's friendship and advice, and many times his emissaries would visit Maizl's house and ask for financial help when the Emperor was in trouble. In exchange Rudolf granted favors to the Jewish population and the Jews of Prague knew very well who their real benefactor was.

Maizl was not able to find a quick solution either but one day, while brain storming, came up with an idea. At first it shocked and frightened them but nevertheless seemed to be the only answer. "The maiden Abishag!" called out Maizl, "Abishag the Shunammite!" The eyes of Horowitz and Gans lit up as they nodded and remembered the story of old king David and the young woman Abishag. King David had suffered from the same affliction as the rabbi and the maiden had sweetened the last period of his life by keeping him warm. And yet there was a great difference between King David and Rabbi Loew. King David had had many women in his life, Rabbi Loew had married once and after his wife's death had remained a widower and been loyal to her memory. There had never been an indication that he was interested in remarrying. Some women had even courted the beguiling rabbi but he always solved the problem by finding a husband for them and marrying them off. In time everybody knew what his standing was. Nevertheless, his friends decided to try. After all even King David did not cohabit with Abishag, he was too old and weak and disinterested, she just rendered him the warmth of her young body and the same could be done for the rabbi. Basically they had to find him a devoted, young woman who would know her duty and obligation, and who would serve him as a warm blanket of life.

It did not take them too long to find the right person. All three of them thought that Eva would be the perfect match. She was a poor, young woman who suffered from bad vision and had to work as an aid in the orphanage. She had once been quite an accomplished seamstress but due to her handicap could not support herself anymore and had to go on welfare. Although she was quite good looking, gentle, and kind, no man wanted her for a wife because of her impending blindness. Even those who sympathized and liked her sweet personality had no desire to have an invalid on their hands sometime in the future. Her father had been the shammes of one of the synagogues in Prague and had taken care of his only child after his wife died, for as long as he lived. Eva was also honest, God-fearing, and quite intelligent. She would be their Abishag. They would explain to her the situation and hopefully help the rabbi live a better life without suffering. But first they had to have Yara's help.

The rabbi's granddaughter agreed that theirs was a good idea. She suggested that Eva come and live with them as her servant for a while and help her out with the chores. Once she became accepted as a member of the household, they would proceed with their plan and tell the rabbi. Eva was happy to leave the orphanage and to find a home in the rabbi's house. She had always admired Rabbi Loew and felt honored to be of help. Within a few weeks the rabbi became accustomed to the silent girl who worked all day long and hardly made any noise. She never spoke unless spoken to and slowly took over some of the many tasks Yara carried out. Yara was hoping that by the time autumn arrived the rabbi would be so very used to Eva that he would not object to what they had to suggest.

The day came when they had to tell the rabbi. The three friends approached him in his study and told quietly and briefly what they had done. The rabbi was very agitated. He got up and paced slowly around the room, leaning on his cane. His face was solemn and drawn. Finally he looked at his friends and said: "I cannot accept your proposal since I have never had impure thoughts and am certainly not going to nurture some now at the age of eighty. I know that your intentions are good and am not angry, but I do not want to discuss this anymore." The disappointed trio left with heavy hearts but returned the next day after they were summoned by Yara. She had disclosed to the rabbi after their departure, who their Abishag was and tried to reason with the rabbi. Rabbi Loew saw them in his bedroom this time since he was feeling very weak that day. He told them that he would accept the offer only under one condition, and that was to marry Eva. He did not expect to live with her as man and wife, after all he was eighty and she was nineteen but, in case people should find out about the arrangement, he wanted things to be proper and according to the law of God. He hinted that, although he was old and weak, he was still a man and Eva was just awakening as a woman. That being the case, he would rather be considered her lawful husband and not sin in the eyes of God.

A few days later a secret wedding ceremony was performed and Eva became the second wife of Rabbi Loew. Nobody, though, knew about it. Eva never went out to talk to other women, nor did she sit in the women's wing during services in the synagogue or engage in gossip while shopping. They were used to her keeping to herself and always regarded her as a servant. She helped with miscellaneous tasks at home and at night she slept in the rabbi's bed keeping him cozy and warm. His health improved and he was able to walk without leaning on his cane as heavily as he used to. His face lost some of the white transparency Yara was so worried about. His eyes were luminous again and the nights stopped being a nightmare.

Then one day things turned for the worse. The rabbi caught a bad cold at the beginning of the winter and barely escaped death. All those days Eva kept vigil at his side and continually nursed him. Yara and Eva had become the best of friends and Yara was grateful for the blessings Eva brought to the house. When the rabbi recovered, Eva seemed to have changed. She was still as pleasant and gentle as before, but she had grown into a mature woman as if overnight. She had blossomed into a full-figured girl and looked healthier and prettier than ever before. The problem was that she also started feeling differently about the rabbi and, since her feelings were very confusing and worrisome, she decided to confide in David Gans whom she considered a close friend.

Eva told David Gans that she had fallen in love with Rabbi Loew and that it was extremely hard for her to control her desire. She lay all night next to him trying to warm him up, yet was not allowed ever to act as his wife. She was despondent and every morning fled to the garden where she embraced a pine tree trying to transmit to the wood the feeling that was burning her up, thus finding relief for a short while. David Gans did not know what to tell her and was just filled with admiration and gratitude toward the rabbi. The wise old man, knowing human nature, had anticipated Eva's longing and saved both of them from a deadly sin by marrying the woman. Gans promised Eva to find a solution and spent a few sleepless nights with his friends pondering what to do.

Maizl again was the one whose suggestion they accepted as the least sinful. Biblical scholar that he was, he quoted the lines from the story of Lot, where his two daughters, knowing that he was the only man alive and not wanting his seed to perish, gave him a lot to drink and slept with him. The father never remembered the incident and in time the two daughters gave birth to his children. Of course, that was not Rabbi Loew's case but, to save Eva from the temptation of committing a horrible sin with some other man, they suggested to her the same path. She had to wait till Passover at which time the rabbi always drank wine. A couple of months after the holiday, she realized that she was pregnant with the rabbi's child. She was afraid to tell him about it since he was unaware of what had happened and kept the secret hidden deeply in her heart not knowing how to handle it. Her fear grew as the days went by since she realized that soon she would be showing, and that her eyesight was becoming worse. She did not want to become a burden and prayed to be able to see her child before complete darkness engulfed her. Eva knew that there was not much time left. Soon enough, though, she thought of a way out and just had to wait for the right opportunity.

The year was 1603 and there were festivities in the streets of Prague celebrating the Emperor's victory over the Turks. The streets were full with excited people, and the rabbi was invited to the Royal palace to a banquet Rudolf had prepared for his friends. On the same day, Yara had to go to the mikveh for her cleansing bath, and with nobody in the house, Eva was able to pack a few of her things and leave without being noticed. She left the Jewish ghetto and followed the crowds along the river heading east. She planned to reach Krakow where the rabbi's daughter lived with her husband and tell them the truth. Then, if they agreed to notify the rabbi about the situation and he would accept it, she would go back to his house once the baby was born. She hoped that the rabbi would be grateful and thank God that he had been blessed with a descendant so very late in his life. She did not want to think what would happen it he refused to accept the child.

Unfortunately, Eva did not have to worry about it since she never made it to Poland. The Emperor's troops were combing the areas in search of revolutionaries who wanted to overthrow Rudolf, and she was caught in one of their traps. Since Eva had no papers and could not prove who she was, they executed her with a number of other prisoners who belonged to the opposition. Thus nobody ever found out about Rabbi Loew's unborn child.

Yara searched for Eva all over the Jewish ghetto and grew more and more concerned as days went by. Rabbi Loew himself had no idea why the young woman, whom he had always treated with kindness and respect had decided to leave his home. He was concerned about her welfare and tried to find her whereabouts for many months. He often thought of her and wondered why she had left and how she was. He went back to his old habits and his health continued to decline. His friends never again mentioned Eva or dared to suggest any remedy for his discomforts and ailments. People speculated for a while as to where Eva had gone and there were different rumors about her all over the ghetto. Soon enough though, since she had always been only in the background and not an important or noticeable person, people stopped thinking about her and Eva was quickly forgotten. David Gans was the only one who suspected why the young woman had left and suffered quietly all his life, regretting bitterly Eva had not come to him for help. In his manuscripts he wrote about the history of the Jews in Prague and described the deeds of the great Rabbi Loew, but never ever did he mention the name of the unhappy, lost Eva.

9

The Blank Face

The mud was deep, sticky, and dangerous. It was deadly for the chicken and geese that used to roam in the yard and look for their food. Even the dogs avoided the outdoors and the cats moved very carefully from roof to roof. The farm consisted of a few dilapidated, wooden shacks that looked gloomy in the dim light of the wet morning. It had been raining for days and the skies were still dark and menacing. Hana wore her father's heavy boots and had much trouble keeping her balance while walking on the slippery surface. She screened the yard looking for an embedded chicken or goose. They had lost about five of them in the last two days. The helpless creatures stuck in the mud, slowly sank into it, and suffocated. That was something the family could not afford and Hana was in charge that morning. She had better eyesight than her three older sisters and was more conscientious and compassionate. Her mother assigned her the task since her siblings had already failed to keep the fowl safe.

Life in the small village at the foothills of the Carpathian Mountains in Ruthenia had never been easy. Hana's was one of the few Jewish families that had lived there for many years, and she knew very little about the world beyond the high peaks she saw in the distance. Fir, oak, and beech forests covered the slopes of the highlands, and Hana and her folks were used to seeing bears, wolves, and even a lynx or two roaming in the area. The land was fertile and provided well for the inhabitants of the valley. Few people crossed the narrow passes of the range and the Jewish villagers with their gentile neighbors experienced a mostly secluded existence.

The village had a small shul, a mikveh, and a couple of stores where people bought their groceries. The synagogue served as a school during the day, and the teacher was also a cantor who led them in prayers. Once a month a few men left the village for the city of Mukach where they purchased staples and miscellaneous tools needed for farming.

Hana's grandfather had once been a rich merchant in the city of Uzhgorod. He had known influential people, and Jews as well as Christians had respected him for his talents and his willingness to aid people in need. He had been very orthodox in his ways and his family had prospered and lived a good life. Then one day he made the mistake of hitting a gentile who dared to eye his wife lustfully, and after that there was no peace left for him or his family. The hurt man swore to get his revenge and Hana's grandfather's life was in danger. One night, taking with them as many of their possessions as they possibly could, he and his whole household left the city and fled into the wilderness of the Carpathian Mountain region. They settled down in a small forsaken Jewish village. The grandfather died in his eighties, a bitter man who became more and more strict as time went by and would not allow his children even the smallest transgression. His only son, Hana's father Jacob, grew up a frightened, weak youngster who could never stand up to his father and seemed to fear his own shadow.

After the grandfather passed away, Hana's capable mother took over the household. She left Jacob alone to follow his way of life at the shul and managed to keep the family afloat while farming. Jacob's four daughters grew up in relative comfort, and when three of them reached the proper age they were married to decent Jewish men in other villages. They were all pretty and smart and married easily despite the fact that the dowries Jacob and his wife could provide were quite meager. Hana was the youngest. She had been born at the time when her parents thought that they would have no more children. She had brightened their days before she came into the world since they thought that God would finally grant them a son. When Hana was born, they were more disappointed then ever. She was not cherished as much as her siblings had been although she was never neglected. She was, nevertheless, the best of Jacob's children. Diligent and pleasant, she also charmed everybody in sight with her enchanting eyes. They were black as coal, almond-shaped, lustrous, and deep as a well. Her long, dense lashes covered them modestly as a bride's fancy veil. They were her finest asset.

At sixteen, Hana was very popular in the village. There were not too many young people around and she, with two of her friends, enjoyed more freedom than girls their age in the city. They used to roam the hills that surrounded the valley and looked as healthy and happy as any of the gentile peasant girls. The five young Jewish bachelors that were available kept to themselves and expected their parents to find them a wife when the time came. Actually, only four of them; the fifth, Shloyme, was a free soul. He talked to the girls when nobody was around and told them funny stories about the inhabitants of the valley. He was not particularly interested in the study of the Torah and Talmud, and planned to leave the village and live in the city where his uncle had a store. One summer, after visiting his relative, he came back a changed person. Hana noticed right away that his behavior was different and that he spent hours reading some newspapers and looking into the void, as if he saw something nobody else could. When asked what was bothering him, he just smiled and looked away as if he was afraid they would discover a secret hidden in the depths of his blue eyes.

One warm autumn afternoon, as Hana was leading the geese back from the pond, she saw Shloyme sitting under a tree deep in thought. She would have loved to surprise and scare him a little but the geese were too noisy. He turned his head, saw her coming towards him and stood up waving and smiling.

"Hanale," he said, "I am so happy to see you alone, there is something I want to tell you but you have to promise not to discuss it with anybody."

Hana sat down under the tree, making sure she would not lose sight of the geese and pleased to be able to rest a bit. She was a short, plump girl and not very agile. Looking up at Shloyme, who kept standing, she asked: "I have noticed how preoccupied you have been since you came back from town. You can tell me, I won't say a word and maybe I can help you, after all what are friends for!"

Shloyme kneeled next to her and began telling her how he had met a group of very special people in the city who had convinced him that it was his destiny and duty to leave the village. He had promised to follow them to the Holy Land and help build a new home for the Jews.

"Hanale," he said, "These are Zionists and they are full of enthusiasm and hope. They do not believe that we have to wait for the Messiah in order to reach the Holy Land, they are positive that we have to create a Jewish country with our own hands and that it is possible. I believe it too and I am going to follow in their footsteps. First I have to go to Moravia where I will be trained. After the Hachsharah, I will join a group of Halutzim and we will depart for the land of our forefathers. Here, take these newspapers, you know how to read after all, look at them and tell me if all this does not sound like an answer to a dream! Imagine, leaving this godforsaken place and reaching Jerusalem!"

Hana was listening to Shloyme with a perplexed expression. She had heard her elders talk about the Zionists but always with a lot of distaste, calling them traitors and disbelievers. Nobody but the Messiah could lead the children of Israel to their land and until then the Jewish people were destined to suffer. That was the belief of all the Orthodox Jews in the valley and nothing could convince them otherwise. On the other hand, Hana's mother had taught her to read and she had learned enough about the history of the Jews to sympathize with the idea of one's own land and going back to one's roots. Yet, all that had been far removed from her own life and now suddenly she seemed to be in the midst of it, not knowing what to say and how to react.

Before she could collect her thoughts, Shloyme was asking her to marry him and join him on his way to Palestine. He stressed that it would be easier for them to leave as man and wife and they did not even have to tell their parents about their real plans, just that they were leaving to work in Shloymes uncle's shop.

Hana looked at Shloyme's flushed face, saw his eyes sparkling with excitement, and sensed that he was asking her to be his wife not because he loved her but out of convenience. She did not know it at that time, but found out later that the people who recruited settlers for Palestine accepted only married couples to ensure a bigger population in years to come. Her heart went out to Shloyme but she did not love him. She had tried many times to imagine the man who would be her husband and each time was able to picture the figure of a tall, muscular man. She could even "hear" his deep, musical voice at times but the face always remained blank, without any features. No matter how hard she tried, the face remained unfilled. . . . One thing she was sure of, she could not fit Shloyme's looks into that empty space.

Two weeks later Shloyme was gone and his parents were devastated. In the end, he had told them the truth and left them immersed in their sorrow, bewailing the loss of their oldest son.

Soon Hana started getting letters from Moravia. At first they were just short notes from Shloyme, telling her how well he was doing in the Zionist retreat in the Bezkyd Mountains and that he wished she was there with him. Later he mailed her fliers, clippings from different newspapers and even a picture of himself with a group of smiling young people, men and women holding hands under tall evergreens. Hana's mother was not thrilled with the correspondence but she did not object to it, hoping that Hana might marry Shloyme after all. She, nevertheless, concealed it from her husband, who was not well and whose temper she feared. As he became older, Jacob developed a tendency to scream and curse if something did not appeal to him, and Hana's mother could not deal with him when he became surly.

Hana had tried to explain to her mother that she could never marry Shloyme since she did not love him but the older woman could not understand what her daughter meant. Love to her was a habit, the responsibility one felt for and the care one gave to someone who belonged to the family, the respect a woman bestowed on the man she was destined to live with. Eventually Hana stopped talking to her mother and became somewhat depressed and desolate. Although Shloyme was not her sweetheart, she suddenly realized that he could help her get out of the valley and escape the same kind of life her mother lived. She wrote to him, telling him that she had decided to join the group.

Hana faced the dilemma of how to travel to Moravia without disclosing to her parents the real reason for her departure. By sheer luck she got an invitation from one of her sisters, who lived in Slovakia, to come and visit over the winter. Her parents did not see any reason for her not to go and within a few days, before the onset of the cold weather, she left her native village. She embraced her mother and kissed her father's hand sadly, feeling deceitful and guilty, yet the urge to leave was much stronger than her conscience. She also knew deep down in her heart that most probably she would never return.

Hana's sister, Rachel, lived in a village in Slovakia, at the foothills of the Tatra Mountains, not too far from the Moravian border. Sučany had a landscape similar to Hana's native village but it was much bigger and so was the number of its Jewish inhabitants. There were a few stores that sold fancy ware that came from as far as Vienna, and Hana's oldest sister, who was a kindhearted woman and pretty well off, bought her some nice clothes. She was somewhat shocked when she heard of Hana's plans to travel to the town of Moravská Ostrava in Moravia to join the group of Zionists at the Bezkyd retreat. However, she promised to keep the secret until Hana reached her destination and only then let their parents know the truth. Rachel admired the courage that Hana displayed, particularly since she could not imagine herself in Hana's shoes. The older sibling was very much the way their father used to be, quiet and of a melancholy disposition, and always anxious not to rock the boat under any circumstances. Hana left Sučany within a few days and this time there was hope in her heart as she felt that nobody but herself was responsible for her decisions and her fate.

The Bezkyd Mountains, where the Zionist retreat was, were covered with deep snow when Hana arrived and she shivered all night in the small wooden cabin that served as a bedroom to the seven girls who had joined the group. The leaders believed in harsh, Spartan training which would be of benefit to them once they reached Palestine. Hana got a thin blanket and no pillow to put on the hard wooden board. Not being able to sleep because of the intense cold, she thought longingly of her bed at home and the heavy down cover she had had since childhood. The days were long and exhausting but the evenings were the worst. She had a hard time keeping her eyes open listening to the lectures and discussions that went on for hours. Some of the topics were beyond her and she was not shrewd enough to pretend to know what they were talking about; discussions about God and the creation of the Universe; the fact that there was something that existed beyond space, since even darkness was not nothing but something; their plans to build settlements in specific places in Palestine; and their loud mockery of the orthodox belief in the Messiah.

Shloyme had become a leader and, although he treated her nicely, did not pay too much attention to her. He had found interest in one of the local girls and Hana felt left out. It was not jealousy that plagued her, just the realization that she had lost a good friend, somebody with whom she had been comfortable in the past and had shared her childhood. When one of the girls happened to mention that her uncle had a grocery store in Moravská Ostrava, and that he was always looking for hired help, she made a mental note of the name of the shop and street where it was located. The next morning she told the leaders of the group that she was leaving. They tried to convince her that she was doing the wrong thing but, adamant as she was, she did not give them a specific reason for her departure, except to say that she felt she would not be a good Halutz and needed more time to decide about her future.

She was lucky to secure a job in the food store the girl had mentioned and even more fortunate to find grace in the eyes of the owner. The old man treated her kindly and helped her find a room in a widow's house. Hana got used to a rather ordinary life in the town of Ostrava. The mining town was far from being glamorous. The soot from the coal mines filled the air at all times, and the snow became black and muddy once it hit the ground. People tried to avoid the outdoors when a strong wind blew from the north but did not hesitate to venture out of their homes when the wind blew in the opposite direction towards Poland, which was only a stone's throw away. Nevertheless, it was a big town, and there was entertainment available, shops to look at, and places to eat, even though she could not afford much and did not dare to go out by herself. Her landlady joined her for walks sometimes, and occasionally they visited the local synagogue where Hana wanted to pray but did not know exactly what to ask for. And then one day, as she was sitting in the women's section, in a secluded corner reserved for unmarried girls, she suddenly envisioned the figure of her future mate and realized that the face was still blank. From that day on, she prayed to meet the man she would love and spend her life with. That became for her a source of great consolation since she had not lost her faith.

He was leaning against the store counter when she walked in one day after lunch. It was a mild spring day and Hana had taken a stroll and enjoyed the fresh air that even the coal mines could not spoil all the time. She quickly put on her apron and approached the customer. As he turned around, and she saw his face for the first time, she gasped. His was the most unusual face she had ever seen. The large aquiline nose was most striking and the dark piercing eyes framed by the heavy eyebrows gave the man a somewhat menacing countenance. His mouth nevertheless was soft, large, and heart shaped. When he looked at Hana, he smiled and she saw the glitter of his flashing white teeth. Her heart skipped a beat when she heard his deep, melodious voice which sounded somewhat familiar although she knew she had never met him before. He introduced himself and politely asked for some items he wanted to purchase. When he left she realized that she had found the features that fit into her image of the blank face.

He came back every day after their first encounter. His name, he told her, was Ivo Kovár and he worked as a salesman for one of the mining companies in town. One evening she found him waiting for her in front of the shop and when he asked whether he could escort her home, she accepted willingly. He gallantly offered her his arm and flashed one of his daunting smiles. He asked her many questions about the Podcarpathian region and listened attentively when she described her life prior to coming to Ostrava. Initially he did not tell her much about himself since he was mainly anxious for her to have a good time and enjoy their outings. The most memorable event for her was the time when he took her to the theater. She had never seen a performance before and could not have enjoyed an evening more. He had a sense of humor that was somewhat out of the ordinary and at first she was not sure whether he was just joking or making fun of her and her previous way of life.

"Do your people in the village still await the Messiah?" he asked her once.

When she admitted that indeed was the case, he asked her seriously if she had any idea when he would arrive. She mentioned that the rabbi of Ushgorod had had a dream and predicted the coming of the Messiah in the following year.

"So now there are two of them," mumbled Ivo with a smirk.

"What do you mean?" asked Hana.

"Well," said Ivo, "the old one and the new. The elderly, tired Messiah and the idea of Palestine. Each an illusion."

"What do you mean?" asked Hana again. She felt that there was something wrong in the way he approached the issue of the

Messiah as she believed that a Jew could not speak with irreverence about something that sacred and basic to the Jewish faith. Ivo would not elaborate and rather continued asking her questions about her family and the two months she had spent training in the Bezkyd Mountains.

Within a few weeks they got so very attached to each other that they had to meet every day. Hana had never been happier and it showed. Ivo complimented her often on the special beauty of her marvelous eyes that sparkled with an intense light each time she looked at him. The day she was hoping for came sooner than she expected. One evening, when it was raining cats and dogs and they found refuge from the nasty weather in a small coffee shop, Ivo asked her to marry him. But before she could react, he told her something so unexpected that her blood froze in her veins and she could not move for a while.

"You must know, my beloved Hanale," he said, "that I am not a Jew."

Hana was speechless, it had never occurred to her that Ivo was not Jewish and all she could do at that moment was to gaze at his big nose. "Only a Jew could own such an enormous nose," she thought. "And what about his black piercing eyes? Those were not the eyes of a goy!! And all his knowledge of Judaism was not something he could have just read about, it was part of his soul, part of his being!" She felt sure of that. There was no mistake on her part. So why was he saying he was not a Jew?

Ivo did not say anything for a while, as if he knew what was going on in her mind and wanted to give her time to sort things out. After a few minutes, he told her that he had been born Jewish but had given up his religion since he had no belief in God. He had been born Isaac Kohn and had changed his name when he left the faith of his forefathers. He could not force her to marry him but knew that she loved him as much as he loved her and that he was a good person. He would never impose his beliefs on her. He was more than willing to talk and explain his views to her but she could pursue her way of life just as before. He just wanted to spend the rest of his life with her and be happy.

Hana got up and ran out of the store. She stood in front of the coffee shop with the rain drenching her uncovered hair and the tears streaming down her face. She knew she could not give up Ivo, she could not ask him to change either, but it meant that she would lose her family since they would never ever accept him as their son-in-law. Ivo had followed right behind her and was looking at her with a sorrowful and worried expression on his face. He looked somewhat grotesque in the dim light of the street lantern, a big, husky man standing immobilized and fretful with the rain gathering on the brim of his hat and cascading down in uneven streams. Suddenly Hana felt as if something had broken and given way inside her and she started to laugh. The sound mingled with the falling raindrops, and before she knew it she was in his arms holding on to him as if for dear life and crying as if her heart was breaking.

They exchanged words of endearment and were completely oblivious to what was going on around them, until they realized that many people in the coffee shop were standing at the windows, watching them, and clapping hands. Some lifted their beer steins and shouted congratulations, and it was obvious they all had enjoyed the unusual spectacle of two lovers making up in public. Embarrassed, Ivo and Hana thanked them with a smile and hurried to their respective homes, deliriously happy and completely soaked. They were thankful they had not caught pneumonia that fateful day when they got engaged.

When Hana met Ivo's parents she was truly touched and fell in love with them immediately. The old couple lived in a nice apartment and shared a wonderful relationship. They constantly helped each other and held hands anytime they felt like it, expressing their deep affection for each other. They were not ashamed to show it to the whole world, Hana thought how different they were from her own parents and how she would have liked it if her mother and father had loved each other the same way. Ivo's father had worked in the same company Ivo now did and had been retired for a few years. They were not rich but comfortable and well taken care of by their son who worried about them all the time. As frail as they looked, they were resilient and independent and hoped that Hana would be able to make Ivo, or Iso as they called him (based on his real name Isaac), realize it and make him fuss less about them. They felt somewhat responsible and guilty that Ivo had turned away from his faith because it was they who had always encouraged him to think for himself and make his own judgments and decisions. They were not religious themselves but kept the tradition and believed in God. They knew that Ivo was an exceptionally bright and fine man, and as such they could not complain and definitely did not want to judge him. Hana had noticed with delight the beautiful silver mezuzah on the doorpost but was saddened to hear that it was empty. The scroll had been removed once when they had the apartment painted and the workers had sealed the openings with the oil paint so that they could not insert the scroll back in its place.

"We have forgotten so many things, my dear," said Ivo's mother. "We have ... but not everything. We still know who we are and so does Iso, although he won't admit it. We still feel Jewish, very much so, although we do know that we are not God's chosen children and He does not love us more than others."

Hana did not respond, she just thought how all this sounded so different from what her father had told her when she left her village: "Always remember, daughter, that you should give due respect to the goyim, maybe even more than they deserve if necessary, but remember who you are. Never forget that you are a princess, a child of the chosen people of God."

Ivo promised Hana to visit her native village and try to get her parents' consent for their marriage. Hana wrote to them about her engagement and that she wanted them to meet her future husband. Her mother responded happily and mentioned that her father seemed to be pleased that she was going to have a good life. He was also relieved since Ivo did not want a dowry which Jacob could not have come up with. It never occurred to them that there might be a problem. Hana had told them that Ivo had changed his name but that did not seem to worry them in particular, since they assumed that he was Jewish.

It was a cold, wintry day when they arrived at Hana's parents' farm and the whole village was frozen under a cover of snow. The trip had been difficult. The last segment was almost unbearable. The old horses could hardly pull the cart, and the driver kept hitting them with the whip each time they stopped. Hana was extremely uneasy and felt that a disaster was awaiting her at home. Ivo did not say much but sat quietly, watching Hana's pale face, and holding her hand. Hana's mother had prepared a festive meal and, when they arrived, initially everything went well. Hana's father had grown old and looked much weaker than he had before, but he was wearing his Sabbath clothes and looked dignified as he greeted them with a happy smile. They spent a pleasant evening talking about different things, avoiding as was the custom the topic of the upcoming wedding.

After dinner the dreaded moment came. Hana and her mother left the men alone while they were busy cleaning up in the kitchen. Soon they heard the father's high-pitched angry voice screaming at Ivo and calling him the enemy of Israel. Ivo had promised to tell Hana's father as gently as he could that he no longer followed the ways of Abraham but news of that kind could not be accepted by Jacob, no matter how well it was put. Hana and her mother ran into the dining room and saw Jacob, as small and as withered as he was, standing straight and proud in front of the towering Ivo and asking him to leave his house. There was no way he would agree to the marriage of his daughter. Even a goy would be preferable since he believed in something, but a person who did not believe in God was better considered dead. Ivo was trying to keep calm. He turned towards Hana's mother and told her that he was not going to influence Hana in any way. She would be always as Jewish as she wanted to be, but there was no way of convincing Jacob. He stood in the middle of the room, his face flushed, his eyes flashing and his finger pointing to the door.

They spent a sleepless, miserable night, sitting up dressed with their luggage all packed. When morning finally dawned they summoned the cart and left with a feeling of doom. The last thing they saw was Jacob, pale and almost transparent as a ghost, sitting on the floor, with the lapel of his coat cut and saying the prayers for his "dead" daughter. Hana's mother was standing in the background, her dark eyes were full of tears and her mouth twisted with sorrow, but she did not tear her clothes nor did she take off her shoes and sit barefoot next to her husband on the floor. She whispered something, but it was not the prayer for the dead, nor was it a curse. Hana read her lips and understood, her mother was blessing her despite all the trepidations and agony. She loved her daughter and that was all that mattered. The horses took off with great speed and Hana closed her beautiful, sad eyes. She did not want to see the landscape, she did not want to see anything at all. She wanted to remember one thing, just one thing, and that was her mother sending her off with a blessing.

10
The Seamstress

Beckie sat at her sewing machine in her small house in Brooklyn. She was in a pensive mood and, as was her habit everyday, she reminisced. She did it day after day, always at the same time in the early morning. She believed that only by recollecting and dwelling on the past—without becoming sentimental, only musing with maybe just a little bit of nostalgia—one could truly evoke the old days. That way she kept her memory active and prevented her mind from becoming sloppy and negligent. Her memories were her magic pill, the herbs that filled her days with a fragrance that only she could detect. If she sometimes had a lapse in the flow of events she would go to the albums and look at the old faded photos. Then the spell would end and she would be able again to access most of the recollections she cherished. Yet lately. . . .

Beckie was worried and her trepidations grew with every passing day. After all she was in her early nineties, a widow and living alone, and knew that one day, maybe sooner than one thought, she would be gone and with her all the memories. She had been in relatively good health for her age and although her life had not been as eventful as those of many of her friends, she wanted her memories to go on living in the hearts of the people she loved—most of all in her beloved granddaughter, Michele. She looked at the old Singer sewing machine, which she hardly used anymore but sat at while collecting her thoughts and reached a decision. She got up and placed a call to her granddaughter asking her to come and visit her as soon as she could. The young woman who was a librarian had just finished her studies at Berkeley and made it a habit to visit her grandmother every week. Beckie explained to her that she was fine and just wanted to talk. She was anxious not to worry Michele unnecessarily, that being the trademark of most Jewish people since time immemorial.

From that day on, Michele listened to her grandmother for many hours and was able to relive the events that the old lady described so vividly. Sitting at the sewing machine which she used as a desk or think tank, Beckie began relating the saga of her life which was the precious gift she offered her granddaughter, the inheritance she possessed and wanted to pass on.

"One of the things I remember most," said Beckie, "are the wonderful challas my stepmother used to bake. Those were no ordinary challas. My stepmother was like an artist when she handled the dough and out of the oven came the most wonderful creations I have ever seen: golden round challas for Rosh Hashanah to symbolize the continuity between the beginning and the end, and ladder-shaped challas for Yom Kippur hoping that our prayers will reach heaven. On special Sabbaths she made a challah that depicted two hands joined in supplication asking God for a succession of good life. Meshka was a good stepmother, the younger sister of my mother Hinda who married my father after his first wife Chia-Basha passed away and later she too died. Chia-Basha had been the oldest of the three sisters and all of them were kind-hearted women. Meshka had eight children to take care of and was very good to all of them. She died of old age after a peaceful and happy life with my father who built brick houses for rich people. He was a kind man and I recall fondly that often I was sent to bring him his lunch in a small pail. He was a big eater and loved his rye bread, herring, and selzer. He was particularly happy on bright, warm days which fitted his sunny disposition.

"The turbulent times following the partition of Poland in 1795 were only a distant memory by now, and things were quite easy on the Jews living in the northeastern part of Polish country where I come from. There was no hardship in being Jewish and I received the traditional education girls were given in those days. I studied in a woman's home and learned Yiddish, arithmetic, history, and geography and what you today call home economics. We went to the synagogue every Friday and Saturday and I had many friends except that all were Jewish. I was not allowed to play with gentiles although there was no animosity among us.

"At the age of eleven I joined my brother Izzy on his trip to Warsaw. He was a shoemaker looking for a job and I became an apprentice to a seamstress. However, the people there did not treat me well. The lady of the house was a domineering woman, so self-centered that she became mean anytime something did not appeal to her. Her behavior most of the time bordered on the ridiculous. If the wind blew in her face, a tree shed some leaves on her hat, or the weather was too hot, she took it personally and became enraged. People tiptoed around her and the only good quality she could be complimented on was that she had excellent taste and was outstanding at her job as a seamstress. Yet I could not communicate with her and the rest of her household were helpless and could not come to my aid when she became abusive. Finally I decided to go back home, to the small town of Amdur, rather than suffer. Izzy would not let me travel by myself and joined me on my way back home. My parents were rather relieved that I had had the good sense to leave a bad situation. Soon after our return I found a position in Grodno and there, thanks to a master teacher, I became an excellent seamstress.

"At the age of sixteen I became independent. I bought a good pair of scissors, a measuring tape, needles and threads, a Singer machine for 90 rubles, and rented a space that became my shop. A year later I had eight seamstresses working for me making linens and underwear for men and women. My business was flourishing and I was satisfied with the outcome.

"My shop was a small place and very modestly furnished. I had a couple of mirrors on the wall, some flower arrangements to make life pleasant for the workers, and a small kitchen in the back where we prepared simple meals. Our customers were mainly Jewish men and women who could not afford expensive clothes but wanted good material and quality workmanship which we provided. Therefore I was very surprised one day when a very well-dressed gentile woman came in and ordered a few sets of female underwear that were out of the ordinary. She had brought her own material which was silk, not cotton and linen, and most of the colors of the cloth were bright and shiny. We accepted the order and worked with that particular customer for a couple of years. She paid very well and needed a lot of the fancy underwear, so we provided her the best of services although I suspected who she was. The elegant lady stopped coming one day and we never found out why. She had been the owner of a house of ill repute and the merchandise was for the girls that worked for her. Some of my friends accused me of bad morals and of helping sinners in their deeds, but I was in need of money and had never passed judgment on other people's actions, particularly those I had no connection with other than business. Then the woman vanished from my life and never again did I make underwear for prostitutes."

Beckie smiled when she saw the look of surprise on her granddaughter's face. "Well," she said, "there must have been a reason for those girls to do what they did, not for the fun of it, I am sure. They probably were in bad need to make a living and the poor souls could not come up with another solution. Some people are helpless and afraid of taking chances while others do not realize that what they are doing is wrong. Once you start sliding, often there is nothing to hold on to and soon you reach the depth of the chasm.

"But . . . do I have a nicer story for you? Do I have a story for you!! A love story at that, my dear, a real, nice, sweet love story that is my own," continued Beckie and her brown eyes lit up while her whole face expressed bliss and the wrinkles seemed to vanish from her face as if her memories erased the years that had passed.

"My store and the apartment I lived in were at the outskirts of town. There were many soldiers who came to Grodno for the weekends and one day two of them passed by my shop. They stopped to look at the display in the small window and saw me working at my sewing machine. It was a very hot, humid day and I noticed they exchanged a few words and then opened the door of the shop and walked in. They asked me politely for some water to drink since there were still far away from downtown and very thirsty. Both of them were Jewish and had enlisted into the army for the required four years. In those days Jews were permitted to do so and some of them even made a career out of their military service. They were very polite young men and after a short, very pleasant conversation they left. One of them, nevertheless, came back . . . more than once.

"Yankel made it a habit to visit me each time he was on leave and soon enough we were the best of friends. He told me stories about his life as a soldier and talked most of the time while I listened. The women who worked in the shop used to giggle behind my back but I decided to ignore them. I loved seeing Yankel and he shared the same feelings. He was not a very handsome man, not too tall or strong looking but I loved to look into his green eyes that had yellow speckles in them and listen to his mellow voice. One day he was unusually silent and stayed longer than was his habit. When the last of my workers left for the day, he looked at me pleadingly and caressing the top of my sewing machine (Beckie put her hand on the polished wood of the sewing machine she was sitting at), he said to me, his voice shaking, 'Will you marry me? You mean the world to me and I do not think I can go through life without you!'

"I had been hoping for his proposal and was delirious with happiness. He had assumed that I would say yes since he had brought me a gift. It was a beautifully embroidered handkerchief, like the ones Polish women in the villages are so wonderful at. It had little red hearts all around the edges and the center chock full of all kinds of wildflowers. When you opened it and put it on your lap it was almost as if one had a field of spring flowers blooming in one's apron. I was delighted, being a seamstress I could appreciate even more than any other person the exquisite beauty of the embroidery. I thanked Yankel wholeheartedly for his very lovely and sweet present.

"We waited for three years to get married until Yankel finished his military service. He traveled to my parents' town to ask for their permission. To prove that he was an honorable man, he donated five hundred rubles to the rabbi in my name and bought me a diamond ring, earrings, bracelet, and a watch on a chain.

"Our wedding was a fairy tale. I had the most beautiful white dress, white shoes, and a red cape covered my shoulders. The wedding was outdoors in the shul's garden and people lined our way and cheered as we became man and wife. I felt like a princess but then this was the happiest day in my life and I would have felt the same even if we were married in a coal mine. After spending two days in Amdur we moved to my husband's town near Krakow.

"Yankel's father had not been to the wedding since he was a very sick man. Yankel's mother had died a long time ago. Despite his illness, my father-in-law was able to have our apartment furnished nicely and ready for us when we came to town. He was quite a wealthy man, owned several buildings, and rejoiced in our happiness. Although Yankel was a rich man's son he had learned a trade and, as soon as we settled down, he started working as a tailor and was very successful at it. Our first child, Anna, was born one year after we were married, and in our little world we thought things could never go wrong. But they did.

"When Anna was nine months old the Russian-Japanese war broke out. Yankel would have been drafted into the army had he not followed my advice. Taking all the money he could, he escaped to America promising that he would send for us as soon as he got things under control. I had been afraid to leave with a small baby since I would not have been able to work initially and worried that the burden of a family in a new, harsh environment would have been difficult for Yankel to handle. I did not tell Yankel the other reason, which was very much on my mind and in my heart, and that was that I loved Poland and my life there and it was extremely hard for me to leave the land I was born in. But I knew I could cope with it when the time came and I had to do it. I took care of my ill father-in-law for a while but unfortunately he passed away soon after Yankel left for America. When times got worse and the army moved some soldiers into our spacious apartment I took the baby and went back home to Amdur.

"Yankel wrote beautiful letters. He was doing very well and asked me to join him in America as soon as possible. I lingered on and on till I became sick, sick because of the continuous stress, longing for my husband, and the dilemma I had created. I was unwell for a couple of weeks and my brother's wife wrote to my husband instead of me. He became extremely worried and insisted I take a photograph with the baby and send it to him as soon as possible since he had had bad dreams that something terrible had happened to us. I sent him the picture and reached the decision to join him, although it was not simple or legal.

"One dark night, in the early winter of 1905, I hid in a farmer's wagon after bidding good-bye to my relatives. I had paid him a handsome sum of money to take us across the border. I held Anna close to my heart and prayed while the covered cart tumbled along the way. The horse that pulled the wagon was a strong, gray one, but pretty old and slow and we had to wait at certain places for long hours in order to continue stealing across the country side. I kept comforting myself knowing that each segment of the trip brought us closer to my husband. I had hardly any luggage but a lot of money hidden in my clothes. God did protect us since the trip was quite uneventful except for the hardship, particularly for the baby, and the fear that I felt all the time. The farmer, though, was very kind and provided us with food, especially fresh milk for Anna whenever he could.

"Finally we reached Belgium, the port city of Antwerp. With some of the money I had, I bought the passage to New York. The ship was not very big but the cabin we got was nice, on the deck, just for the two of us. It would have been pleasant if I had not been sick for the whole journey and suffered quite a bit, particularly since I was unable to take care of Anna and worried about her continuously. People, nevertheless, were very helpful and the baby never lacked anything. I felt somewhat better after thirteen days and at that time we were already approaching Ellis Island where Yankel was waiting for us. That was the second happiest day of my life when he was able to hold us in his arms and we felt again safe and sound. When people ask me about my voyage and I am not able to tell them much, I feel somewhat ashamed, especially when I hear the stories of misery and agony many of my friends experienced while traveling in the bottom of the ship under really harsh conditions. I think that maybe God granted me a favor and being sick I did not have to live through all that. I am grateful I had had the means to suffer less."

Beckie paused and looked at Michele lovingly. "Are you getting tired, my dear?" she asked. "This is quite a long story but I am almost at the end. You actually know the rest. Since the day Anna and I arrived and a ferry took us to Manhattan, we had a very happy life. Grandpa worked all the time and lost his job making velvet collars for men's overcoats only during the strike of 1913. Still, we had enough money saved for a rainy day. We lived in several apartments on the East side and moved each time our family grew. Finally we bought this house in Brooklyn where all five kids grew up. Your mother Rose, my sweet, had a happy childhood just as her siblings did. We had some bad times but mostly good times and never lost our love and faith in each other. We have always kept our Jewish tradition and our Friday dinners were special. Yankel loved my roast chicken and carrot tzimmes. He always ate everything and anything I cooked. We knew that some others had more than we had and others had less. We did what we could for ourselves and also for others. We managed to bring a few relatives from Russia and did mitzvot wherever we could. I still do."

Beckie had prepared some tea and was drinking it Russian style, putting a sugar cube in her mouth and sipping the tea from a small saucer. "Ah, Ah," she said, "This is delicious!" Suddenly tears came into her eyes as she continued her story.

"Yankel died young from emphysema when he was fifty-nine. I have been without him for thirty-four years. I still miss him tremendously and feel quite lonely. Most of the time I am by myself despite the fact that my family is very good to me and relatives visit me often. Also," she said and smiled naughtily, "I should say that I have a permanent companion. Last year they put a pacemaker into my body and he takes good care of me! Drink up, drink up sweetheart, do not feel sad, I have had a good life, I am content and I am still around. I love America and have been very proud to be a citizen. I have voted in every single election since women got the vote! I also do think a lot about the country of my birth and feel only sorry I never went back to visit. It is too late now." She paused and thought for a while, "Maybe one day, in another life, I will be able to go back, when I am different, when God will extricate me from this form and I will be free. . . ."

Beckie died in October of 1977. A few days after the funeral Michele received a very special gift from her grandmother. When she opened the crate that was delivered to her apartment, she found in it the old Singer sewing machine and on top of it, nicely folded and wrapped in tissue paper the same handkerchief, somewhat yellow and faded, that Yankel gave his beloved bride many years ago.

11

The Abyss

In a small Moravian town, towards the end of the sixteenth century, there lived a rich Jewish jeweler who had a lovely daughter. Abraham Mendel had been a widower for many years and his only child was the apple of his eye, his most precious possession, the crown jewel he cherished more than anything in the world. And indeed Miriam was very beautiful. Her skin was white and lustrous as a pearl, her lips red as a ruby, her hair the color of onyx and her eyes deep green as the most valuable emeralds. She was also blessed with a very pleasant disposition and delighted everybody with her sweet singing. No wonder her father wanted to find for her the best of all husbands and nobody seemed to fit the picture he had created in his mind.

One day a carpenter came to see the jeweler who needed a good craftsman to fix some of the old, valuable furniture in his house. The young man appealed to Abraham Mendel when he saw how well an ancient chest had been repaired. It had belonged to Mendel's wife and was very precious to him. The carpenter was a very gifted artisan and the jeweler entrusted the task to him with confidence. Miriam noticed the buoyant handyman, whose name was Rupert, and they exchanged long looks although they never dared to speak to each other in her father's presence. It did not occur to the old man that these two young people might feel attracted to each other since he knew that Rupert was a humble Christian and as such regarded him as one of the servants who would pose no danger to his darling daughter. Yet, Rupert was so very different from the other young men Miriam had seen and she liked his tall frame, his blue smiling eyes, and the way his large, strong hands handled the wood and polished it. Soon they became good friends and talked to each other, whenever the father was absent. Rupert's work was long term since the jeweler had neglected his home after his wife's death and wanted to have everything fixed nicely before his daughter's marriage. Rupert was in no rush to finish his assignments, and the jeweler, who wanted the best of quality work, never pressured him with deadlines. Things had to be done right and Rupert was the best carpenter Abraham Mendel had ever hired.

One summer evening, Abraham Mendel returned home earlier than expected and saw his daughter and Rupert talking and laughing. They were so absorbed in each other that they did not notice the livid old man standing behind the rose trellis where they were holding hands. The jeweler was speechless with anger and a deep feeling of fear overcame him. He left the place unseen and sat down in his chambers to recover from the shock. In his eyes, Rupert's treachery was the greatest, meanest crime and he could not tolerate that. It never entered his mind that maybe they had fallen in love with each other without Miriam being forced into it. The jeweler's priceless pearl had been stolen from him and he had to recover what was his. He had heard the devotion they expressed for each other and swore that those glowing feelings had to be extinguished. Miriam had promised Rupert to follow him wherever he went even if it meant forsaking her belief. She was angry with the faith of her forefathers that would not permit her to marry a man outside her religion. Her father was devastated that she was so bewitched and did not realize what it meant. He knew deep down in his heart that he had to save her from falling into the bottomless pit.

Some time passed. The jeweler did not terminate Rupert's work and behaved towards him the same way he had before. Then one day he asked him to leave on an assignment to inspect and purchase for him a piece of antique furniture in a neighboring town and bring it home. Rupert brought the beautiful old chair back with him but he seemed to be ill at ease. The day after his return he collapsed at his work bench and fell seriously ill. The doctor who was summoned did not know what was wrong with him and within a couple of days Rupert passed away.

The whole town followed his casket to the cemetery since he had been liked by many people. He had no family of his own but was very popular thanks to his good nature, warm personality, and wonderful workmanship. The only person who was not present at the funeral was Miriam. She was petrified as if she had turned into a stone statue. From the moment she heard the horrible news, she could not move, speak, or cry. Grief and anguish, such as she had never experienced before, overcame her completely. Joy had been taken out of her life, and neither her father nor anyone else could console her. She spent her days in her room gazing vacantly into space as if her spirit had departed from her body.

About a week after the burial, the day of All Saints was celebrated by the Christian population of the town. That same night Abraham Mendel could not sleep. He kept tossing and turning in his bed hearing a voice telling him over and over again: "Miriam is not yours to own, she is not yours, she is not yours . . . not yours, not, not . . . " Finally, feeling exhausted and in pain, he got up to pray. As he was putting on his shawl, suddenly he saw a translucent Rupert passing through the closed door and approaching his bed. In deadly fear, Abraham held on to his prayer book but Rupert did not stop and, crossing the room, disappeared into the adjacent one which was Miriam's. Abraham's knees gave way and he fell to the ground. He thought he heard Rupert's voice as well as his daughter's echoing from the other room as if in a void and then he fainted. The next morning when they resuscitated him and he rushed to his daughter's room, he found her lying dead on her bed, her body already cold.

The news of Miriam's strange demise traveled quickly through town and the authorities started investigating. Abraham told them about the apparition he had seen that ill-fated night, and rumors of his daughter's and Rupert's love began circulating. The judge ordered Rupert's body exhumed and asked Abraham to be present at that time. The old jeweler was still in shock and hardly made it to the cemetery where the dismal event was taking place. The casket was already open and the cadaver exposed when he arrived. As he approached the grave, Abraham suddenly noticed that the eyes of the deceased had opened and that they were following him wherever he turned. In despair and panic, he admitted to all present that he had administered to Rupert a slow working poison that had taken his life within a couple of days. He had been forced to do so because Rupert had robbed him of his daughter and sentenced her to eternal damnation. They carried the old man to jail to await his trial.

The Jewish congregation of the town refused to bury Miriam in the Jewish grounds since they had found a cross hanging around her neck at the time of her death. Her tomb is in the Christian section of the graveyard, next to Rupert's. Abraham Mendel is not buried in the Jewish cemetery either. He could not bear his sorrow and guilt knowing that he was standing at the very same abyss from which he had tried to save his daughter. He committed suicide while in prison and was buried on the other side of the fence, an outcast to his people as well as everybody else.

12

The Hunchback

A poor young hunchback arrived one Friday evening, just before the Sabbath, at a little village in the heart of Hungary. He had been traveling for many days and once he found the synagogue, all he wanted to do was to lay his head on a bench and sleep. His stomach was crying out for food but his legs could not support him anymore, and he barely made it through the door. He collapsed in a corner of the temple and almost lost consciousness. He dreamed that he was back at home in the city with his parents when they were still alive and that his mother was cooking in the kitchen. He smelled the wonderful aroma of the chicken soup and the dumplings she prepared so well. And then again he saw himself in the hospital when his father lost his fortune and had a heart attack just after his mother had succumbed to a severe cold and died.

Within a few days he found himself on the streets without a home, exposed to the cruelty and mockery of people who laughed at his deformity and were afraid to have anything to do with him. His parents had shielded him from the world and made him believe that the hunch on his back was no big deal and he was praised for his intelligence and diligence. A young scholar used to come to his house to teach him and convinced him that one day he would make a very fine rabbi. They had not too many friends and hardly any connection with the Jewish community so that when disaster struck, young Job was on his own.

Suddenly somebody was shaking him and he opened his eyes with difficulty. An old Jew was leaning over him asking him who he was. He was the shammes of the temple and invited him to his house for the Sabbath dinner. Job had slept through the services and since he had been hidden behind a bench, the shammes had discovered him just before locking up the shul. Job accepted the invitation with gratitude and followed the old man down a twisted alley. He thought his mind was playing tricks on him since he saw, as if through a veil, that the old man also had a hunch on his back. When they arrived at the shammes' home, Job realized to his amazement that not only the shammes but his wife and two daughters, all of them were hunchbacks.

He ate their simple dinner thankfully and told them about his misfortune. They insisted he spend the night in their house and in the morning, the shammes made him an offer to become his helper and work for him. As compensation Job would get his meals and a bench to sleep on in the synagogue as well as time to study. Job accepted without hesitation. He had no place to go and felt relieved to stay there at least for a while. The shammes and his family were very kind to him and he craved for their sympathy which, no doubt, they extended to him since they all were in the same boat.

Nevertheless, Job had second thoughts about his decision when he discovered that all the inhabitants of the village were hunchbacks. He could not believe his eyes, but every person he saw was misshapen. Initially he thought that fate had played a cruel joke on him and that he was doomed to see in front of his eyes continually what he wanted to forget about. Yet later when he realized that the people of the village lived their lives calmly without being concerned about their gnarled backs, he told himself that maybe it was a blessing that providence had led him to the one place where he was no different from others and where disfigurement was normal. In time he got used to the community and his new life although he promised himself that, no matter what, one day he would leave and go out into the world once again.

Time passed and Job became well known and respected by the community. His brightness, knowledge, and quick wit were admired by all. He was released from his duties as the shammes' helper and asked to teach and coach young men at the shul. The local rabbi, who was in his eighties, learned to rely on Job and hinted many times that he saw him as his successor. It was at this point that Job decided to leave. He liked the people and felt obliged to them but he did not want to become their rabbi and mainly he was set against marrying the shammes' older daughter. Although nothing had been said about it, Job knew that the shammes expected him to do so and he had trepidations just thinking about it. It was not that he disliked the girl. She was a very pretty and sweet lass and her hump did not bother him in particular, but it was this very deformity of hers and his own that prevented him from committing himself. He did not want his children to be born like that. His parents had told him that he had been crippled due to a fall when he was a baby, not because it ran in their family. He knew that if he married the shammes' daughter the child could be misshapen and he wanted to avoid that by all means. So one night, after writing a lengthy letter to the shammes and the rabbi explaining his departure and asking for their understanding and forgiveness, he left quietly, just as he had arrived two years earlier.

Job still had his hump when he left the village but he had become a different person. He had matured considerably in those two years and aged somewhat. His hair had turned almost gray and, despite being a young man, he looked much older and distinguished. Wherever he went the Jews looked at him with respect and it did not seem to matter anymore that he was disfigured. People did not seem to see his body but rather his mind and the intelligence that shone in his deep, dark eyes. Finally he settled down in a small community, not too far from Budapest, where he became a very well-respected rabbi.

It so happened that there lived a poor widow in that very same town whose daughter was very beautiful. The girl was not very young anymore but remained unmarried since she refused most of the young men in town. Nobody was good enough for her and so in time Judith was in danger of becoming an old spinster, particularly since she also had the reputation of being irascible.

Job saw her once in the synagogue and lost his heart to her. He was a reasonable man and knew she would not want him but he could not help but be smitten by her beauty. The matchmaker was sent to visit the widow who was ecstatic at the prospect of her daughter marrying the revered rabbi. The young woman though, as was her habit, refused with a smirk. Her mother tried to reason with her, pointing out all the benefits of her future life and the handsome face of the rabbi. If she avoided looking at him from the side or the back, the widow emphasized, she would not even know he had a hump. Finally, after days of supplication, tears, and moans, Judith agreed to meet the rabbi before she made up her mind.

The rabbi received her in his study, and she was somewhat impressed by his manners and dignified looks yet, when he turned his back to get her some refreshments, she could not but gasp. His crooked back gave her the shivers. She impatiently cut him off in the middle of a sentence and told him that she would not become his wife because he disgusted her. The rabbi remained silent for a moment and then told her: "As you wish. I cannot force you to become my wife but I must warn you that there will be consequences. I have been told that if somebody refused me in marriage solely because of my hump that particular person would be punished while I, although despondent, would be relieved of my burden. Please go look in the mirror behind you and you will see what I mean."

Judith turned around and looking in the mirror saw to her great horror that her frame had become bent and on her back she had a hump. She screamed and, twisting her body, tried to shake off the load she was carrying. But it was to no avail. The hump stuck to her back like glue. The rabbi had not moved but when she looked at him and at his back she realized that he, unlike her, stood straight and tall and there was no sign of any disfigurement. She kept jumping and hopping around, using tart and contentious words the rabbi had never heard before. But he kept his peace and, after a while, the exhausted Judith sank into a chair and begged the rabbi to help her. She promised to marry him if only he took back his hump and she became the way she had been before. And lo and behold, the instant she uttered her consent, things returned to the way they had been. The rabbi was a hunchback again and Judith's back was as straight as an arrow.

Judith married Job and was always in awe of him. She calmed down and although she remained spirited, lost her crabbiness and sharp tongue. They had a happy marriage and three children who were all good-looking and suffered no deformities.

One day a stranger arrived in town. He was an old rag merchant who traveled from hamlet to hamlet selling and buying merchandise. The rabbi, as was his habit, invited him for dinner, and the old man told him about his wanderings. He had been all over Hungary and knew the country like the palm of his hand. Job listened to him carefully and then asked him about the village of hunchbacks where he had spent two years of his life. The merchant looked at him with surprise. He had never visited a place like that. In all his years of extensive traveling he had never, ever, been to a place where all the inhabitants had been deformed. Such a place just did not exist.

13

The Treasure

One autumn day at dusk it was very silent in the depth of the woods. Only the sounds of some birds in their nests, the chirping of eager crickets, and the rustling of shriveling leaves falling to the ground disturbed the stillness. Suddenly the noise of a carriage drawn by two horses abruptly penetrated the quietude of the forest. Rabbi Isaac, the mayor of the Jewish ghetto of Prague, was on his way home from visiting a family in a nearby village. Since the day was coming to an end, the coachman had suggested taking a shortcut through the woods to get to the city before nightfall. Unfortunately he was not very familiar with the terrain and lost his way. They were traveling back and forth in the same area looking for a way out, and the rabbi was getting very tired and anxious. Daylight was fading and suddenly the rabbi noticed a bluish gleam ascending in front of them. He ordered the frightened coachman to a halt, got out of the carriage, and asked him to wait while he found out where the glow was coming from. He ventured a few yards into the thicket and suddenly came to a clearing where he saw a most unusual sight. Two dwarfs were busy collecting gold coins and glittering jewels that were dispersed all over the ground. They were gathering them into a sack and seemed to be in a great rush.

The rabbi watched for a while without being noticed and then he called out asking them what they were doing. The older of the dwarfs, who had a very long gray beard, looked at him angrily and replied: "It is none of your business!" and without further ado, vanished into thin air. The second imp was young and did not seem as hostile as the first one. He lingered, looking helplessly at the rabbi and then at the pile of gold and precious stones, and seemed to be at a loss as to what to do next.

"To whom does this belong?" asked the rabbi gently, anxious not to anger the dwarf and make him disappear.

"Not to you!" yelled the imp. The rabbi pleaded for an answer. "To one of your people," lashed out the little man, "and now that you interrupted our task you have created trouble!"

"Please, please tell me who that happy man is, I beg you!"

"I am not allowed to disclose that," snapped the dwarf.

The rabbi was really becoming frustrated but implored once again: "Could you at least give me a tiny hint, an idea what he looks like or when he will receive this magnificent gift?"

The little man looked at him mockingly and said: "When your daughter marries!"

The rabbi was greatly surprised to hear that and continued questioning the dwarf who would not say anything beyond what he had already told him. At the end the imp allowed him to exchange three coins from the pile of gold for three ducats which the rabbi took out of his purse. As soon as he picked up the coins, everything vanished from the clearing, the blue light faded until it was gone completely, and neither the dwarf nor the treasure could be seen. A strong wind started blowing. The rabbi hastened back to the carriage and ordered the coachman to speed up and get to Prague as quickly as possible. Suddenly a road appeared in front of them and dusk seemed to hold on for a while until they got out of the woods and saw the outline of the city in the distance.

Back in the Jewish ghetto, Rabbi Isaac was constantly plagued by a nagging concern. Why did the dwarf mention his daughter, his only child? How was she connected to the treasure? He pondered about it for days. One night, when the rabbi was falling asleep, he sensed something at the foot of his bed. He opened his eyes and to his delight saw the younger dwarf standing there and watching him. Before he could utter a word, the little man said: "Wrap each of the coins you took in a piece of paper and throw it out of the window into the street. Do this for three consecutive days and you will learn more." With that he disappeared and the rabbi woke up. He realized that it had been a dream, most probably a figment of his overworked imagination but, nevertheless, he decided promptly to follow the instructions.

He sat at the window the whole day watching the small packet lying on the street but, despite the fact that lots of people passed by, nobody seemed to notice it. He almost gave up, feeling tired and silly, when suddenly out of nowhere a young lad appeared. He was dressed in weather-worn clothes and looked haggard and pale. He walked straight to where the wrapped coin was, picked it up, and ran away. The rabbi was completely confused, worried, and somewhat angry. Was this the future owner of the treasure? This good for nothing, this beggar? Was he destined to marry his daughter? He threw the second coin out of the window the next day, and the boy appeared again and picked it up. Exactly the same happened the third day, and Rabbi Isaac knew by then that this was a real sign, not just a coincidence. His heart went out to his child destined to marry a pauper and to himself too, of course, since he did not want this to be his precious daughter's fate.

He had to find that lad! So what did he do? He had a notice posted all over town stating that he had lost three coins and asking the honest finder to return them to the rightful owner. The young boy came to the rabbi's house that very same day. He apologized to the mayor of his town and told him that he had had a strange dream for three successive nights. A little man had appeared and told him that he would find a wrapped coin under the mayor's window. The shocked rabbi did not doubt anymore that the lad was meant to be his future son-in-law and the proprietor of the great treasure. The boy returned only two of the coins, asking the rabbi to forgive him since he had already spent the other coin to buy some food. Rabbi Isaac, despite his trepidation, was touched by the boy's truthfulness and praised him for it. A few days later he visited the lad's home and talked to the parents about his future. The father was Solomon Maizl, a poor, half-blind Jew whom his son led every day to the synagogue to attend services. The mother ran a small hardware shop where she tried to make a living selling miscellaneous tools. Mordechai was their only child and the apple of their eyes. Good-hearted, diligent, and very bright, he was well liked in the whole neighborhood.

It was not very hard for Rabbi Isaac to convince Solomon Maizl and his wife to allow him to take care of their son but, it was the youngster who refused to forsake his parents and stop helping them. The rabbi hired a guide for the old man and a helper for the mother, and only then did the lad agree to take up the course of studies that the rabbi had suggested. In time he became a scholar and his talents were praised by all his teachers. He also endeared himself to the whole family of the rabbi and especially to the young daughter, but not Rabbi Isaac himself. The whole town praised the rabbi for his good deed and although nobody knew his secret, at times he felt quite uncomfortable because of his ulterior motive and dismissed the praise quite angrily. That made people admire him even more, and he was considered not only a benefactor but a very modest and pious one as well. Rabbi Isaac was pleased with the success of the young man despite his reservations and when Mordechai was twenty years old, he had him marry his daughter who was two years younger. The couple was very much in love and they were extremely happy.

Shortly after the wedding, Rabbi Isaac invited his son-in-law for an outing. He had visited the clearing in the forest a few times and knew exactly how to get there. He had even learned how to drive the carriage and control the horses so as not to reveal it to the coachman or anyone else. Mordechai followed his father-in-law's wishes without asking any questions. He felt immense reverence for him and respected him greatly. When they reached the woods and the spot was empty and forsaken, the rabbi decided to wait and spent the whole night sitting in the coach hoping for the treasure to reappear. When nothing did happen, he drove back before dawn and spent the next two days sulking in his chambers. Mordechai had no idea what it was all about and did not confide in his wife. The rabbi repeated the trip a few times and each time in vain. He had to admit to himself in the end, that he had been fooled by some nasty, evil forces, and that he had married his daughter to a poor man for nothing.

His dislike for Mordechai grew and the young man became despondent. He was fearsome that his father-in-law had become somewhat irrational and unstable. The trips to the forest and the long silent sessions among the tall, dense trees, made him suspect that Rabbi Isaac was looking for a communion with God through nature and that he wanted to share it with him. Later on, though, he did not know what to make out of it and often worried about his father-in-law's mental health. When the situation became unbearable, Mordechai decided that he and his wife should move out of the rabbi's mansion and live in the small house he had restored for his mother. Solomon Maizl had passed away a few years earlier, but Mrs. Maizl continued managing the store and, with her son's help, became quite prosperous. The house she lived in was small, but very pleasant and cozy. Mordechai's wife agreed to go and live with her mother-in-law. She had noticed her father's hostile behavior toward her husband and thought that the time had come to be on their own. Mordechai Maizl became one of the leading merchants of Prague. His hardware store grew in size and soon he was one of the richest men in town. His wealth, nevertheless, did not make him vain and he was very generous, helping as much as he could and doing it gladly with an open heart.

One summer day, just before harvest time, an old peasant, bent and with a long gray beard, came to his shop and asked for some tools. He urgently needed a scythe and a sickle, but had no money and asked Mordechai to defer the payment for a short while. Although Mordechai had never seen him before, he felt sorry for the old, withered man and thought he could trust him. He gave him the tools and the grateful farmer promised to return soon. A few days later, the old man reappeared and brought with him a big, old rusty trunk. Looking at Maizl thankfully, he said: "My dear sir, you have been very good to me and, since I do not have the money yet, I thought that I might give you this old trunk to hold till I come up with my payment. I do intend to pay, but if for some reason I do not return within a year please consider this yours!" Maizl weighed the heavy trunk and told the poor farmer: "This old iron trunk is worth much more than the tools I gave you. We could use the metal, if necessary. I will advance you some money. When you come back, you can pick up the trunk and we will adjust the payment!"

A year passed and Maizl had actually forgotten all about the deal. One evening, in a hurry to go home to his family, he was about to leave the shop when something made him stop. He suddenly caught a glimpse of the old rusty trunk in a corner of the shop and felt a strong urge to look inside. He thought it might be almost impossible to open it, but, as he touched the tarnished lock it opened up by itself as if by magic. And inside . . . Oh inside! Maizl could not believe his eyes: the number of golden coins was almost countless and the gleam of the precious stones made him breathless. When he overcame the shock of discovery, he sat down for a while to think what to do. He realized that the treasure was his, the old man had not claimed the trunk and Maizl had a strange feeling that it was meant to happen. He went to see his father-in-law and told him all about it. The rabbi, whose attitude over the years had softened considerably, was delighted with the news and told Maizl the whole story. He apologized for his silence, greed, and bad behavior and the two made peace.

Maizl disposed of the treasure very carefully. He invested a large amount of it very cautiously and contributed a large sum to the poor of the ghetto. He also built a new synagogue for the congregation and asked his father-in-law to keep it secret. However, Rabbi Isaac was remorseful and, on the opening day of the temple, declared that Maizl was the real benefactor and builder of the synagogue. Since that day it is known as the Maizl Synagogue and is one of the great treasures of Jewish Prague. Maizl continued to prosper and his wealth grew. He became one of the richest and most influential people in the land, sought by nobility and kings, and his reputation as a philanthropist spread far and wide. He built an orphanage, a mikveh for women, and a city hall. He had the narrow, dirty streets of the ghetto paved and the Jewish cemetery restored. He died in 1601. The street that bears his name still exists today in Josefov, the Jewish section of modern Prague.

The old iron trunk found its way into the cellar of the Maizl house and there it rested for years. When the story of the treasure leaked out and people began talking about it, one of the maids of the household noticed it in the cellar. For a while she avoided it but then her desire to open it up became stronger and stronger and finally one day, making sure she was all alone, she lifted the heavy lid. There was nothing in it except in one of the corners, almost completely hidden there was one small, forgotten coin, all by itself. The maid visited the cellar a few times hoping that by some miracle she would find additional money. Finally she had to accept the fact that it was not a magic trunk and that it would not produce coins or precious stones on its own. She stopped descending into the cellar and nobody looked into the trunk again. The old Maizl home has been destroyed since then and another house stands in its place. And where is the trunk? Does anybody have an idea? Who knows? Perhaps Mordechai Maizl's friend, the scholar and astronomer David Gans? If he had known where the trunk was and had seen it with his own eyes, maybe he would have believed the story, but as the tale goes he had not. Mordechai Maizl himself told him the real story of how he came into his great fortune. Old David Gans related his version to his friends one winter night as they sat around reminiscing about past times.

Mordechai Maizl did come from a very poor family and a very religious and devoted one. His father had been a butcher and was well respected by the community. When he became sick and half-blind, his widow had to make a living and worked for a rich man who owned a hardware store located in the best section in town. It occupied a whole floor of a corner building and sold different tools, regular as well as unusual ones, to the entire population of Prague. The proprietor of the shop was Jacob Saar who came from a family of successful merchants and was a benefactor of the Jewish community. He had been blessed with good fortune and his business prospered. Only in one area was he unlucky. God had not given him any descendants, and he and his wife Rebecca longed for children more than anything else in life. When he died early in his fifties, his widow remained all alone and that was the hardest ordeal she had ever had to bear. Since she had loved her husband deeply and spent most of her life with him, she felt extremely desolate and forsaken. Her wealth did not comfort her, neither did the relatives that suddenly appeared from nowhere and began courting her to find grace in her eyes. She spent her days in misery, mostly at home pacing the many rooms of the mansion, and sometimes wandering the streets of the old town like a body without a soul.

Mordechai Maizl was a young man in those days and had just opened a small hardware shop of his own which was doing well. His mother helped him as much as she could, but mostly she was confined to her bed because of rheumatic pain. Mordechai had known Jacob Saar and had been advised by him on how to deal with different aspects of the trade. The older man had treated him kindly and helped him establish his business despite the fact that he was a competitor. Mordechai saw how grief stricken the widow was and, contrary to the majority of people, did not think that she was going insane. He sensed that she was just very lonely and with nothing much to do except wallow in her sorrow.

Maizl went to visit Rebecca one day and asked for her help in the shop. She had assisted her husband for years and knew a lot about hardware. Rebecca consented happily and since that day spent most of her time helping Mordechai in his store. She refused to be given a salary since she did not need money, and Mordechai donated it to the orphanage upon her request. Rebecca worked with Mordechai for a couple of years until she became sick and died within a month after her initial illness. She was happy towards the end of her life, particularly since she was looking forward to seeing her husband again in after-life, and that happened much sooner than she ever thought. When she was on her deathbed, she summoned Mordechai, thanked him for his help, and asked him to take home a large bundle she had left for him in the corner. She had loved him for his sensitivity and kindness and considered him almost a son. She knew that he had not really needed her help in the business, but wanted to ease her suffering at the worst time of her life. She pressed his hand lovingly and passed away peacefully with Mordechai, her only true friend, at her side.

When he reached home that night, carrying the heavy sack on his back, and opened it in his chamber, he was astounded to find a large number of golden pieces. Once he finished counting, he realized he had inherited eighteen thousand golden coins from Rebecca. Since that day his wealth grew until he became one of the richest men of the area. He never forgot those who were less prosperous than himself, those who had not come into fortunes, those who were not blessed by God and suffered poverty and affliction.

And that is the true tale of Mordechai Maizl's treasure.

14

The Gilded Slippers

Once upon a time there was a Jewish milkman who lived in a small village, far away from any city and any other Jews. In those ancient days hamlets were dispersed among dense forests, deep valleys, and high mountains. There was hardly any access to bigger towns where many Jews settled down and lived their lives according to the laws of Moses.

The Jewish milkman was fortunate to serve a nobleman who was both kind and generous. He, his wife, and child did not lack anything. They kept busy taking care of the five hundred cows that belonged to their master and lived a peaceful and healthy life. Their only son, a sixteen-year-old lad, was a joy to behold. Tall and strong, he had a ruddy complexion and a cheerful personality that was liked by all. The milkman and his loyal wife should have been pleased with their lives but they were not. Amidst all the bounty they had, amidst all the plenty they enjoyed, they could not but worry that their only child was not growing up as a young Jewish man. They were mainly concerned how and where they would find the right wife for him.

They were decent folks, followed tradition as best they could but nothing much beyond that. The husband did not study the Torah since he was not an educated man and they did not dwell among people of their own faith. They did pray to the God of Israel with all their hearts but had doubts whether, under the circumstances, God even knew about their existence. They felt that there was only one mitzvah they could perform properly and that was being good hosts to visitors who passed through the village. But since they were so secluded and out-of-sight, not too many people came by and the milkman and his wife were disheartened that there was so very little opportunity to carry out the one good deed they could.

One cold winter evening the husband had just finished his rounds and they were getting ready to go to sleep. Heavy snow was falling, the earth was frozen, and a light wind was picking up. The milkman was about to close the door to his house when he noticed something moving at the edge of the forest where they lived. He stepped outside trying to discern what or who it was. His wife was fluffing up the pillows in the bedroom and when he failed to come in, she looked through the window to see whether he was still outside. She could not see much through the frozen glass and knocked on the white, hard panel a few times trying to get his attention. When he did not respond she followed him outside. She saw him standing in the middle of the yard, all covered with snow, his eyes fixed on the trees in the background.

And then she noticed it too! It was a person, or rather something like an image of a woman, coming towards them. Floating over the fallen snow without leaving footsteps, the creature looked more like an apparition and both the milkman as well as his wife sensed an intense fear that took over their bodies so that, for a moment, they stopped being aware that it was freezing. Yet when the figure came closer they realized that it was a living human being, clad in fancy clothes, wearing a Turkish turban on her head and covering her shoulders with an opalescent scarf more as a decoration than as a means of protection from the bitter cold.

They invited her to come in. The milkman and his wife were so thrilled that God of Israel had found them worthy of taking care of a guest that they did not know what to offer their visitor first. The wife ran into the pantry and brought many delicacies into the kitchen, foods they had saved for special occasions, and began preparing a splendid meal. Yet their guest stopped her and told them that all she wanted was to rest for a while. She had a mission ahead of her and it was still a long way to go. The milkman and his wife were very disappointed but honored her wishes. The wife showed her into a beautiful chamber with an inviting bed covered with an embroidered spread and snow-white down pillows. The guest again insisted she did not want to sleep but just to relax a little before continuing her journey. Seeing how upset the milkman's wife was, the strange lady smiled at her sweetly and asked her whether she could compensate somehow for their kindness and hospitality.

The milkman's wife felt insulted and hurt when the woman uttered those words. They were delighted to have her since she enabled them to claim the only mitzvah they could and that was all the fulfillment they were looking for. The lady soon found out that they had no wishes except for the one that was causing them so much worry and distress: to find a good and righteous Jewish girl for their precious son. When asked what they intended to do about it, the wife told her that they prayed every single day and begged God to grant them their request.

"And so it shall be," commented the guest. She reached under her lovely shawl and pulled out a magnificent pair of gilded slippers, covered with tiny pearls that glittered in the dim light of the candles like stars in the sky.

"Here," she said, placing them in the wife's hands, "this is my gift to your future daughter-in-law, may you all be blessed!"

And she was gone.

It was the milkman's turn this time to look for his wife.

He waited for a while for her to come out from the guest room. Nothing happened. It was very quiet in there and he felt some trepidation, not knowing who that woman really was. He knocked on the door a few times and when there was no answer, opened it slightly. In the flickering light of the candles he saw his wife standing in the empty room with her mouth open and her eyes protruding, holding in her hands a pair of small exquisite slippers, such as he had never seen before.

It so happened that in a neighboring forest, not too far away, there lived a Jewish charcoal maker with his young daughter. He had been a widower for many years and had taken care of his child all by himself. The girl grew up and became not only a lovely lass but a very bright and diligent one. She knew how to read since her mother had taught her before she died and the charcoal maker, who was a simple man, relied on his daughter to read to him from the Bible as well as other books they kept at home.

The father toiled long days, summer and winter, and whenever he came home dirty and tired he found clean clothes and a hot meal awaiting him. He treasured his daughter, yet in addition to the deep sadness he had felt all those years since his wife's death, the charcoal maker carried within himself a nagging, perpetual fear. Since they lived in such seclusion, far away from a Jewish settlement, he was concerned that his beloved daughter would not find the right mate.

The young girl loved to take care of her aging father but at times felt lonely and within her heart yearned for a friend. Her feelings became stronger as time went by and she got into the habit of praying every evening, asking God to help her find a soul mate.

One wintry night, while her father was sleeping and she was reading her books as usual, the door to the cabin suddenly opened and a woman walked in. She was dressed in a magnificent, flowing dress and on her head there sat a tall, shiny turban. It was hard to say whether she was old or young but the light that shone from her eyes filled the room with silvery, blue light and the whole place smelled of roses and violets. The young girl was about to wake her father not knowing whether to feel frightened or just amazed but the woman placed a finger on her lips, motioning to her to keep quiet.

"Do not fret, my child," she said, "no harm will befall you. I heard your voice and listened to the words and have come to help you."

The bewitching lady pulled out a piece of velvet cloth from among the folds of her dress, as well as some silver and golden threads and a needle which she gave to the young girl.

"Let me show you how to make a beautiful bag that will hold your future husband's tefillin," she said, and within a few minutes she had the young girl stitching away as if she had been doing it all her life.

So immersed was the charcoal maker's daughter in her labor of love that she did not notice that her visitor had disappeared. When she lifted her head she saw the first light of dawn and on her lap the finished bag which she had embroidered to perfection.

On his seventeen birthday, the milkman's son was given a horse and a cart and told to go in search of his bride, the one on whose small feet the gilded slippers would fit.

He traveled through forests and valleys, visited cities and small hamlets but wherever he went he could not find a girl whose feet were so tiny as to fit the exquisite shoes.

"A girl like that just does not exist," he told himself when two years passed and he felt discouraged and disappointed. In the end, heartbroken, he headed back home, hoping to reach his father's house before the first snow fall.

It was a Friday evening when he was quite close to his home, yet he knew he would not make it before the Sabbath since he had lost his way in a deep forest. He decided to stay among the tall trees and pray there as if he were in his house. Night fell. The horse was resting next to the cart and he was almost falling asleep when he saw through some dense branches a glimmer of light. He approached it carefully and coming close to a small cabin knocked gently asking if a Jew dwelled there. The old charcoal maker opened the door and invited him to spend the Sabbath in his house although he admitted with sadness that he could not provide him with a hearty meal as he would have wished. The young man was happy to share with the charcoal maker the food he had in his cart and in a while they were both sitting at the table, celebrating the Sabbath.

The milkman's son noticed after a while that the old man was carrying some of the food outdoors and, not being able to control his curiosity, asked him if he had any pets. The charcoal maker smiled unhappily and told him he had no animals to take care of. It was his own daughter who refused to step into the room since she had no shoes and was embarrassed to appear in his presence barefooted.

The young man took out the gilded slippers from his bag and, with his heart beating wildly, asked the charcoal maker to give them to his daughter and ask her to wear them.

It was a perfect match!

The wedding took place at the nobleman's farm with great joy and excitement. The bride and the bridegroom were deliriously happy and the young man's parents as well as the charcoal maker shared their great happiness. The wine was flowing and food was plentiful, and among the many guests one could notice, just for a short while, an elegantly clad lady, who wore a shiny turban on her head and an exquisite, silvery shawl around her shoulders. She smiled sweetly at the couple but when they tried to find her among the crowd, they did not succeed. She had vanished and never appeared again.

15

No Miracle

My name is Ari, yet when I was living in the country of my birth Hungary, they called me Arpad. I liked the name and, as a child, often times imagined I was the Magyar chief who hundreds of years ago led his people across the Danube river and built settlements in the lowland. In a way, I thought then, he was almost like Moses leading his people to the Promised Land. Somehow I felt that he had been very unique and, since in my heart I wanted to be special too, the name of the great leader that I had inherited made me feel precious.

I needed that kind of escape from the drudgery of everyday life since I spent most of my time studying the Talmud in the little local shul. My family lived in Polgar, a little village near the town of Miskolc. My father died when I was one year old and my mother worked hard to support us and make a decent living. Her embroidery was so exquisite that people from near and far came to buy her creations. She was an artist in her heart and, had she chosen a different media, she would have been a great painter or sculptor. Her colorful hand-crafted articles mainly showed the traditional Hungarian touch but often she would embroider prayer shawls, kippahs, and covers for the Torah, if so requested. Then, the artifacts became alive with different scenes from the Bible and I could not keep my eyes away from them. She would put all her heart into her work and sing beautiful niggunim while she was sewing. I remember her best, sitting at the table with her head bent and her glasses sliding slightly down her nose, concentrating on the small, delicate stitches.

At night after we had eaten our dinner, she would tell me miraculous tales of great rabbis and stories that had been forgotten long since then. Even though I do not remember all of them, what I do recall is that she was deeply religious and her belief in God and the love He felt for his people was boundless. She used to tell me that no matter what, God will always be there for us and things will happen the way they are meant to. The good will always gain victory even though sometimes it does not look like it. In the end God sets things right and He always has his reasons. This deep faith filled my soul and for years I carried it with me, finding in it a source of strength and fulfillment.

Time went by and I grew up. I left my small village to study in a seminary for Jewish teachers in the capital Budapest. My mother was truly happy that I wanted to become an educator, particularly since my main interest was music. Although she had no formal musical training, she had talent and a perfect pitch. Her voice was mellow and soft and the songs she sang still vibrate in my heart, as if she sang them just yesterday.

One wintry day in 1944, the gestapo collected all the Jews in Polgar. My mother was among them and she was taken to Auschwitz in the only transport that left the small town. She never came back. She was standing with other Jewish women in a long line and the German officer, playing God, told each of them which line to go to. My mother was ordered to step aside into line A. She did as she was told, yet could hardly stand on her feet that were swollen and blue, almost frozen due to the harsh cold and the biting wind that blew that day. She looked around and saw that on the other side, where the second line was stationed, there stood a wooden bench. She glanced at the soldier and pleaded with him to let her sit down since her legs could not carry her anymore. The soldier smiled, his eyes lit up with a strange light, and there was an amused smirk on his face when he graciously allowed my mother to step into the other line. She followed the others into the gas chamber that very same day.

I have asked myself many times what was God's purpose in making things happen the way they did. The woman who came back and told me the story does not have an answer either. Did God want my mother to suffer less? Was that an act of mercy on his part? Could he not have wrought one of those miracles my mother believed in so much? And what about me, her son? Did I not deserve to see her again? I had never known my father. Was that not enough? Would she have thought twice before asking the soldier to switch her if she had known the outcome? Was she so tired that it did not matter anymore? Since we had lost contact for a few months, did she think I was not alive anymore and gave up? Where was her faith? Did she lose it or did she cling to it with all her might to overcome her ordeal? I never found a reply to these questions.

Yet, I do believe I have an answer to one query: Does my mother live on? I know she does. Not just in me, in my children and grandchildren, and in all of Am Israel. She lives on each time a niggun is sung, each time I play a song, each time I hear a melody that she carried in her heart. I know she will always live on.

16

Kytička

In a certain place, on the left bank of the river Vltava one can spot a deserted, empty lot. Years ago there stood in that place a small house belonging to a widow and her daughter. The tiny parcel of land has since been abandoned and is overgrown with thick weeds and dense bushes. There is only one area on this stunted plot that is bare and barren, the shrubs grow around it as if trying to avoid the ground, struggling to stay away from a soil that carries with it desolation and disaster. This section is dark and grim, and a pile of smoldering coals keeps sizzling and emitting a hazy smoke that makes the whole place gray and blurry. Even the waters of the Vltava that occasionally touch and even overflow that parcel have not been able to extinguish the fumes and the smoggy vapor always comes back.

The widow who used to live in the little house was an honorable Jewish woman who excelled in her work. She was an artist and painted a variety of designs on pottery and other materials. Once she even designed a pattern for the queen who had it embroidered in living colors on her royal, velvet cloak. The widow was a meticulous craftsman and very knowledgeable at that. She knew how to treat the colors she mixed so that they would not fade, and her workmanship always reached a degree of perfection that was a marvel to those who purchased her creations. Despite her success, she remained modest and humble and lived happily with her young daughter in the small cottage on the banks of the river.

One cold, wintry evening she was painting a beautiful design on a Torah scroll meant as a wedding gift for the family of a rich merchant in town. Her daughter Kytička was at her side helping her, when suddenly the mother realized that the girl had turned, as if overnight, into a lovely young woman. She paused and said to her: "My dear child, you have become exactly what you are called, a kytička, a small beautiful flower that has blossomed and opened up its petals to the sun."

The girl blushed and indeed, in the light of the lamp, she looked like a fragile white lily, delicate and sweet. Her frame was lean and slight and her long neck gracefully supported a small head surrounded by a multitude of auburn curls that enhanced the beauty of her face. Her movements were sheer delight as she mixed the colors her mother needed and cleaned the brushes with her dainty fingers.

The mother stopped her work and opened an old chest that stood in a corner of the room. She pulled out a small sack and untied the cord. She motioned to Kytička to approach the table and, to the girl's great amazement and elation, poured out a large number of golden and silver coins that glittered in the light.

"This is all yours, my dear," said the mother, "I have saved it over the years for the day of your engagement. It is sound money I earned by working hard and with much pleasure for you, my child. With God's help we shall find you a fine groom who will love and cherish you and be a good husband to you."

Kytička laughed happily. She was thrilled to hear that she was about to have a mate and clapped her hands with great excitement, just the way she used to do when she was a small child about to get a new toy.

The evening was still young and the widow, who suddenly felt an urgency to consult the matchmaker about her daughter's prospects, left the house. Kytička remained sitting in front of the roaring fireplace dreaming about her future spouse.

The fire was burning brightly and Kytička, bundled up in a warm shawl, kept looking into the playful shimmering blaze, trying to imagine how beautiful her married life would be and mainly the looks of her desired bridegroom. So intensely and feverishly was she gazing into the brilliant glow that she began to imagine that there existed a world within the burning fire. The twinkling flames parted to let her catch a glimpse of a incandescent garden where the flowers, trees, and bushes, all crimson, seemed to thrive and grow while being part of the surrounding red splendor. She saw a number of fine ladies and proud gentlemen strolling along the shining paths of the radiant park, and in a corner, under a scarlet tree leaning on a carmine sofa, she saw a young man resting. His beauty took her breath away. He was reading from a book with flaming letters and suddenly lifted his eyes and looked straight at Kytička. He got up and made his way slowly toward where she was sitting and, stepping out of the fireplace, greeted her charmingly. He wrapped his long red velvet cloak tightly around his body as if he was cold. Kytička noticed that the bronze curls that adorned his high forehead were almost the same color as hers and surrounded his temples like a glittering halo. His amber eyes flashed passionate looks at her and he said: "Kytička, nobody, but nobody, in my fiery kingdom can compare to you. You are the most beautiful of all maidens I have ever seen and the sweetest and kindest of them all."

Taking her hand in his, he added: "You are meant to be my wife and I will come and take you with me as soon as I make the wedding arrangements." He was about to say something more but, at that moment, Kytička's mother opened the front door of the cottage. The gallant young man kissed Kytička's hand and vanished into the flames of the fireplace. The blaze died and the dark coals kept sparkling and flaring up while Kytička sat in the same place dazed from what had just happened and what she had seen.

Kytička's mother was pleased to convey to her daughter the good news of who her future husband would be. She reminded her of young Jacob with whom she had played as a small child and of whom she had always been very fond. Jacob, a handsome lad, was the son of the local goldsmith and a gifted craftsman as well. The matchmaker had promised to settle matters by the end of the week, and a meeting was arranged between the two families.

Kytička was still sitting quietly next to the extinguished fire but her mother did not notice anything unusual about it. Kytička had never been a talkative child and in their house it was always the mother who did most of the conversing and the daughter the listening. Kytička was staring at the palm of her hand that the fiery young man had kissed and where she saw a crimson mark that was gleaming in a bright reddish-orange color. She felt there a tingling, slightly burning sensation yet it was not painful but rather pleasing to her. When her mother approached and hugged her, she closed her hand and hid it under the shawl. She did not want to share the experience she had just gone through. After a while she calmed down and felt happy again listening to her mother's description of all the great qualities young Jacob possessed and how lucky she would be to become a member of the goldsmith's prosperous family.

That night Kytička could not fall asleep. She felt joy since she knew Jacob and liked him a lot, but was also perturbed thinking of the fiery prince and his amber eyes. She lay in her bed for hours and, as the night advanced, her trepidation seemed to subside. Finally, exhausted from the events of the day, she sank into a deep slumber. As soon as she closed her lids, the coals in the fireplace ignited and became crimson red. Flames sprung up and Kytička could hear the familiar crackling of the burning timber. Once again she saw the stunning prince strolling in his garden with his courtiers following him at a distance. He stepped out of the fireplace and approached her bed. He lifted her gently and wrapped her in his soft velvet cloak. Without uttering a word he walked into the blazing flames and carried her into the garden where many damsels and gentlemen curtsied in front of her and greeted her as their queen.

A lady in waiting took her to a scarlet chamber where she was dressed in a brilliant glittering dress with a flaming veil, and on her head they placed a golden crown adorned with magnificent rubies. In the blink of an eye she found herself in a cathedral, standing next to the prince who wore crimson clothes and a crown exactly like her own. A priest appeared from nowhere and Kytička realized that she was facing a wedding ceremony. She wanted to tell the prince that she could not marry him but she was not able to move or say a word. It was as if she had become a stone statue without a will of her own. All she could do was to watch as if it was not herself to whom all this was happening. Her soul was hovering outside her body and desperately trying to stop the event but to no avail.

A light appeared in the distance and it became more and more intense as it came closer. Kytička noticed it was a star, and for a moment felt comfort since she thought it was her star, the familiar star of her people, the star of David, but soon the glare became so strong that she could not look at it anymore and closed her eyes. When she opened them again she found herself in her own bed at home, and the prince was kissing her hair with his ardent lips. He was whispering to her that soon he would come and take her to his kingdom where together they would worship fire and light forever after.

Kytička's mother was very concerned the next morning when she found her daughter running a high fever. The young girl was mumbling incoherent words and burning up. Her face was flushed, and she kept asking for the star of David and begging her mother to extinguish the fire in the fireplace. The widow treated her with a herbal tea and nursed her for a couple of days till Kytička recovered and felt as good as new. Being basically of a cheerful disposition and positive nature, she soon came to the conclusion that her troublesome dreams had been a result of the fever. She tried to forget about the prince and helped her mother to prepare special food in honor of her betrothal.

The day the goldsmith and his son came to pay their respects was a particularly beautiful wintry day. Fresh snow had fallen the previous night and the sun shone brightly as the groom and his father knocked at the widow's door. Supper went well and Jacob could not take his eyes from the beautiful face of his future bride. The matchmaker, who had also been invited, smashed a precious goblet on the floor, a sign that the marriage was a done deal and that nobody could undo it just as nobody could glue together the many broken pieces of the colorful glass. Towards evening the rabbi arrived, lit two festive candles, and witnessed the signing of the covenant. He addressed the young couple and asked them to be faithful and love each other for the rest of their lives. Kytička was truly happy, yet became tense and fearful whenever she looked at the shimmering flames in the fireplace.

That night, after the guests had left, an extreme feeling of gloom and sadness descended on Kytička. She sat quietly at the table while her mother went on happily chattering about the events of the day. When they bid good night to each other, Kytička hugged her mother and clung to her in a way she had never done before. Her mother though was not surprised, she assumed that Kytička was just as excited and happy as she was and together they joined in prayer thanking God for their good fortune.

Kytička did not lie down for a while. She felt the urge to recite the psalms she knew by heart, and did it a few times till she felt more at peace. In bed she closed her eyes tightly and tried to think of Jacob and the upcoming wedding. Everything was quiet for a while but when the clock struck midnight, the fire in the extinguished fireplace suddenly ignited and Kytička woke up from a restless sleep. Trembling she sat up in her bed and saw the prince approaching with an entourage of six men, all dressed in flaming red suits. The young man was not smiling this time. His eyes were flashing as usual, but this time it was anger and fury not passion and love she saw in them.

"You are just like the others!" he screamed. "You deceived me just like all humans have done before, and now you will not rule with me in the kingdom of fire. You do not deserve my love and your fate has been sealed!"

His voice broke down and, standing at the foot of the bed, he slowly spread his arms in front of him. Terrified Kytička saw flames springing from the tips of his fingers, and in a minute she was engulfed in a ferocious fire.

Kytička's mother woke up at that moment and immediately realized something was wrong when she saw flames and smoke coming out of her daughter's room. She was not able to open the door to Kytička's alcove no matter how hard she tried. In desperation she kept hammering at the smoldering wood with her fists screaming and calling her daughter's name. The smoke overcame her and she collapsed at the threshold.

The cottage was in a remote, somewhat wooded area and far from the gates of the ghetto. The closest neighbors noticed the fire only when most of the house was already in flames. They ran over, as quickly as they could, to help the inhabitants but were able to save only Kytička's mother. The house burned down to its foundations. A party of men went there the next day, and all they discovered were some blackened wooden objects but no sign of the young girl. No matter how hard they looked, they could not find any remains of Kytička. In time a thick vegetation covered the entire grim lot. The scars the fire left vanished almost completely except for the black area where the fireplace used to stand.

Kytička's mother ended up in the house for the poor where the Jewish community provided her with shelter and food. For a while she was still able to make a meager living with her art, yet was never herself again. In the last year of her life she started drawing pictures of her deceased daughter and refused to do anything else. She painted the face of the young girl on a big canvas and kept it hanging on the wall next to her bed. People used to say that there was something uncanny about the picture. The girl looked young and happy, as beautiful and delicate as a flower, yet there was an expression of deep sadness in her eyes and a touch of bitterness in her sweet smile. One day they found the widow dead in her bed with hundreds of her drawings dispersed around the room and her daughter's portrait calmly looking down at her.

II

Light and Shadow

If not for the light, there would be no shadow.

—Yiddish proverb

17

Kaddish

An old woman was dying. As she lay in her bed, she saw the angel of death approaching and raised her hands in supplication.

"Please, wait!" she said.

The messenger from the other world paused, and whispered: "Why and for what? I have to do my job, you know. You have been around for a long time and now you have to come with me. Do not be afraid, you have lived a pious life and many of your relatives and friends are waiting to welcome you!"

"Wait, please!" repeated the woman.

Tears were streaming down her face and she was shivering all over. The people who stood around her bed were strangers. She had lived alone for many years and had had nobody to take care of her. She was so very old that nobody really knew anything about her family. They had all passed away and she never talked about them. She had worked as a cleaning lady at the rabbi's house for a decade and, after she became unable to do so anymore, the congregation had taken care of her. Now she was about to embark on her last journey and all the faces around her were somber and sad. She knew them but they were all strangers, kind people no question about it, but not her own flesh and blood. She wanted one of her own to say the kaddish for her.

"I want my great grandson to say the kaddish for me!" she told the angel of death, "and he is so far away, I do not even know in which town. He is the only one who can say it after I am gone. Please give me a few days to find him, please!"

The messenger from the other world answered kindly: "That is not possible, you do not have any time left but there are other ways to let your relative know. Do not worry, it shall be done!"

The people standing around the old woman's bed saw how her lips quivered for a moment, then she smiled at them thankfully, and closed her eyes never to open them again. They buried her the next day.

Her great grandson Joseph lived in Germany and had cut off all contact with members of his family years ago. He was somewhat of a recluse, lived by himself in the woods, and followed his own ways rather than those of a Jew. The first night after the old woman's death he had a strange dream, yet he rarely ever had any dreams! He saw an old woman, all dressed in white, approaching his bed and caressing his face.

"Josele," she said, "I am your great grandmother and I just died yesterday. I wish I had known you but, even though we never met I have not forgotten you. Now you must do something for me, otherwise I will not rest in peace. You have to say the kaddish after me, there is nobody else but you, nobody else . . . nobody . . . nobody . . . nobody . . ."

Joseph woke up trembling and spent the next day trying to forget the odd dream. He had a vague recollection of having an old great grandmother living in the ghetto of Prague but, since he never saw any relatives, he had forgotten about her altogether. He wanted to do the same again. Yet, the following night the same dream recurred and so it happened every night afterward.

Finally Joseph gave up. He found his old tefillin in a box and walked for a few hours through the forest till he reached a small town where they had a tiny synagogue. He approached the rabbi and explained to him what he wanted to do. The rabbi was very understanding and arranged for Joseph to say the kaddish everyday after the morning prayers. Joseph did it faithfully for a year and his great grandmother never appeared again in his dreams. That experience, nevertheless, had an impact on him. It changed his way of thinking and he found the way back to his people. Joseph remained in the obscure shtetl hidden among the high mountains. He worked with the shammes at the shul, and eventually married and had a family of his own. Thus, the angel of death had kept his promise, helped the great grandmother rest in peace, and perform a great mitzvah even after her death.

18

The Dancing Maiden

In Prague, during the time of Rudolf the Second, there lived in the Jewish quarter a tailor who, although poor, was well respected since he had the reputation of a God-fearing and loving man. His wife and young daughter were seen every Friday following the tailor to the synagogue to attend services and mingle with the congregation. The daughter was a nice, pretty young woman, yet despite all her positive attributes the matchmaker could not find her a suitable groom. She even had her dowry set and ready to go since she had been lucky to inherit a sum of money from a distant, childless uncle. Yet all this was to no avail and the girl remained a spinster well beyond the right age.

The women gossiped that there was something strange about her and that her dark eyes shone with an odd bright light each time she saw a young man who was not Jewish. They had seen her looking at the hired help who came into the ghetto and observed the smile that appeared on her face each time a hefty young man worked in the yard, cleared the debris from the sidewalk, or sat on a bench in the square eating his lunch. She sneaked out of her house and hid in the little alleys following the workers and sometimes her mother did not know for hours where she was. Despite her interest in men, she never even glanced at the Yeshiva students whom she could see walking to the synagogue every morning. She spent all her time at the window waiting for the gentiles or roaming along the crooked streets of the Jewish ghetto. Some people even said that they saw her leaving the ghetto in the dark of night and disappearing outside the gate.

But all this was hearsay and nobody could prove she was a sinner until one evening the wife of the shammes provided them with the evidence they needed. On her way to the bathhouse, through an open window she saw the tailor's daughter dancing around half-naked in her nightgown. She was holding onto a broom and singing to herself softly and happily while whirling around continuously. The shammes' wife decided that this was too important to ignore and, forgetting about her cleansing bath, ran to a friend's house that was nearest. Soon there were about a dozen women in one room discussing the unusual sight of the dancing maiden and arguing whether the rabbi should be notified about it or not.

The rabbi was familiar with the problem of the tailor's daughter. Her parents had confided in him and had asked for his help. He had talked to the young woman, tried to find out what was troubling her and gave her some guidance on how to keep herself occupied and satisfied by reading sections of the Torah. He sat there, listening to the group of women who talked all at the same time, describing the voluptuous dance of the young girl and their suspicions that she was either demented or had sold her soul to the devil. He sent them home, promising to look into the matter and urging them to calm down and not spread any unnecessary gossip so as not to damage the girl's reputation even further. They promised him that. Yet, he was not sure he could believe them, seeing the glitter in their eyes and the saliva dripping from the corner of their mouths. He was truly worried about the fate of the tailor's daughter.

The next day he summoned the parents to his house and talked to them for a long time. Within a week after that particular conversation an older man arrived from out of town and stayed with the rabbi as his personal guest. The rabbi had invited this poor widower he knew from a small village in Moravia. The stranger, who was a butcher by profession, had no family or property of his own and was ready to help the aging butcher of the ghetto to serve the congregation. He was far from being a handsome man, thin, short and bent. He made a sickly impression but had the reputation of an honest man and was ready to marry the tailor's daughter.

The young woman was not introduced to her future husband, just told that her wedding was to take place soon and that she was fortunate to marry a decent man who could make a living. She kept quiet. The intense light in her eyes became a constant glow and she managed to cast a look at her groom when he accompanied the rabbi to the synagogue. Her reaction was quite peculiar. She broke into loud laughter and continued till she fell exhausted on the floor as if in a fit of rage. That evening she danced for a few hours behind closed windows and drawn curtains. Yet everybody knew what she was doing and hoped that the groom would not change his mind. They all believed what the rabbi had told them, that she would settle down after the marriage.

On the wedding day she appeared calm and timid. When they led her to the chupe, she walked slowly with a little smile on her lips. The rabbi started the ceremony and the whole congregation stood there watching her. Suddenly she began twisting her arms, pulled the veil from her face, released the pins and combs from her dark, thick hair (she would not let them shave it), tore the sleeves of her dress, and began dancing in front of all of them. With a fiendish laughter she whirled around, making lecherous motions towards the men and vicious comments at the women. They all stood transfixed as if in a trance without being able to move. Finally the rabbi screamed, his voice hoarse and filled with anger and disgust: "Dance you want, dance you shall . . . forever after till eternity. . . ." The young woman stopped, stood still for a while, and then ran out of the room into the street. They tried to follow her but she was too swift for them and disappeared around the corner of one of the twisted streets.

They looked for her for many hours and several following days but could not find her. Friends in other parts of town were notified and joined them in the search, all in vain. The parents and congregation mourned, and the groom after a short while returned to Moravia and his old way of life, not knowing whether he should feel fortunate or miserable.

It has been told that the dancing maiden's ghost dwells close to the Old-New Synagogue in Prague, just next to the burial society's building. One can see her dancing away on moonlit nights and beware the man who happens to go by and cross her path. She will engage him in a furious dance whether he wants it or not and dance him to death. The only people who are safe from her savage embrace are the Yeshiva students whom she ignores, but just to be on the safe side even they do not walk around that part of town at night.

19

Ice Candles

One wintry afternoon when it was freezing outside and the cold was so harsh that it was almost impossible to breathe outdoors, the disciples of the Baal Shem Tov were expecting the return of their rabbi. He had been on an extended trip and they wanted to welcome him as nicely as they could. They lit a fire in his alcove and were able to prepare a good meal regardless of the scarce provisions they had. They were quite pleased with the outcome of their efforts when they realized that there was only one candle in their possession and that, come night, it would be very dark in the house. They felt sad and frustrated since one of the things the rabbi liked and would not compromise about was to have a lot of light. Nevertheless, there was nothing they could do anymore to change the situation and, when the rabbi and his wife arrived at dusk, they greeted them feeling very embarrassed.

"Jews, Jews," exclaimed the rabbi, "there has to be light!! My whole purpose in life is to bring light to the Jewish people! We need light!"

"Dear Rabbi," responded his followers sadly, "we are so sorry to disappoint you, but we have only one candle to light the whole house."

The Baal Shem Tov sat down for a while and, looking at the descending darkness outside the frozen windows, motioned towards the hundreds of icicles that were hanging all around the roof.

The Hasidim brought in as many icicles as they could and the whole place lit up gloriously. The ice candles continued burning for many hours and there was light and a warm glow throughout the house.

The hasidic followers in later generations often used to tell the story of the Baal Shem Tov's ice candles to illustrate that, wherever there is fire in the soul that glows like a memorial candle, even icicles can be lit and so can cold hearts.

20

Bella Ella

Hundreds of years ago, in the city of Prague there lived a rich man whom everybody held in high regard. He was famous for his wisdom even in remote areas of the country. His wealth supported the community in many ways and for his generosity he was not only respected but also loved. Since the name of this man has not been preserved in the memory of the people we shall call him Gershon.

Gershon had many visitors all year long and he was a very gracious and outgoing host indeed. Not only did old, long bearded rabbis come to discuss issues with him but he was also sought out by young men who flocked to his home continually. The reason for this overwhelming number of young guests was due not so much to his knowledge but for the fact that he had a most fair and unusual daughter. Ella was a real beauty, graceful and slim as the cedars of Lebanon, with the most enchanting pink cheeks and soft white skin. Her dark eyes flashed whenever she looked at a young man and made him forget all the troubles of the world. They called her Bella Ella, Ella the beautiful, so as not to confuse her with other maidens who bore the same name.

The most educated and richest young Jewish bachelors asked for Ella's hand in marriage but she rejected them all. Her answer was always the same: "My heart belongs to father." Her father had been a widower for many years and Ella had taken care of the household ever since she was a very young girl and seemed to worship the ground her father walked on. Gershon refused to interfere in his daughter's decision, always emphasizing that it was her choice and that he would not force her to marry anybody unless she wanted to. The suitors were so heartbroken that each of them died of sorrow shortly after leaving Gershon's house and returning to their homes.

If Gershon had not been a devoted son of Israel, and his daughter a God-fearing lass, people could have said that she had a pact with the devil and therefore was able to destroy those young men who courted her so lovingly. Despite her sinister reputation Ella continued to attract suitors. They knew that it might lead to their demise but they could not resist her beauty and the charm of her black eyes. They were lost once they reached Gershon's mansion.

One hot summer a terrible pestilence befell the Jewish Ghetto. First it was the children who died one after the other, so quickly that there was no time or space for a multitude of graves, and they had to bury many of them together. Then the adults started succumbing, some because of the illness and some because of the grief of losing their children. When the God of Israel punishes his people so harshly, a terrible sin must have been committed amongst them. The whole congregation went into mourning, asking for God's forgiveness and his mercy. But the Angel of Death did not stop his morbid task and every day many lives were lost.

What horrible crime had the people of Prague perpetrated that they had to suffer such a deplorable fate? Why did God not listen to their plea?

The rabbi went on a continuous fast and prayed day and night asking for a sign. How could they correct the wrong done if they did not know what it was?

One night, when the weak rabbi was in a state of semi-consciousness in his room, he thought he heard faint voices calling his name. He opened his eyes and made an effort to listen but collapsed in his seat. The voices became louder and stronger and, pulling himself up with the last of his strength, the rabbi opened the door of his house and followed the sound to the close by Old-New Synagogue. Inside he found the faint light of candles flickering and a congregation waiting for him. He took his place as usual behind the podium and blessed the congregation as was his habit.

The blood froze in his veins when he lifted his head and realized that all of the present were walking dead, their skulls covered with prayer shawls, their eye sockets empty and dismal as an abyss, their skeletal fingers holding onto the prayer books. And at the entrance standing much taller and menacing than any figure he had ever seen, stood the Angel of Death holding a long curling list in one of his glittering hands while in the other there was his mighty sword dripping blood from its pointed tip. The chanting had stopped and there was silence, silence heavy with the chill of death, of fear and doom. A small figure of a pale child appeared suddenly and the Angel of Death carried him off in the flicker of an eyelid.

The next morning the rabbi had no recollection of how he had made it back to his house. He invited all the elders to help him solve the dreadful situation the ghetto was in. He understood from the previous night's experience that some horrendous wrong had been done to a child or by a child and they all agreed that time was of the essence and they had to find out who the perpetrator was before it was too late. How could they save the rest of the congregation? The rabbi suggested the only possible solution: to summon one of the departed children and force him to tell them the name of the sinner who was the source of all their mishaps.

They decided to bury a little boy who had just died without the customary white sheet. That night while they were waiting in the synagogue, as expected the child appeared in the shadows and plaintively demanded his sheet without which he could not rest in peace. The rabbi promised to give it to him but demanded first to be told who the sinner amongst them was, the one who brought the pestilence on them.

"Cleanse your homes from abomination," said the child, "and this too will pass."

"Tell me, where does this evil dwell," requested the rabbi.

"In the house of Gershon!" the child answered.

"In the mansion of that God-abiding man?" whispered the rabbi with great surprise.

"Yes," said the child, "in that house there lives a poisonous snake, the cause of our misfortune. Gershon and his daughter Ella are the exterminators of the children of Israel. Now that you know, give me my sheet!" The rabbi threw the white cloth over the child's head and it disappeared immediately.

The rabbi summoned Gershon to his chambers at once, but he was nowhere to be found. Instead of him, his messengers brought the beautiful Ella who was shivering as if suffering from a deadly malady and was as pale as death itself. So frightened was she that her knees buckled and they had to help her to sit down.

The rabbi talked to her softly, trying to convince her to tell him what had happened. The tears flowed in torrents from her dark eyes and her lips quivered as she tried to speak.

"Rabbi," she said, "I have sinned, I have sinned so badly that there is no salvation for me and I just want to die. God will never forgive me. I have gone too far."

"Do not doubt God's mercy, my child," said the rabbi, "never doubt!"

"My crime is worse than the darkest secrets of hell!" she screamed. "Your hair will stand up on top of your heads, your hearts will stop beating, and your bones will not support you anymore when you hear what I have done! Listen to me and turn away in disgust: I have been my father's lover!"

With those words Ella fell on the ground, covering her face in shame while the shocked men looked at each other in utter disbelief.

"Woe to the home and the community where such atrocities take place!" moaned the rabbi.

Bella Ella sat up and said: "You do not know it all. I was a child and did not know what was right and what was wrong. My mother had died and I believed my father's vicious teachings and his devilish upbringing. Only when I grew up and young men started paying attention to me, it occurred to me that something was wrong. When I expressed my misgivings to my father, he talked me out of it. He was very convincing and I believed him. Each time a suitor came looking for me, my father was filled with such jealousy and hatred that he administered a slow working, tasteless and odorless poison to the beverages the young men drank, causing them to die in a short time."

The horrified elders could not hold their dismay anymore and with loud screams, demanded the punishment of the pervert Gershon. They were all set to go to his house and stone the depraved man. But the rabbi put a stop to their wish for revenge. "Brothers," he said, "we are just foreigners in an alien land. We cannot take the law in our hands. We must hand Gershon to the Christian court. Go and bring that servant of Ashmadai to me!"

The same messengers that had brought Ella to the rabbi went to look for her father once again. They searched the house but he was nowhere to be found. Finally, as they were about to leave the premises, they heard deep groans coming from the basement and when they descended they beheld a horrible sight. The cursed Gershon, knowing that his secret had been uncovered and that punishment was soon to come, had decided to take his own life and cut his throat. He was lying on the floor in a pool of blood looking like the devil himself.

The rabbi was notified and he, as well as all present, lowered their heads, deeply shaken since another terrible transgression had taken place when the miserable father had decided to commit suicide. Only Ella stood there disinterested and as if removed from the whole incident, her eyes without expression, her lips tightly closed.

The rabbi spoke to the elders: "The name of this sinner will be erased from memory, he is where he belongs and has received the just punishment. But this child of Israel, although a sinner, has been wronged. Will God forgive her? Will he extend his mercy to her? Can she hope for redemption or is she doomed to be Satan's bride?"

Some of the elders wanted her to pay for her sin, yet those who hoped for mercy won and Ella was asked if she was ready to undergo a test and accept God's judgment. She lowered her head and whispered: "I am ready to suffer all the pain in the world in order to save my soul."

Ella was instructed to return to her home. Women came and prepared her as if for her burial. They cleansed her like a deceased, wrapped her in tachrichim and placed her in a coffin. She had to spend the night in the burial society's building adjacent to the cemetery. In the morning, if she survived, all would know that God had forgiven her and she still had a chance for a pious life.

Despite their curiosity, nobody dared to stay outside the burial building that night. In the morning the whole congregation accompanied the rabbi to that place. The coffin where Ella had been laid was empty and all over the cemetery they found torn pieces of her flesh. They assumed that she too, just like her father, had been taken by the devil.

Since that day the pestilence subsided and the sick recovered quickly from their illness. The mansion in which the sinners used to live remained empty, nobody wanted to live there. In time Gershon's property was destroyed, the abandoned dwelling was torn down and no sign remained of it. The street where the house used to stand was considered cursed for a very long time and people went out of their way to avoid it. They called it Bella's Street and that is the name by which it was always remembered.

21

The Descending Ceiling

One spring day, when Emperor Rudolf was in a good mood, he decided to visit Rabbi Loew in his home. The rabbi fascinated him and he always liked to pick his mind, particularly since he had never been disappointed. The court astrologer, Tycho Brache, joined him on that particular occasion and Rabbi Loew humored both of them by creating the illusion that they were not in his humble house but in the grand hall of the imperial palace. The Emperor was delighted with the rabbi, desired more of the same, and asked the rabbi to come visit him in the royal residence shortly. Although the rabbi did not like to perform his magic unnecessarily, he had no choice since he knew how volatile Rudolf was and did not want to anger him.

On the chosen day Rabbi Loew was shown into the presence of the Emperor who wished to see all the Jewish patriarchs that afternoon and asked the rabbi to summon them from the other world. Rabbi Loew grew pale and uneasy and tried to warn Rudolf of the danger of that particular venture, but Rudolf insisted. He was in a playful mood and wanted to be entertained. Sighing, Rabbi Loew asked only for one thing, that no matter what, the Emperor should not talk when the patriarchs appeared and absolutely not laugh. Rudolf gave his word.

The rabbi closed his eyes, the elegant chamber where they were sitting became engulfed in semidarkness and, out of the shadows, one by one the patriarchs emerged. The Emperor marveled at the height and strength of these revered figures and kept quiet, not daring to utter a word. Yet, when redheaded, freckled, Naftali appeared, dragging his shorter leg behind him, Rudolf could not contain himself anymore and burst into loud laughter. The apparitions disappeared at once and the high ceiling of the hall started descending. It would have continued doing so and would have crushed the Emperor if Rabbi Loew had not used his kabbalistic knowledge and, with raised arms, commanded it to stop. They say that till today that chamber is locked and nobody goes there since the ceiling never regained its original height.

In any case, that is the tale the Jews tell each other.

22

The Rebirth of the Maharal

The Baal Shem Tov often wandered from village to village with his devoted second wife Hana, the daughter of the rabbi from Brody. She had been a rich man's daughter, used to the best things in life and very spoiled and moody. Yet all that changed once she married the Baal Shem Tov. She would have followed him to the ends of the world regardless of being subjected to poverty and discomfort. She toiled in the garden, grew produce for their food, cleaned and washed his clothes, and mingled with other paupers at the outskirts of the village where her husband used to preach. She admired the way he treated sick people with different herbs and flowers he collected in the woods and how he used the right words to soothe those who were suffering. She rejected the accusations of her learned brother Gershon that she had married a fake sage who knew nothing. Hana tried to persuade him that he was mistaken and that, although the Baal Shem Tov seemed to be a simple man, he was nevertheless a great tzaddik. Gershon hated the Baal Shem Tov and tried to convince his sister to divorce him, particularly since he saw her needs and did not want her to share the misery that her husband had forced on her. Yet all that was to no avail and Hana remained devoted to her husband.

It so happened that once while they were traveling, they encountered much trouble and their hardship became very acute. Their old horse refused to continue pulling the cart and collapsed on the side of the road. The Baal Shem Tov tried to help and treat the poor animal but it was too late and the horse died within a short time. Not being able to handle the situation, the Baal Shem Tov and his wife asked the advice of some beggars who were passing by. They saw them as birds of the same feather. Calling them brother and sister, the paupers suggested they seek out in a neighboring town a rich man by the name of Rabbi Baruch. He was known as a great philanthropist and never refused help to a man in need.

After a long and painful trip, the couple reached Rabbi Baruch's house and was greeted with sympathy and compassion. Upon hearing about their misfortune the rich man gave them one of his own horses and invited them to spend the Sabbath in his house since they were exhausted from their ordeal. The Baal Shem Tov and his wife Hana accepted the kindness with gratitude and relief.

When night fell and the Baal Shem Tov and his wife retired to one of the guest rooms in the house, Rabbi Baruch was not able to sleep. Feeling restless and uneasy, he decided to get some fresh air and walk around in his garden for a while. He spent a short time looking at the dark sky and meditating when suddenly he noticed a strange, yellowish gleam coming out of the guest room where the paupers were sleeping. It was late, close to midnight and that kind of light was different from any brightness he had ever seen. It could not be the reflection of the moon on the window panel, since it was a black, moonless night. It was not a fire either. Curious, he approached the window but the resplendence was so strong that he could not see a thing. He could hear a muffled voice singing and the sound of somebody weeping. He hesitated for a moment but then drew near the door and looked through the key hole.

What he saw at first was nothing extraordinary. The Baal Shem Tov was sitting on the floor chanting the midnight prayer, the Tikkun Hazot, his hands stretched upwards and tears streaming down his cheeks. Yet Rabbi Baruch looked again and his heart almost stopped when he saw a very tall figure standing just next to the Baal Shem Tov with a long silvery beard and a face that was beaming light. Rabbi Baruch lost consciousness out of sheer fright and collapsed next to the door.

The Baal Shem Tov heard a noise and tried to open the door. Since Rabbi Baruch had collapsed in front of it, he was not able to do so. He tried a few times and succeeded in pushing the inert body of Rabbi Baruch aside so that he could squeeze through the narrow opening and assist him. When Rabbi Baruch came around, he apologized to the Baal Shem Tov for not realizing he was a tzaddik and for not paying homage to him. Yet the Baal Shem Tov dismissed it and also turned a deaf ear when Rabbi Baruch kept asking him who the other man was. When he would not take no for an answer, the Baal Shem Tov finally agreed to let him know the identity of the secret visitor under one condition. Rabbi Baruch had to keep it secret under all circumstances.

The mysterious apparition Rabbi Baruch saw was none other than the illustrious Rabbi Loew who appeared in front of the Baal Shem Tov, in that particular place, that particular night, to let him know that it was time for his soul to be reborn. It would descend and dwell in the future son of Rabbi Baruch, whom he should call Lev, after the Maharal. Rabbi Baruch's eyes filled with tears and he did not know how to express his deep gratitude. He wanted to take care of the Baal Shem Tov's worldly needs from then on, yet the Baal Shem Tov graciously but firmly declined the offer. Rabbi Baruch had to continue treating the Baal Shem Tov and his wife just like all the other beggars whom he helped out.

The Baal Shem Tov and Hana left as soon as the Sabbath was over and Rabbi Baruch never saw them again.

In a year's time, Rabbi Baruch's wife gave birth to a son who was called Moshe Lev. When the child grew up he became a distinguished rabbi, also known as the famous grandfather from Shpola.

23

The Bartered Song

The Great Plain of Hungary is a flat region of the country. God sprinkled small hills, sand dunes, and little valleys here and there to make it more interesting and not be envious of the other parts of the land that are full of thick forests, spectacular mountains, and unusual rock formations. The Great Plain can also boast of having the most fertile soil of Hungary, of producing the richest crops, and of being a dreamland for cattle, horses and, particularly, grazing sheep. That is the way it is today and that is the way it was during the lifetime of Rabbi Yiztchak Taub, the tzaddik of Nagykallo.

Rabbi Taub (1781–1821) lived in the little village of Nagykallo, near the town of Nyiregyhaza in the county of Szabolcs. He was very knowledgeable and had the reputation of a saintly man. It was his habit to travel around the Great Plain and provide services such as teaching, advice, and support to the small Jewish communities dispersed among the many villages and small settlements in the area.

One summer day early in the morning, as soon as the rooster finished his call, the rabbi set out in his carriage to visit a sick man who needed his help. It was a long ride to that particular village and the old horse did not heed the orders of the reinsman. It was just too weak and made its way slowly and sluggishly. The coach rattled and heaved along the dirt road and the rabbi, who had spent most of the night studying the Talmud, dozed off. He woke up when the coach stopped abruptly and he heard the curses of the driver. The coachman was an impatient man and did not seem to be able to quit his bad habit despite the rabbi's reprimands and his own frequent awkward apologies.

The rabbi descended from the coach and rested in the shade of a tree while the coachman was tending to the tired horse. It was a lovely spot where they had come to a halt and the rabbi enjoyed the landscape, the gently rolling hills, the scent of the grass at midday, and the sight of a shepherd and his grazing sheep nearby. He felt very much at peace and relaxed and thought that that place was definitely a little slice of heaven. He saw a bird fly by and he could have sworn that it had green wings and blue legs, of a color and tint he could have only imagined in his dreams. The feathers sparkled as if the bird was covered with emeralds and precious stones and before the rabbi could have another look it disappeared behind the tree.

Suddenly he heard the sound of a melody and almost stopped breathing for a while. It came from the direction where the shepherd was grazing his sheep and the tune did not just reach his ears but touched his soul. It sounded so familiar, yet he knew he had not heard the melody before. The shepherd stopped playing on his flute and began singing the same song. The words he used were simple and the verse plain, yet the impact it had on the rabbi was immense. He jumped up like a young lad and as fast as he could approached the shepherd who was very surprised to see the rabbi coming towards him. He got up and respectfully greeted the stranger.

The rabbi said: "My dear man, where did you learn this song?"

The shepherd explained that the song was a very old one. The shepherds passed it from one generation to another and he had been singing it since his childhood. He was flattered that the rabbi liked it so much and offered to teach it to him.

The rabbi said: "Please do, but I want to buy the song from you so that it belongs to me and my people."

The shepherd was quite amazed to hear such a request. "Sir," he said, "the song is not for sale. I receive money only for my labor and I could not accept anything for a tune that belongs to whoever wants to sing or listen to it."

The rabbi sat down on the grass and asked the young man to sing the song again. The shepherd happily complied and sang sweetly about his poor sheep that had been suffering, asking him to beg God to provide for them. The shepherd honored their request and implored God to help them in times of trouble. Soon—the song continued—there arrived a messenger riding a donkey, delivering the tidings that God was going to take care of his sheep and protect them from harm. Rabbi Taub's tears ran freely down his cheeks while he listened to the sad melody delivered so beautifully by the plaintive voice of the shepherd. The coachman approached them in the meantime and also listened to the song with an open mouth.

When the shepherd finished, the rabbi turned to the carriageman and said: "Reb Shlomo, do not look so surprised. God works in amazing ways. You have noticed that this is undoubtedly a song about the coming of the Messiah sung by a gentile shepherd in the middle of a distant Hungarian meadow. We have to take this song back to our village."

The shepherd listened attentively to the rabbi who in the end convinced him to accept a small sum for teaching him the song. He explained to the young man that teaching is labor and as such he is entitled to a reward. He thanked the shepherd, mastered the song, and left the place with joy in his heart.

The shepherd's song became very famous among the Hasidim. They sang it often and with fervor, and they had only one regret, that despite their enthusiasm and intensity, the Messiah did not come, no matter how many times they sang the song. Why did the Messiah refuse to come? Why did he not hear the song of the Rabbi from Nagykallo? The answer is buried in the fact that the original song was sung in Hungarian and not in Hebrew, God's sacred tongue.

Rabbi Taub's grave is visited every year on the anniversary of his death which happens to be the same as that of Moses. Hundreds of people flock to the cemetery to honor the memory of the great tzaddik and to sing together the famous bartered song.

The shepherd lived a long and simple life, happily taking care of his sheep and singing his songs. Despite his exceptional memory and good ear he forgot just one song, the one he loved most, the one he sold to the rabbi. As soon as the rabbi left that day, he could not remember it anymore and no matter how hard he tried, the tune never came back to him.

24

The Headstone of Anna Schmidt

Only Jews were buried in the Old Jewish Cemetery in Prague, yet there was a grave that bore the name of a woman who was not Jewish by birth but a convert. The gilded headstone was that of Anna Schmidt. It had an engraving of a broad meadow with three stars in the horizon. Two ferocious lions shielded the borders of the field as guardians of the property.

Legend tells us of the unhappy, abused wife of the King of Poland who was a tyrant and took pleasure in Anna's suffering. He had married her when she was still a teenager, innocent and trusting. She was from a small Polish town where her father, an impoverished nobleman, had practically sold his dazzling, beautiful daughter to the king to find grace in his eyes.

The king was twice as old as the young girl and had no understanding of her love of life, her eagerness to explore all there was to be seen, and her sunny disposition. He forced her to spend her days in the dark rooms of the castle, not allowing her to participate in any of the festivities he enjoyed. In time Anna became withdrawn and sorrowful and aged fast. She would have become an old woman way before her time had it not been for a young page who saw her suffering and wanted to help her. They fell madly in love and kept their passionate affair secret for a very long time. Then one day the word was out that they were lovers and Anna as well as the page were sentenced to death.

Anna's salvation came the night before she was to be beheaded. She was sitting in a dark corner of the dungeon, crying bitterly, knowing that her lover was already dead and her only solace the thought that she would be able to join him soon. Suddenly she heard voices outside the cell and, when the rusty, creaking door opened, her maid rushed in carrying a bundle. The old woman fell to her knees and confessed that she had told another servant about the queen and the young man and felt responsible for the whole disaster. The guard of the dungeon was her long-time friend and was ready to help the queen escape. He was waiting outside the tower with a carriage and a horse to take them across the border towards freedom. At first the queen stubbornly refused to listen to her maid's supplications and assured her she held no rancor against her. Yet, when the old woman kept insisting that she should escape, describing all the wonderful things that could still be hers in life, the queen mellowed and decided to follow her maid's advice.

In the deep darkness of a moonless night, the three fled south towards the Czech land. While sitting in the cart, the servant disclosed to her queen that she was Jewish and so was her friend, and that they were going to take her straight to the Jewish Ghetto of Prague where all of them would be safe.

And so it happened. The queen lived among the Jewish people of the ghetto all her life. She was at first apprehensive of their habits, but soon learned all their customs and got attached to many of the inhabitants who became her friends. She did not need charity. Her maid had managed to bring along with her most of the queen's jewels which she felt were rightfully hers, since the king had treated her so despicably. In time the queen decided to convert to the Jewish faith and spent the last years of her life as a devoted member of the Jewish community. After her death, the Jews buried her in their cemetery under the name Anna Schmidt, which became her assumed name. They were afraid that the Polish King, who was still alive, would desecrate the grounds and dig up her grave if he ever found out that his wife was interred there.

Many years have passed since then and nobody knows were Anna Schmidt's tomb is. Yet the legend of her tragic life lives on.

25

The Eternal Punishment

It is believed that the deceased of the Prague ghetto rest in peace in the Jewish cemetery close to the right bank of the river Vltava. The graveyard which is also called the "garden of life" in reality resembles an old, somewhat desolate and neglected plot where the bushes grow sparingly and the trees have twisted branches and protruding roots.

Only one departed cannot rest in tranquillity. He, who renounced his faith, is forced night after night to leave his grave. Although born and brought up in the ghetto, he left his religion, became a Christian, and spent his life serving Jesus as the chaplain at the cathedral of Saint Vitus. Only on his death bed did he remember his origin and felt an uncontrollable desire to return to the "good place" of his forefathers. The desolate man also knew that the girl he had loved once was buried in the Jewish graveyard. The convert repented just before he died and having accepted once again the faith of Abraham, was allowed to be interred in the Jewish cemetery.

On the surface the supplicant's wish was granted, but the dead man could not escape the eternal curse of those who forsake their faith. He was fated to leave his grave every night at the strike of eleven o'clock. At that time he rushes to the bank of the river Vltava where a boat with a skeletal rower awaits him. He has to be at the same place every single night, regardless of the seasons or the weather. Once in the boat, the skeleton transports him to the other side where both get off and race along the streets of the sleeping town uphill to the church. The former chaplain then sits at the organ and plays while his bony companion pushes the pedals. At the stroke of midnight both leave the church in haste and rush back to the banks of the river. When the boat hits the right bank the deadly rower disappears in the darkness. The desperate eternal wanderer returns to his grave where he is doomed to wait for the next night when he will embark once again on his never-ending journey.

26

The Magic Ring

Elohim, the Eternal God of Israel, wore a most exquisite ring on his finger. Many precious stones were attached to it: amethysts, opals, emeralds, sapphires, jaspers, and granite gems. Each of them flashed thousands of sparks and lit the firmament with a dazzling glow that twinkled as millions of stars on a clear enchanting night.

One day God in his infinite wisdom set his heart to create the most extraordinary land which is the land of Israel. Till then it was bare and deserted, just a range of mountains, desolation, and utter chaos.

Elohim turned the ring on his finger and thousands of multicolored sparks flew and descended over the pinnacles of the Galilee and Ephraim as well as the valley of Jordan. They landed as far as the Dead Sea, the desert, and the high-reaching peaks of the Negev. At once the mountains wore the insuperable bluish gleam that covers the range at dawn and dusk. At the very same time, bands of luminous glittering circles surrounded the Jordan valley. They looked like flaming rings or sparkling chains that had joined hands in a dance of joy and exultation.

God saw that it was good and turned the ring again and a multitude of fiery specks covered the range of Jehudah with a pink glimmering tallith. At times it reappears on a melancholy autumn evening over the skies of the Galilee in the shape of a glowing cluster of purplish clouds.

God moved his hand upwards and downwards and a particle from a precious stone flew over the mountains of the Negev and crashed with such force that it melted at once and became the sea of Eilat. It sparkles and shines as an emerald day and night, and the land surrounding it is adorned with an unbelievable display of colors that came from God's ring.

Elohim's gaze turned to the north and He saw the mountains of Galilee turning misty, dark, and sad toward nightfall, and He felt like cheering them up and enhancing them with brightness. He turned his ring once more and the most beautiful of the sapphires fell toward the earth and embedded itself between the mountains of the Galilee. It is the sea that bears its name or Kinneret. It is embraced by the Golan range in the east and the crest of the lower Galilee in the west. Its starry eye is forever turned upwards longing for the place it fell from. Its loyalty and love of God is as deep as its waters that shine and glitter, hinting at the majesty that is Elohim's eternal glory. And thus it came to pass that the most beautiful of God's precious sapphires became the sea of Galilee.

27

The Wandering Jew

There is a small town in the southeastern part of the Czech land, where a traveler can admire till this very day a majestic bell that hangs resplendent on the church's tower. It chimes every hour on the hour and its deep resounding ring seems to traverse the ages. At times, while watching it rock mightily from side to side, one gets the feeling that if it could, it would lift itself from bondage, leave the tower it is attached to, and fly away. The fastened bell, as magnificent as it might be, is a slave doomed to serve the church and its people for as long as it is meant to do its work. This has to do ironically, in a twisted way, with the story of the Wandering Jew. Unlike the hitched bell he is free to roam all over the world, yet in a way he is in captivity too. Just like the bell, he is unable to unchain himself from his fate.

The bell has been in its place since 1505, a gift presented to the town by Vaclav Kohout, a linen merchant. He had found a treasure under very unusual circumstances and wanted to commemorate the event.

In the spring of that particular year, Vaclav Kohout, his wife, Martha, and their two children went for a stroll. It was a lovely, sunny Sunday, and the couple watched as their children frolicked and ran along the streets of the town at first and later across the beautiful green fields that surrounded it. After a while they reached the spot they were aiming for. It was a lovely meadow in the midst of which stood a gigantic oak tree. Its branches spread far and wide as if the tree was willing to protect the whole world. Sitting in the shade, the happy family unpacked their basket and enjoyed their lunch. Suddenly, out of nowhere, a beggar appeared, slowly making his way towards the oak. He was a very old man, somewhat bent, with a long drab beard, shabby clothes, and a hat that had a number of holes in it. Martha noticed him right away and was particularly puzzled by his outfit, since it seemed so old fashioned as if it belonged to a different age. Nevertheless, she greeted him kindly and offered some of their food.

"God bless you, my child," said the old man and sat down to eat. He was very hungry but ate slowly and with grace. He smiled at the children who were somewhat apprehensive and watched the stranger from afar. "You must have been traveling for quite a while," said Vaclav, looking at the man's dusty clothes and the worn out shoes. "Oh, yes," answered the guest, "I have been on the road for a long, very long time, all over the world and have not been able to find the peace I am searching for." He paused for a moment and exclaimed with a doleful voice: "Will I ever find it?" The soft-hearted Martha wanted to give the stranger a few coins but he refused, explaining that he could not accept money, nothing but some food and water to sustain himself. He thanked them humbly and they followed him with their eyes till he disappeared in the distance.

That was the last carefree time the Kohouts had for many years to come. Within two weeks after their encounter with the beggar, a terrible fire broke out in town. Many people lost all their property and belongings, and the Kohouts were among them. When everything was reduced to ashes, they packed their meager bundles and headed towards Germany, thanking God that their lives had been spared. Vaclav Kohout worked diligently for many years to save some money to be able to return home. No matter how hard life would be in their hometown, they wanted to go back to their place of origin and struggle there rather than remain in a foreign country. When they reached their town, it was autumn and all they found was the burned lot, the ruins covered with weeds, and some wild animals roaming around. They set up their tent hoping to be able to rebuild the house with the small amount of money they had saved.

Soon afterwards they went to visit their favorite oak tree and there was no limit to their surprise when they met the same old man with whom they had shared their meal that sunny day in the past. Martha told him about their misfortune and that, regardless of what the future would bring, she would rather sit under her beloved tree than anywhere else in the whole wide world. She loved the oak so much because her great grandfather had planted it back in his day. He had been the wealthiest man in the area and a vast section of the town's land had belonged to him.

"What was the name of your great grandfather?" asked the old wanderer, and there was an urgent note in his voice.

"There was no richer man in town in those days," answered Martha, "He was known as affluent Dudyk."

"Dudyk!" cried out the beggar. "Do you know when he died?"

"Sometime during the Hussite wars!" said Martha, thinking that the stranger was asking, indeed, very odd questions.

"Blessed be God!" exclaimed the old man, "Your troubles are over!"

The astounded Kohouts listened to the story that the old man told them. Eighty years ago, while wandering in the countryside, he met Martha's great granddad Dudyk who was in the process of planting the oak tree in that very same field. Dudyk had greeted the wanderer kindly and guessed who he was. He asked him for a favor at that time and the old man was ready to oblige. Dudyk was a very cautious man and knew that riches do not last forever. He wanted to ensure that his offspring would not suffer in times of misery and, therefore, buried a chest of coins under the oak. He asked the wanderer to reveal the place to his family only if he should not return alive from the war. And so it happened. Yet the wanderer did not reappear in the area for many long years, and when he did and found out about Dudyk, he was not able to locate the descendants.

Initially, the Kohouts were thrilled with the news but at the same time very suspicious since it seemed almost impossible for the wanderer to have known Martha's relative so many years ago. Vaclav did not hesitate and asked the old man point blank: "How could you have know Martha's great grandfather when you are at most eighty years old?" The stranger smiled bitterly and answered: "I am many times eighty years old, dear sir, many, many times. Even when I met Dudyk I looked just the way I do now, and that was the way the first kings of the Czech Land, the Premysls, saw me. I have many more years to wander till I will find the peace I long for!" Martha was gazing at the old man in amazement and whispered: "Then you must be the man people tell stories about, the perpetual wanderer, the eternal Jew!" "Yes, that is me," sighed the old man and he disappeared into the thicket.

When the Kohouts recovered from their shock, they sat down for a while and thought things over. Vaclav was very skeptical and sure that the old man had pulled their leg. Martha, on the other hand, wanted to find out what was buried under the oak. They brought some spades and started digging. A long time passed and Vaclav was getting angrier by the minute. Finally he threw his tool away and told his wife that he was fed up and that the wanderer was probably somewhere nearby roaring with laughter. Martha, though, was not satisfied and continued working while her husband was grumbling and fuming. Suddenly the spade hit something and they both heard a metallic sound. When they continued digging they uncovered a small trunk all rusty and eaten up by the passage of time. The lock was rotten and fell off as soon as they touched it and they were able to open it without any effort. And inside, just as the old man had told them, there were the golden coins that had belonged to Dudyk. They both fell on their knees and thanked God and the eternal Wandering Jew for coming to their aid.

The money served them well. They were able to build a lovely home and live prosperously for the rest of their lives. Thus the wish of the great grandfather was granted and the stranger never came back to that part of the country. But the tale of the Wandering Jew has been passed from one generation to another.

28

Dust Is Not Just Dust

Hard times fell on the Jews of Russia. The Czar had issued a decree according to which all merchants, who had not been born in the country, had to leave Russia. A Hungarian Jew who had made his home and fortune in the city of Lodz was desperate and wanted by all means to prevent disaster from striking his family. He knew that there was one way out but was reluctant to follow that path since he was an observant Jew and did not want to sin. He decided to visit the local rabbi and ask his advice on the matter.

"Dear rabbi," he said when he stood face to face with the respected sage. "I am a good Jew and as such I need your guidance. I cannot leave this country unless I want to lose everything and turn my whole family into beggars. There is only one way out, as you know, and that is to convert to Christianity. Of course, the conversion is not going to be a real one since I intend to remain a Jew at home and in my heart and will use Christianity only as a means to an end. How can a few drops of baptismal water make me a non-Jew when I will always be loyal to Adonai?"

A shadow of a smile appeared on the rabbi's face and the worried merchant thought that he had pleaded his case well and saved himself from ruin. But the rabbi did not agree with him. He answered: "God blessed Jacob by promising him that his offspring would multiply as dust. It says in the book of Genesis (28:14): 'Your descendants will also be like the dust of the earth, and you will spread out to the west and to the east and to the north and to the south; and in you and in your descendants shall all the families of the earth be blessed.'"

The rabbi continued, "Have you ever asked yourself, my dear man, why God chose dust to illustrate the seed of Israel? Have you? The truth is that dust resembles Jews in more than one way. The wind carries dust from place to place without destroying it, and the people of Israel are chased from country to country but are not wiped out. There is only one element that will eradicate dust in its original, purest form, and that is water. Even a few drops will turn it into mud and its form and substance will be all gone. And the same will happen to you and your family. Just one drop and you will lose your identity and invalidate yourself and yours as true Jews."

The merchant asked the rabbi for forgiveness and returned home despondent yet feeling a certain amount of relief knowing the truth no matter how bitter. He had to choose between bankruptcy or the destitution of his soul, and either way face the harsh destiny of the children of dust.

Whether he returned to Hungary or remained in Russia is unknown.

29

The Borrowed Life

A shammes and his young daughter lived in a small house adjacent to the temple. One night the shammes thought he heard a faint knocking on the door. It sounded like the clank he made with his cane when summoning the congregation to the synagogue.

"That cane will not let me sleep," he told his daughter who also had been awakened by the sound.

"Somebody is dying," she whispered and a shiver shot through her spine. "Oh, my God, it must be the rabbi!"

At that very moment the muffled sound stopped but at the same time they heard somebody knocking vigorously on the door. A sorrowful voice demanded: "Get up! Get up! Take the cane and knock on each and every door! We all must recite the psalms, our rabbi is dying!"

The shammes went out into the dark night and his terrified daughter heard the three knocks that struck each door of every single dwelling. When the noise stopped she was sure that the rabbi had passed away. She began weeping bitterly.

Yet . . . the rabbi's demise was delayed. Thanks to the recitation of the psalms, the shadow of death had retreated temporarily. The saintly man was, nevertheless, still in great danger and his pupils were already mourning and weeping. They measured the length of the rabbi's body and using a barrel of wax made a huge candle. They wrapped it in a white sheet and carried it to the cemetery where they buried it among the dead. They knew that it was a fleeting solution and it would not be possible to cheat death for long and so they purchased pine wood to build the rabbi a casket.

"God, dear God," they prayed. "What can we do to keep our rabbi alive?"

"Let us go and collect some years for him," said one of the followers. "Maybe God will assist us."

One pupil started walking from house to house writing down on a piece of paper the years, months, weeks or days of one's life a person was ready to give up for the rabbi's sake.

The young man passed by the house of the shammes. The lovely daughter was standing at the door and when asked whether she would offer a portion of her life to the rabbi she answered, crying bitterly: "All of it, all my life!"

"Should I write it down?" asked the pupil. She emphatically urged him to do so, and he did. At that very moment the rabbi recovered from his illness.

The next day they buried a young girl who had suddenly died. It was the shammes' daughter.

Initially the rabbi rejoiced in his new found health and vigor, but as time went by he became sullen, sad, and grew pale and morbid. Nobody knew why this was happening. They did not know that the rabbi, while studying the Talmud late at night, heard a plaintive voice singing softly. When he opened the window and looked out into the yard, he saw the image of a beautiful young woman with a frightening deadly smile watching from the darkness of the night.

"She could be alive, sing and rejoice," he thought to himself and tears fell on the yellow pages of the ancient volume he was reading. Once he heard the cheerful tunes of a marriage procession and within a few months the doleful moaning of a woman in labor. Sweet lullabies kept filling his sleepless nights for a few years and, when one night he heard the joyful melody of a bar mitzvah being celebrated, he mourned that he had also taken that pleasure away from the daughter of the shammes.

For a few years there was a pause and, when the sound of an ecstatic voice was heard again, the rabbi knew that the shammes' daughter was leading her own child to the chupe. "I also took that away from her," he mourned. "She would have been such a happy mother!" From then on the voice was always sweet, blissful, and void of any pain. The rabbi continued living the girl's life and he often wished that there would be some grief and sorrow in her life so that he could feel that he had at least spared her some woes. But that never happened.

The happy songs made him wish he could die. He longed for death but could not pass away. He was a very old man, weak and frail, who had lived longer than any of his contemporaries and outlived even the children he had blessed at their *brits*. Everybody was dying, except him.

"When will the time come, girl?" he asked often. "How much longer do you want to live?"

Finally one night, around midnight, he heard the heartbreaking sound of a dying person. "She is dying," he said. "Blessed be the God of Israel!"

In the morning his pupils found him dead, crouched over his books.

30

The Last Tear

Most of the time, the Golem was a faithful servant to Rabbi Loew and followed his instructions to the letter. At times he seemed to be perturbed and moody, and only after the rabbi took out the shem and let him rest over the Sabbath did he, at least for a while, return to his quiet and unobtrusive ways.

The rabbi's wife Pearl learned her lesson when she sent the Golem shopping for fish and apples. She also remembered very well the incident when her friend's kitchen had been flooded. The Golem was told to fetch a couple of buckets of water from the well. Yet when the containers were filled he would not stop and kept bringing more and more till half of the kitchen was under water. If the rabbi had not interfered, the damage would have been great. Since that day, Pearl never again asked for the Golem's assistance. But other women were not so cautious and thought to themselves that it was a pity and a real waste to let the hulky, strong creature sit at the synagogue day after day without doing anything. And so, without the rabbi's knowledge, they secretly summoned the Golem and asked him to perform different tasks that they either could not or were too lazy to do themselves.

Rebecca was the wife of the shammes and very assertive and energetic. She asked for the Golem's help often and got his attention more than others since she lived near the synagogue. She used to bribe him with the foods he liked most, the shoulet, dumplings, and during Purim the hamantashen. Rebecca was an excellent cook and the Golem, who nobody thought had any food preferences or ate at all, seemed to appreciate it a great deal. He also enjoyed looking at Sarah, Rebecca's beautiful, dark-eyed daughter who was always helping her mother in the kitchen. At times he followed her like a dog and turned his muddy eyes adoringly towards her when she brought him some food. Sarah's friends noticed the way the Golem admired the girl and teased her about it, but also warned her not to play with fire. Yet Sarah, who had her mother's disposition, laughed it off.

One Friday afternoon, the rabbi forgot to take out the shem. The Golem seemed to be agitated that day and proved to those who had had any doubts till then that he could think or at least had feelings of his own. He rose from the bench where he was sitting and started smashing everything in sight. He entered the shammes' house and began demolishing the kitchen where Rebecca stood aghast, unable to utter a sound. Sarah came running from her room when she heard the commotion and stopped short at the door, terrified at the sight she saw. She was, nevertheless, a brave girl and confident she could handle the Golem. She screamed at him and ordered him to stop. He merely turned around and grabbed her in his arms, lifting her from the floor and holding her close to his body. At that point, Rebecca woke up as if from a trance, picked up a broom from the corner of the room, and began hitting the Golem with all her might. When that did not work, she ran panic-stricken to the synagogue next door to ask the rabbi for help. In the meantime the Golem was trying to kiss the horror-struck maiden but was not very successful and kept crushing her in his deadly embrace. She was gasping for air and thought that her last hour had arrived. At that very instant though, the rabbi crossed the threshold and only when the Golem saw him and heard his angry voice did he release Sarah and walk humbly back to the bench outside the house where he sat down.

Rabbi Loew asked the Golem to follow him and led him to the attic of the synagogue. There he told him to lie down. The Golem trembled and looked at his master as if asking for mercy, knowing that his time had come. The rabbi understood his plea and told him: "Your strength is of no use to us anymore and it has become a menace to the whole congregation. Your job is done. Lie down and sleep forever!" At that moment the rabbi thought that he saw on the Golem's face an expression of deep sorrow as if imploring the rabbi to spare him. So human and sad was the supplication that for a moment the rabbi felt his heart stop and he was overwhelmed with pity. Yet, he did not give in and, once the Golem lay down, he removed the shem for the last time. The Golem crumbled into a big mass of soil, only the head remained intact, and the rabbi saw a tear slowly emerging from the closed eyelid. That saddened him immensely and he pondered about it in the days to come.

Leaving the attic, Rabbi Loew descended to his congregation to sanctify the Sabbath with the singing of the psalms.

31

Two Skinny Goats

In the midst of a forest, close to a town in Poland, there lived a poor Hasid and his wife. Every Sabbath the husband went to pray in the synagogue and study the sacred books. Nobody knew what he did during the week, yet it was common knowledge that he was the owner of two very skinny goats that provided him with a meager amount of milk. Every morning the wife untied the goats and took them out to pasture and in the evening she tied them again to a pole. The milk was sold as well as the bit of cheese and butter they were able to get out of it and that was their sole livelihood.

One evening the wife forgot to tie the animals to the pole and in the morning they were gone. The woman began crying and bewailing the harsh fate that took away from them the very little they had. Yet the husband stopped her and told her that it must have been determined in heaven. The woman pondered over her husband's words, and looking into his eyes, understood that there was more to it than she could grasp. Her husband had used the same words the day they bought the tiny does. Surely he must have been aware of something she did not know.

The goats returned the same day before dusk and gave plenty of milk, much more than on any regular day and it was rich and sweet as never before! The Hasid and his wife stopped tying the goats during night, and each day the animals came back from their pasture with their udders almost bursting with the wholesome milk. Whoever drank it knew bliss and those who were weak or sick recovered in no time and felt strong and healthy.

Six days passed and on the seventh the Hasid decided to follow the goats to their destination and discover the secret pasture. The goats strode along a path in the forest for awhile. When they approached a pile of broken branches lying at the end of the narrow trail, they paused for a short while and then continued through a passage that led under the stack of wood to a tunnel. The Hasid did not think twice and went underground after them. Suddenly he found himself in a dark place that was haunted by demons and devils of all kinds. Yet he went on and did not look right or left. The noise was deafening but he forced himself not to pay attention and went on. He did not look right and he did not look left. Naked, luring women blocked his way and huge, menacing stones started rolling from the sides of the passage. He felt tremendous fear, yet he did not look right, he did not look left, and continued walking. As he went on, the noises subsided and the frightening images dissipated as well.

Suddenly he saw a light at the end of the tunnel and when he emerged into the brightness, he saw a dazzling, beautiful landscape. The sun was shining and the scent of orange and lemon blossoms was felt in the crisp air. A young shepherd was sitting on the grass, playing a heart-warming melody on his flute. He addressed the stunned Hasid asking whether he too had moved to the countryside. It seemed that the youngster had just arrived at Sefad from the outskirts of Jerusalem. The Hasid's knees almost buckled with awe and his heart filled with joy when he realized that his feet were standing in Eretz Israel.

When he recovered from the shock, he kissed the soil and gave his thanks to God. At once he wrote a note to his wife and the people of his town about the events that had transpired. He suggested they do the same as he had done and follow the goats to the land of milk and honey. He warned them of the dangers they would encounter along the way but promised them that they could overcome them with their faith and love of God just as he had. When he finished, he addressed his letter to the rabbi of the town and placed it in a fig leaf. Then he tied it to the neck of one of the goats and sent them back home.

When the goats reached the Hasid's house without him, the wife became extremely agitated, fearing the worst. So great was her concern that she did not notice the fig leaf that was tied to the goat's neck. She waited for a day, two . . . and by the end of the third day felt sure that her husband had been killed by some bandits in the forest. She mourned deeply and being all by herself, decided to leave her home in the woods and move to the town to be near all the other Jewish inhabitants. She would have no use for the goats there since she planned to find a job, so she sent them off to the shochet, hoping to get some money for their meat.

After the shochet performed his task, he found the letter tied to one of the animals and rushed it to the rabbi. The rabbi was devastated. The goats were dead, there was no way to bring them back to life and no way to find the path leading to the Holy Land without them. The rabbi ordered the congregation to go on a three-day fast and pray with their whole souls. He was positive that they had missed the once-in-a-lifetime opportunity because of their sins and transgressions and they would have to continue and wait in the diaspora for the Messiah to come.

For many years the letter was kept in a secret place in the synagogue till the whole building was burnt down. It turned into ashes and was scattered to the wind. Only the tale remains.

32

The Cat

It was summertime, toward dusk, one of the hottest days of the season. Yemima was sitting near the open window trying to get as comfortable as possible. There was not even a single wisp of breeze in the air and it felt as if the whole world was on fire. She could not remember such a torrid summer in the Old City of Prague, and God knows she was not a spring chicken. Her husband Yankel and she were living alone since their daughter had married some years back and moved out of town. They were getting old, yet Yemima thanked God everyday for the blessing of being capable of taking care of herself and her husband. Yankel continued going to the shul regularly and was considered one of the most respected people in the ghetto. Not only had he served his community well as a carpenter and people praised the furniture he built for them, but he was also known as a scholar and a true believer in God.

From her window Yemima could see the narrow, twisted street of the old Jewish Ghetto where they lived and there was no living soul in sight. "No wonder," she thought, "Who in his right mind would venture out!" Most people kept indoors, although the sweltering heat made it difficult to breathe inside as well. Yankel had to lie down to rest. He was not a very healthy man and suffered from intense headaches quite often. Such was the case that day and Yemima kept changing the cold, wet cloth she placed on his forehead. She was grateful he had fallen asleep a while earlier and could escape the scorcher that way. She touched his forehead and it felt cooler than before when she had feared he was feverish. He looked flushed but was breathing evenly and sleeping peacefully. Feeling relieved, she changed the towel once more and returned to her seat at the open window.

Suddenly she noticed something dark perched on the roof across their house. It moved a little and she realized it was a black cat. It was odd it would be sitting on the blistering tiles and not seeking some shade away from the heat. Yemima got up and moved to another window to have a closer look, and to her great surprise and concern she saw that the cat was in labor, about to give birth. She froze for a moment and then called out to the cat to come to her so that she could help her. There was no way she could reach her on the roof and she was afraid the animal would die there right in front of her eyes. The cat, nevertheless, turned her head as if she understood what Yemima was asking her and made an effort to move. The labor pains must have subsided since she was able to crawl from the roof and make it across the narrow ledge to Yemima's window sill. Yemima picked her up gently and carried her carefully to the kitchen. She placed her on a clean towel in a wicker basket where she stored coal in the winter. The cat meowed painfully for a while and gave birth to three small black kittens.

Yemima and Yankel took good care of the small family and the cat seemed to express her gratitude constantly. She meowed whenever she saw them and rubbed her body against their legs showing her affection. One day she brought a dead mouse and placed it at Yemima's feet which made the surprised woman scream and run out of the door. Yankel disposed of the dead animal and realized that it was a "gift" the cat meant to offer them. The intelligent feline understood what had happened and never again brought in mice. Instead, Yemima found a yellow field flower on the kitchen table one day. She placed it in a glass container, and caressed the cat thanking her for the present. She appreciated it greatly, particularly since the cat had to travel far away from the ghetto into the open country to find such a lovely meadow flower.

Then one morning the cat was gone and so were the kittens. No matter where they looked, Yemima and Yankel could not find them. Nobody had seen them in the neighborhood, and after a while the couple gave up their search and even stopped talking about it. When winter arrived and they were about to fill the basket with coal, their surprise knew no limits when they discovered a few pieces of gold on the bottom. It was possible that the previous winter, Yemima might have forgotten a few pieces of coal inside the basket, but gold? Finally they came to the conclusion that it was the cat's doing and that it must have been some magical animal with supernatural powers. When, after a few days, the gold remained solid, they took it to the rabbi and asked him to use it to restore the synagogue which was so precious to all the Jews of Prague. The rabbi accepted the gift and did as requested.

This, though, is not the end of the story.

Yankel had prayed all his life to be granted the great privilege of dying and being buried in Jerusalem. He thought, as a young man, that perhaps there was a chance he could travel to the Holy Land, but when he got old and ill he knew that he would never be able to fulfill his dream. He accepted his fate and prayed fervently for the coming of the Messiah. One day, Yemima was sitting at her window darning Yankel's old socks when the cat reappeared on the roof. Excited, Yemima called out to Yankel that their cat was back. The cat though would not come close to the house but kept meowing as if calling them to come out. Yankel decided to see what that was all about and followed the cat on his own while his wife stayed at home to fix dinner. He promised Yemima to return promptly, hopefully with the cat. Some time passed and neither Yankel nor the cat were back. After a couple of hours, Yemima became worried and went out in search of her husband. People told her that they had seen him following the cat in the direction of the synagogue. At the shul, the shammes assured Yemima that her husband was inside praying and promptly went to call him. He never found him and neither did Yemima or any other member of the congregation. Yemima was heartbroken and could not find solace. Finally, when all hope had been lost, her daughter came to take Yemima away to her home where she mourned her husband's disappearance till the day she died.

And Yankel, where was he? He had followed the cat to the synagogue and indoors. The cat continued meowing, leading him toward the back of the shul where suddenly Yankel discovered some stairs leading underground. Without thinking twice, he followed the cat into a long tunnel that became narrower and darker until he saw some light at the end of it. As he emerged from the semi–darkness he found himself in an unknown land. People around him were going about their daily business. The sun was shinning. The sky was pale blue and a pleasant breeze was blowing from the east. When Yankel asked a passer-by where he was, he was told that he was standing in the Holy Land, in the city of Jerusalem. Yankel's surprise was so great that his feet gave up and he fell to the ground. So intense was his gratitude to God that his body could not deal with it and his soul departed at once. Thus his dearest wish was granted. He was buried in the sacred soil and richly rewarded for his lifelong devotion.

33

A Billy Goat with Human Eyes

Not too far from the town of Kotsk in Poland, there lived a sock knitter by the name of Leyb. His mother had taught him this skill and he had learned to make different kinds of socks at a very early age. He seemed to have a special talent at that and worked very fast and efficiently. When his widowed mother died, he was still a very young boy and continued to make his living following his mother's profession. So busy had he been all his life that he never received any education and spent his days without being able to study, just knitting away in his little cottage that was all the property he had. Every day he got up at dawn and by noon he finished knitting three pairs of socks which he promptly took to the local market and sold. His life was quite monotonous and Leyb was not a happy man. He felt that he had missed his real calling because of the lack of learning. He believed that he could even have been a rabbi if only . . . if only.

Yet, there was one thing that brought joy to his bleak life and that was his tobacco pipe. After he finished his work, sold the socks, and bought some more wool with the earnings, he also purchased some tobacco and filled his little smoke box to the rim. Then, at home, lighting his pipe and puffing away, he dreamed his dreams and felt content for a while as long as there was tobacco left in his box.

One afternoon he sold his merchandise for a very good price and felt very happy about it. He purchased a better brand of tobacco and headed home, already envisioning himself sitting in his chair and enjoying the pipe. It was getting quite late since he had lingered choosing the special tobacco and Leyb was whistling happily, smiling at the full moon that had just risen, and feeling less miserable than usual.

Yet, when he reached his cabin and was about to pull out his precious tobacco box, he almost fainted out of sheer despair. The box was not in his pocket and no matter how hard he tried, looking for it everywhere, all around the cottage and even in front of the house, he could not find it. He sat down on the porch and tears of grief rolled down his cheeks.

"Dear God," he said loudly. "We Jews have such a terrible destiny, what kind of life do we live? Our Temple was destroyed. We have been wandering from country to country and wherever we go we are mostly shunned and mistreated. The only joy you left us is the sacred Torah and its study. But I have never had time to learn anything that would lead me to the Torah. All I do is knit, knit, and knit and sell socks. I cannot enjoy the sweetness of Your wisdom and my only pleasure has been tobacco. Why have You denied me even that little bit of happiness? Why have I lost my tobacco box?"

Leyb cried his heart out for awhile and then he started walking, not knowing where his feet led him. He left his cabin behind, crossed some fields and a wooded area, and finally collapsed in a grassy meadow. His sorrow was so deep, his desperation so intense, that he could not proceed and he felt that his heart was going to burst. Suddenly he heard a horrific sound, as if thousands of hoofs were galloping through the meadow. Terrified he fell on his back and when he recovered from the fall, sat up, and opened his eyes. He saw towering in front of him a gigantic billy goat. His legs were as thick as tree trunks, his body as mighty as a fortress, and his straight horns reached the skies. Leyb thought that his end had come but suddenly he heard a wonderful melody that seemed to originate from within the stars and voices praising the wisdom and love of God. His trepidation vanished when he gazed into the eyes of the goat that stood above him motionless and saw in them the affection and concern of a loving human being.

The goat addressed the sock knitter and asked him: "What is the matter? What causes you so much pain?"

Leyb gathered as much courage as he had left and told the goat about his bad luck and how he had lost his tobacco box.

The goat listened patiently and then shook his head.

"Is that all!" he said. "I can easily help you fix that. Cut a piece of my horn and it will serve you as a very good box to store your tobacco!"

Leyb did not have to be asked twice. He pulled out his little pocket knife and, when the goat lowered his head, he cut a small piece of the hefty horn.

The next day he filled his pipe from the new box he had and smoked to his heart's content. A strange thing happened. No matter how much he smoked, the tobacco kept coming, it never ended. The unusual box was never empty. Besides that Leyb noticed something even more marvelous. The more he puffed and puffed, the clearer his head became. His mind seemed to have lost its simplicity and he began thinking deep thoughts. He felt as if he were in the temple in Jerusalem inhaling a heavenly scent. He sensed that the box was like a great magical sage that taught him the mysteries of the Torah and each additional puff seemed to add to his learning.

His new found wisdom did not remain a secret for long and Leyb became a famous and well-sought man. He was able to conduct discourses and answer questions that even the wisest rabbis could not tackle. In the end he gave in to pressure and revealed just to a few people how he had acquired his unbelievable knowledge.

And so Yankel the tailor, Pinchas the shochet, Simon the cart driver, and a few others were also able to get a piece of the goat's horn and the wisdom of the inhabitants of the town grew like mushrooms after the rainy season. One day, just before the High Holidays, the goat disappeared. No matter how hard they tried and how much time they spent looking for him, they could not find him. He had vanished once and for all, maybe forever. Leyb was approached by his friends who wanted him to tell them whether he knew where the goat was, but Leyb was in the dark just as they were. He also agonized about it, worrying that he would never again encounter the magnificent animal.

Then one night he had a dream. He found himself in a tiny narrow room in which there was an old man. He looked at Leyb and told him to go to Kotsk the next day and visit Menachem Mendel, the local rabbi, who would tell him where the billy goat was. When Leyb woke up he did exactly as he had been told. For the first time that he could remember he did not knit socks and rushed empty-handed into the town to see the rabbi.

When he approached the rabbi's house, the door opened even before he had a chance to knock and the same old man he had seen in his dream opened the door. He invited Leyb to step in and took him to the same room he already knew from the previous night. And there sitting in a row were all his friends, the ones that also had gotten a piece of the horn of the billy goat with the human eyes. Leyb marveled and asked himself whether all of them had had the same dream. They all pulled out their special tobacco boxes and filling their pipes started puffing away. The smoke became thicker and denser by the minute and suddenly all of them realized the secret behind the billy goat's horns. The mist cleared and they saw the rabbi standing in front of them, looking at them with the same deep, green eyes the goat had. They realized that the rabbi was the billy goat, the secret teacher and guide who had comforted them and taught them all they knew.

The rabbi addressed them quietly: "You who met the billy goat should know more than others. There is no more knowledge left. The horns do not reach the skies anymore, they are all gone, used up. I gave you all I had." The rabbi's voice sounded weak and tired. "Now, go tell others all you have learned."

Silently he blessed each of the men and when they left he locked himself in his room. Shortly afterwards he passed away.

34

The Healthy Patient

The Rambam, Rabbi Moses ben Maimon, dwelled in Egypt after his family escaped the Islamic persecution in Spain, the country of his birth. Most Jews revered him because of his knowledge and the many treatises he wrote on Jewish law and philosophy. Yet his greatest success was his medical ability to treat and heal patients. The Sultan of Egypt asked for his services and in time the Rambam's reputation became legendary. As such he had many admirers but did not lack enemies either. Those who envied him and hated him most were other doctors at the court who wanted to destroy him. They failed many times but in one instance they were pretty sure they would be successful, or so they thought.

One day a man was sent to see the famous Maimonides. He was a relatively young man who looked sturdy and healthy, yet the expression on his face was that of discontent and pain. He complained of aches in different parts of his body as well as sluggishness, nausea, and not being able to breath. The doctor examined him thoroughly and left the patient sitting for awhile in the waiting chamber. After what seemed to the young man as an eternity, the great physician returned and told him, with sadness and concern, that his condition was very serious. The man wiggled uneasily in his chair and asked the doctor what the problem was. Maimonides refused at first to give him the information and used a few Latin words nobody but a doctor would understand. Nevertheless, when the man insisted on knowing the truth, he had no choice but to give him the gloomy news that he had only six months to live.

That night Maimonides' hostile colleagues had a party. When the conspirator whom they had hired to seek Maimonides' advice gave them the famous physician's diagnosis, they laughed as much as they possibly could and embraced each other jubilantly. They were hoping to embarrass Maimonides after the six fateful months passed when he had predicted that the man would die. The so-called patient was not sick but strong as an ox and had agreed to take part in the hoax for a large sum of money and also since he had feelings of animosity towards the Jewish doctor. Yet, while the men who hired him were partying and drinking joyfully, he went home somewhat confused and uneasy.

The healthy patient did not live for long. He was dead within the period of time that the Rambam had predicted.

The Rambam's adversaries were all frustrated and humiliated although they did not admit it and washed their hands of the whole matter, being afraid of becoming a source of laughter to the whole court. The Rambam did not spread the story of their deception. Yet a few close friends of his heard about the matter and wondered how he knew that the healthy man would die. When asked, he looked at them gravely and said: "The man knew he was not sick, yet once I planted the idea into his head he started to believe in it. In time his body followed the suggestions of his mind. He did not die of a disease but because of the strength of human conviction."

35

The Postmortem Bath

Once late at night, Rabbi Eleazar, a famous teacher and expert in the kabbalah, was deeply immersed in his studies reading the Talmud. It was very quiet in the synagogue and the only sound was that of the rabbi's breathing. Suddenly the rabbi heard a heart-breaking moan coming from the small yard that encircled the old temple. He opened the window and saw in the moonlight a white clad figure that was stretching its arms towards him in agony as if begging for something.

"What are you asking for?" asked the rabbi. "I am the wife of the glass cutter," the apparition answered. "They buried me yesterday. Nevertheless, I have not been cleansed properly since I forgot to go to the mikveh the day before I died. Therefore I had to come back. Rabbi, dear rabbi, please be so kind and give me the keys." The rabbi did not think twice and threw the heavy bundle of keys to her from the window.

Soon afterwards he heard the sound of flowing water coming from the adjacent building where the mikveh was located. He could hear the faintest sound, he heard for a while the motion of the woman getting into the water, splashing around and rinsing her hair. After some time it became very quiet again and the rabbi fell asleep over the book. Early in the morning he woke up and saw the bundle of keys hanging on its usual place over the doorstop.

36

Rabbi Loew and the Rose

Once, and not just once, did Rabbi Loew save his own life thanks to his great wisdom.

It so happened, as it had many times before, that the Jews of Prague were inflicted by a terrible plague. The pestilence affected young and old and the corpses were piled up in the cemetery since there was not enough space to bury them all. Rabbi Loew was a frail man at that time, about a hundred years old and his hair and beard were as white as snow. He studied day and night, looking through his books and manuscripts, searching in vain for the cause and the cure for the disaster that once again descended on the Jews. When his distress became unbearable he suddenly remembered a dream he had once under similar circumstances. And so, in the dead of night, he and his loyal followers left the old synagogue and approached the rear gate of the graveyard.

The rabbi reached into his pocket for the key to unlock the gate when it opened on its own. A tall, bony and pale man, holding a scroll in his skeletal hands, walked out. The wise rabbi realized right away who the stranger was and with a swift motion pulled the list out of the skeleton's hand. That lean, emaciated creature was Death itself. On the list were the names of all the people meant to die the next day, including the rabbi and his companions. Rabbi Loew's knees started shaking, yet as quick as lightning he tore the paper into tiny pieces.

"Tonight you have escaped," said Death. "Just watch out for next time!"

Rabbi Loew did indeed watch out. He knew that Death was lurking for him at every corner. Once again he submerged himself in his studies looking for a solution, at least a temporary one. Since he was very handy with mechanical gadgets, he prepared a little device for his own protection. He carried this item with him wherever he went. If Death happened to be near by, the small machine began ringing quietly like an old watch and the rabbi was able to elude the deadly traps.

Death tried many disguises to deceive Rabbi Loew, but the clever scholar noticed it each time. Sometimes Death chose the image of a greengrocer. Other times it appeared as a fisherman offering his catch for the Sabbath, an old beggar asking for alms, or even a young disciple searching for a tutor. Death could appear also as a dignified visitor who came to pay his respects to the famous rabbi. Yet each time the little gadget warned Rabbi Loew in time and he was able to save himself from the pending disaster.

A few years passed and the rabbi was celebrating another birthday. His disciples, friends, and relatives were all gathered in the main chamber to convey best wishes and to show the dear rabbi their love and respect. The rabbi was touched and in his excitement forgot the small gadget in his bedroom while he rushed with a happy smile to greet his well-wishers. The last one to approach him was his youngest granddaughter. She hugged him tenderly and gave him a lovely red rose. The rabbi kissed the child and inhaled deeply the sweet fragrance of the intoxicating flower. At that very moment he fell dead on the floor since Death had been hiding and waiting for him among the soft petals of the rose. In vain did the tiny machine play its silvery chimes over and over again in the adjacent room. It rang for a very long time till the strings broke and the bell stopped forever. Nobody noticed that on one of the petals of the fated rose there shone a drop of dew where the image of death was mirrored.

Rabbi Loew is buried on the western side of the Old Jewish Cemetery. He lies there with his beloved wife under a monument that resembles a temple. A lion is carved into the headstone. His resting place is surrounded by thirty-three graves of his most beloved disciples who guard him in death the way they did when he was alive.

37

The Gilgul of the Baal Shem Tov

The Baal Shem Tov, the illustrious founder of Hasidism, spent his life traveling in the Carpathian region, healing and helping the ill and restoring faith to the lost souls of Israel by means of prayer rather than study and pilpul. His followers worshipped him and, as time went by and he grew old and frail, nobody was ready to accept the fact that one day he would have to leave this world. They worried constantly about what they would do and what would happen once their sage would not be with them anymore.

"Rabbi, dear rabbi," they complained. "What will the world be without you if you have to leave? How will we live? How will we survive without your leadership? We are all going to be lost like sheep without a shepherd!" The rabbi comforted them gently and asked them to pray and put their trust in the God of Israel who would not forsake his children.

Years passed and the time came when the Baal Shem Tov was on his deathbed ready to join his forefathers in the next world. He bid good-bye to his loyal friends and believers and asked them not to despair. He promised to come back within a hundred years if by then the Messiah should not come.

A hundred years passed, the misery of the Jewish people continued, human nature and people's transgressions would not allow the Messiah to appear. Yet, by the end of the hundredth year, Benjamin Zeev Herzl was born. The great soul of the Baal Shem Tov descended into his body and it continued to toil towards redemption.

The Baal Shem Tov had kept his promise.

38

Rabbi Rashi

The year was 1140 and the town of Prague was celebrating the coronation of Vladislav who ascended to the throne of his father. Everybody seemed to be rejoicing except for some inhabitants of the city who quietly crept through the streets with sadness in their eyes anticipating more suffering. Those were the Jews who expected the worst from the new ruler.

In those days of anxious upheaval, a foreign rabbi arrived in Prague and became a messenger of hope to the depressed Jewish population. This was the very famous Rabbi Shlomo son of Issac, called Rashi. He was only thirty-six years old at that time but thanks to his knowledge of the kabbalah, astrology, and medicine, he was one of the most outstanding scholars of his time.

He came from his native town of Troyes in the county of Champagne. In the past, while studying in Barcelona, he excelled in the study of Greek and Arab philosophy and gained the admiration of many. At that time he was particularly interested in the works of Aristotle, the Babylonian Nathan, and the Arab Ibn Sin. When he reached the age of thirty, the wise Rashi set out on a worldly pilgrimage. From Italy he traveled to Constantinople. He visited the land of Canaan, mourned at the tombs of the prophets and kings, wandered through the ruins of Zion, and marveled at the ancient sights. He discussed the Talmud with Moshe Ben Maimonides in

Alexandria and, richer in knowledge and experience, traveled across Persia and the Mongolian steppes to Poland and the Czech land. He planned to return to the country of his birth after his visit to Prague. Wherever he went he was greeted with genuine warmth and great admiration.

While in Prague, Rabbi Rashi was the guest of Rabbi Jonathan, the oldest and most revered Czech rabbi in those days. The news of his arrival and the enthusiastic welcome given him by the Jews soon reached the ears of the ruler. Vladislav was of a suspicious nature. He feared the Jews and mainly Rashi who, he thought, could be the false Messiah. Four days after his arrival, Rashi was arrested and taken before the king's tribunal.

Vladislav was seated on his throne in the ancient hall. The bishop Zdik and the advisers Nacherad and Velislav stood close by ready to provide the king with their expert counsel. Nacherad, who owed the Jews a large sum of money, suggested to take advantage of the situation and banish the Jews from the land.

"Who are you?" roared Vladislav staring at Rashi.

Rashi calmly returned the gaze and said: "I am a Jew," and looking at the bishop added, "whom that priest will protect."

Puzzled, Zdik approached the prisoner and, when he looked into his face he recognized his friend Rashi. With great excitement he explained to his master that Rashi was the wise rabbi he had told him about, the same one who some years back had healed him from a sudden illness and saved him from death while he was visiting the Holy Land.

Vladislav immediately gave orders to release Rashi and asked him to tell his story. At that moment a messenger arrived with the news that the people of Prague, incited by the arrest of Rashi, penetrated into the Jewish ghetto ready to start a pogrom. Rashi humbly begged the monarch for help which was granted to him willingly and the danger of Jewish bloodshed was prevented.

Since that day Rashi's esteem grew in the eyes of the monarch who often asked for his advice. The bishop Zdik, Velislav, and Rashi became friends. They shared a relationship uncommon in those days and an understanding that surpassed the differences in their religious views and social position. Only Nacherad felt left out and planned his revenge.

In the meantime Rashi fell in love with Rabbi Jonathan's oldest daughter Rebecca and asked for her hand in marriage. The Jewish community saw the wedding as a good omen, hoping that Rashi would settle down in Prague permanently. Rashi, nevertheless, began planning the return to his native land and only on his father-in-law's request agreed to stay in Prague a couple of months longer.

Shortly after Rashi's wedding, Vladislav and bishop Zdik left for Moravia, leaving the advisers in charge. This was a golden opportunity for Nacherad, who obsessed with his desire for revenge decided to carry out his darkest plans. He had a number of murderers-for-hire and assigned to one of them a most heinous task. On the eve of Passover, while Rashi was chanting the habitual prayers, the assassin stormed into his house and struck him with a hatchet in the head. He was able to disappear into the darkness of the night before the shocked family realized what had happened.

Funeral preparations were underway the next day and the time came when each of the mourners, who had washed and prepared the body for burial, had to drive a nail into the coffin. Before they could accomplish that, the grief-stricken Rebecca stormed into the chamber begging them to let her behold her husband one more time. Unwillingly, and with great sorrow, the men opened the lid. Before they realized it Rebecca quickly poured a purple liquid over the dead rabbi's head. She had been searching for the miraculous potion her husband had told her about and found it before it was too late. The dead man's limbs began quivering, the wounds on his head began healing, and the breath of life flowed into his body. Soon he was able to sit up, embrace his wife and thank his friends and doctors who stood there petrified and unable to utter a word.

As soon as they got over the shock, they began worrying that the murderer would come back to finish the job if any news of Rabbi Rashi's miraculous recovery leaked out. They decided to hold a fake funeral while in reality Rabbi Rashi would return to his native land. They dug up the grave and buried a coffin filled with dirt. Rabbi Rashi though, before leaving Prague secretly, warned his friends of the unusually dangerous situation they were in. Quoting sages of old times he said, "Into the grave which carries a name no other remains may be placed but the owner's, otherwise great shame and suffering will befall the people of Israel. Therefore, I want you to keep this grave for me till the God of Abraham calls me to my resting place. Then you will transfer my remains from the other land and bury them here in my rightful place." Having made that declaration, he left Prague with his beloved Rebecca.

As long as he had dwelt among them, the inhabitants of Prague showed Rashi great respect, but as soon as he was gone, the high regard he was held in dropped surprisingly. One particular rabbi, who had been jealous of Rashi but, nevertheless, had praised him to the heavens while he was there, lashed out with venomous anger and spread filthy gossip about the famous man. Rabbi Eliezer's followers bent easily to any new directions from which the wind blew. The situation became so bad that Rashi, who was almost worshipped before, became an object of hatred to many who spoke of him as an outcast. Some went to the extreme of spitting each time Rashi's name was mentioned and that was not just to please Rabbi Eliezer. When things reached that level, Rabbi Jonathan was forced to leave Prague and travel to Champagne where he lived with his daughter and son-in-law for the rest of his life.

Rabbi Eliezer's rage did not subside with Rashi's departure. He had Rashi's grave destroyed over and over despite the fact that a higher force was at work. Each time the monument was vandalized it was restored overnight and Rashi's inscribed name shone brighter than ever.

In the year 1161 the Czech land was hit by a terrible plague. The Christian population was aware that the Jews were not as badly affected by the pestilence and, as was the habit in those days, blamed the Jews for the catastrophe. Two physicians were assigned by the king to look into it, and they came to the conclusion that indeed it was the Jews' fault since they had poisoned the wells. About a hundred Jews were taken to prison and, while being tortured, admitted to all the "crimes" for which they were being blamed. It was odd that all of them named Rabbi Eliezer as the cause of their misfortune. He was arrested and soon afterwards burned at a stake together with eighty-five of his followers in front of the gates of the Vyšehrad castle. Their ashes were thrown into the waters of the river Vltava.

Nineteen years later Rabbi Rashi passed away, and with the help of loyal followers, his remains were transferred to the original burial place. For thirty-nine years the headstone miraculously bore his name as if untouched by the passing of time.

A few weeks after Rabbi Rashi's burial, a Christian child's body was retrieved from the Vltava and once again the Jews were blamed for the crime. In the months that followed, the Jewish population was subjected to unbelievable suffering. Many of them were tortured and killed while others were banned and chased away from their homes. The synagogue was completely destroyed and the cemetery erased from the face of the earth. When the Jews were allowed back after a few years, nobody knew exactly the location of Rashi's grave. They did not try to erect another headstone in his name but the spot where he had been buried was not lost. They knew it because each time a body was interred at that particular site, the corpse was found cast outside the grave the very next day. The place were the monument had stood would not accept any other body and in time it became sacred.

Time elapsed, yet Rabbi Rashi was not forgotten.

Four centuries later, an old rabbi by the name of Simon the Righteous, a follower and great admirer of Rashi, died and was buried in the same spot. Since he had been a man of many good deeds, exceptional wisdom, and faultless reputation just like Rabbi Rashi, miraculously the plot did not reject him. As matter of fact, when the burial procession arrived at the cemetery and looked around for an appropriate spot, they found the name of Rabbi Simon already inscribed in gold on a headstone as a sign of acceptance. The legend tells us that the two rabbis were so much alike that their golden hearts found each other after death and became one. In the spring a multitude of bright golden flowers adorns the gravestone and they bloom again and again every year without fail.

39

Rabbi Loew's Tomb

In the ancient Jewish Cemetery of Prague, Rabbi Loew's grave is visited every year by thousands of people. Just as in the days after his death and in all the years that followed, people stood at the foot of the famous rabbi's resting place and paid their respects. They placed small pebbles and larger stones on the tomb to let him know they were there. They inserted small notes in the crevices of the old sepulcher to beg him for favors and ask for his protection and advice. Some received no indication that the revered sage heard their outcry, others swear by everything sacred to them that he has aided them in times of trouble and supported their plea from beyond.

Once, during the initial days of the World War I, a young woman brought her small daughter to pay their respects to the rabbi. They were from a small village outside Prague, and it had been a hardship for them to travel to the city during those difficult days. But when the young woman stood at Rabbi Loew's grave, a sudden peace descended upon her and she felt as if her troubles and concerns had vanished. Her small child was at first apprehensive and very silent, standing among the old and tumbled tombstones, and held on to her mother's skirt with all her might. The young woman tried to calm the child and told her once again the story of the rabbi, how wise and kind he had been and how loving, particularly to tiny children and especially to those who were not well. The child was very pale and thin. Only the mother knew that she was dying of tuberculosis and the doctors had given up on her. When her husband was drafted into the army and left her alone with her daughter, she decided to do the only thing she could think of and went on a pilgrimage to the rabbi's grave to ask for his help.

The mother took a small stone from her pocket and placed it on the grave and asked the child to do the same by handing her another one. The littler girl, nevertheless, refused to do so. She did not like the stone and wanted to pick another, a bigger one from an adjacent grave. When the mother prevented her from doing so, explaining that it belonged to a previous visitor and it was not hers to take, she began crying and, pulling her hand away from her mother's, ran away towards the entrance to the cemetery. The worried woman followed her at once but the small child disappeared quickly around the bend and was nowhere to be seen. It was already late in the afternoon and there was nobody around. The mother was livid with fear. She did not want to scream in the cemetery yet she had to find her daughter. She began calling her name softly and the sound of her voice increased with her worry. Soon she was shrieking and it seemed to her that the echo of her call was coming from all sides of the graveyard.

Then suddenly she saw her daughter. Nothing sinister had happened. The little girl was sitting in the dirt at the entrance to the cemetery, smiling happily, and in her hand she held a perfectly round, green pebble that was almost as big as an egg. "Where did you go," the relieved woman asked quietly. "Where were you? Why did you not answer my call? I was so worried about you!" The child looked up at her mother and said: "I did not hear your voice, Mother. I did not hear you. I was looking for a nice stone and I found one right here at the gate. Is it not nice? I like it, I like it! . . . and now I am going to put it on the rabbi's grave, the nicest pebble of them all! He will like it too, you will see!"

Indeed, Rabbi Loew did like the little girl's stone. Whether he heard the mother's plea, or whether he was grateful for the small child's devotion and good will, he did listen to their call for help. And so, regardless of the doctors' grim prophesy, the girl recovered from her illness and grew up to be a healthy maiden. Her mother never forgot the visit and what the rabbi had done for them.

They say that the rabbi is still involved even after death in the fate of the Jews, not out of choice but necessity. He will continue to study in his grave as long as needed, till the Messiah comes. He will protect his people and continue mourning the destruction of the Temple day after day, the way he used to when he was alive. One can hear his lamentations every day around midnight, except for the Sabbath, Rosh Chodesh, and eves of holidays, coming from the Old New Synagogue adjacent to the cemetery.

The rabbi's beloved Pearl is buried next to him as well as his grandson. His only son died in the town of Kolin and had to be buried there. When Loew's grandson passed away, the elders of the community visited the rabbi's grave hoping for a sign. When they arrived at the site, the plot where the rabbi was buried had widened considerably to accommodate another member of his family. Once the grandson was buried there, the plot shrunk again so as not to crowd the others who were resting next to the rabbi and his wife. Rabbi Loew's generation used to place gifts and money on the rabbi's tombstone that were meant for the poor and desolate. Although this does not happen any longer, the hundreds of stones and pebbles that have accumulated over the centuries and crumbled into dust express the ongoing love and reverence that Rabbi Loew has always commanded.

40

The Unblessed Child

There was once a child who would not let his father bless him either on a Friday evening or during the Sabbath. Whenever the father came back from the synagogue and called his children, the two older ones came running and lowering their heads let their father place his hands on them and bless them. The third child was either too busy to come to greet his father or even hid to avoid the ceremony. He died early in his childhood.

The first Friday evening after the child's death, when the father came home from the temple as usual, the two kids came running asking for his blessing. When he placed his hands on their heads he had a feeling that he was touching a third one. In consternation, he removed his hands and tried to bless each child separately. Again he had the sensation that a third head was reaching forcefully for his hands. The same thing happened on the Sabbath and during the first thirty days of mourning. Distraught, with his long beard and mustache still unkempt, the sorrowful father sought the advice of the rabbi. "If it should happen again," said the rabbi after a long silence, "hold your hands over the imaginary head and bless it. It is your child."

The next Friday the father did as he had been told. He held his hands in the air over the little head he felt yet could not see and blessed it using Jacob's words for his son Josef. Since that day the unblessed child slept peacefully in its grave.

41

The Spilled Soup

Very few rabbis were as beloved as Rabbi Elimelech. Years ago he dwelled in a small town in central Poland and everybody knew that he was a true tzaddik. Not only was he a man of great wisdom and insight but he also had a golden heart. Rabbi Elimelech was ready to share his knowledge as well as his earthly goods with anybody who asked for it. He would, as the saying goes, give the shirt off his back to the poor and never think of it twice. God had also granted him a special gift to be able to sense way ahead any misfortune that was about to strike the Jewish community and he succeeded many times in averting disaster.

On Sabbaths after the services, the followers of the rabbi were always invited to his house where his devoted wife Faygel would have prepared a sumptuous lunch. She had the reputation of being a wonderful cook and her heart was as big as her husband's. Those were always joyful occasions for the scholars and they flourished in the warmth of the rabbi's home like rare plants pampered in a hothouse.

Yet happy times do not last forever and one day, in mid-winter, terrible news reached the small peaceful community. One of the emperor's ministers, who hated the Jews with passion, had managed to convince the ruler that he needed more soldiers for his wars and that he could find them among the Jewish population within his domain. Also the rabbi had been somewhat under the weather for a few days and his congregation had been concerned not just about his well being but also apprehensive as to what it could mean.

The Jews were petrified with fear. If the decree was signed by the emperor, their young men, as young as fifteen years of age, would be drafted into the army and would be lost among all the other soldiers as drops of water in the sea. There was not only the danger of death but the unbearable agony that they could lose their identity as Jews, not being able to follow their tradition, even basic things like revering the Sabbath and praying three times a day. Instead of all that, they would have to march, fight, kill, and just hope to survive. The whole community was in mourning and the synagogue was full of parents who continually lamented their fate and prayed to God to help them overcome the latest imminent catastrophe.

Some of the inhabitants of the village began collecting money to buy a present for the wicked emperor's adviser and convince him to help them out, but Rabbi Elimelech forbade them to do such a thing as bribe an enemy of Israel, knowing that it would only cause more trouble. The congregation did as told and put their last hope and complete faith in their rabbi. The decree was to be signed to their dismay on a Sabbath, an additional little touch that the vicious adviser had managed to arrange to his great satisfaction.

The fateful day arrived and, as was their habit, the rabbi's students were all sitting at the table in his house waiting for lunch to be served. This time though, their faces expressed despair and there was no joy in their hearts. A sorrowful Faygel brought in the hot soup and began serving it. She poured the first bowl for the rabbi who was sitting quietly at the head of the table with a pensive look on his face. He looked at the soup and, after a few seconds inadvertently pushed the bowl only slightly, but the soup spilled all over the table.

Everybody was surprised. The rabbi was always very meticulous and tidy and such a thing had never happened before. Faygel quickly cleaned up the mess and faithfully brought another dish to serve her husband, an additional bowl of soup. The rabbi did not react at first. He just stared into the hot liquid and suddenly spilled the soup again. The thick liquid was all over the tablecloth, dripping from the sides onto the floor. Faygel was devastated but she did the same as she had done before and cleaned up without uttering a word. The students were truly concerned this time and worried that their rabbi was in real trouble, maybe ill, maybe losing his grip, and may not be able to eat for some reason.

The room was quiet. There was a feeling of intense panic. Nobody dared to move. The rabbi motioned to his wife to serve him the soup for the third time and this time she had hardly any left in the pot and could fill the bowl only half way. The rabbi was breathing heavily. His eyes were half closed, yet his look of intense concentration was cast again on the hot liquid in the bowl in front of him. Suddenly he spilled it once again and while his followers were wondering whether he had lost his mind, the rabbi lifted his head, opened his eyes widely, and smiled broadly at all present.

"Do not be afraid, my children," he said. "Our troubles are over. God has helped us to prevent the disaster. Our youngsters are safe and free to follow the teachings of the Torah. Come, let us rejoice and celebrate the Sabbath!"

If the events of the day had been quite unusual in the rabbi's house, they had been really out of the ordinary in the palace of the emperor. His Majesty sat down to sign the decree against the Jewish population at the same time the rabbi was having lunch. When he was handed the pen to dip into the inkwell, the container spilled all over. The attendants quickly cleaned the mess and the wicked minister handed the emperor a different inkwell which also promptly turned over as soon as the ruler dipped the pen into it. The emperor's face became red with anger and he looked snarling at all the people surrounding the table. Still he controlled his temper and tried to sign the document for the third time. Once again the same thing happened. The black ink spilled all over the gilded table, covering the paper as well as other items on it, and dripped onto the polished wooden floor. The emperor jumped up from his seat, his royal garment was stained as well. He furiously grabbed the document, tore it into little pieces, threw it at his minister, and ordered him to disappear from his sight.

When the Jews found out what had happened at the emperor's court, how the advisor had spilled the ink three times, and that the ruler had destroyed the document and banished him from the palace, they rejoiced and celebrated for days. The menacing decree was a thing of the past. They could continue following their tradition and not worry, at least for the time being, about an impending calamity.

After all Rabbi Elimelech was alive and well! God willing he would stay with them for a very long time.

42

Rabbi Loew—The Guardian Angel

Rabbi Loew lived on Wide Street in the Jewish section of Prague. At that time there were many Jewish newcomers who came to the city from Spain and Portugal fleeing the Inquisition. Prague, nevertheless, was not the asylum the fugitives were looking for. It could serve them as a hideaway for awhile but it was far from being the safe port in the storm.

All this was due to the mood swings of Emperor Rudolf the Second and his advisers. Rudolf had decided to expel all the Jews from Prague and this decree was served to the Jewish population without any explanation. When Rabbi Loew requested an audience with the emperor to present his plea, he was chased away by the guards. This happened more than once and Rabbi Loew realized that he had to use other means if he wanted to speak to the capricious ruler.

Every day the emperor's carriage, pulled by four graceful Arabian horses, passed through the Old Town. One evening Rabbi Loew mingled with the crowds on the Stone Bridge and awaited the emperor's arrival. When he saw the royal coach approaching, he stepped into its way with his arms outstretched. The onlookers grew very angry when he refused to move aside and engulfed him with a torrent of curses as well as stones and mud. The rabbi did not budge and the crowd froze in awe when they saw the stones and clusters of mud thrown at the rabbi turn into roses and violets. The horses halted and stood still in front of the rabbi as the emperor looked out of the window to see what the commotion was all about. The courageous rabbi bowed deeply in front of the ruler, handed him a letter, and asked for an audience. Rudolf hastily looked at the paper and the rabbi, and then told him not to leave his home for seven days. On the seventh day a splendid carriage stopped in front of Rabbi Loew's house ready to take him to the palace.

The rabbi spent a long time in the emperor's chambers and finally convinced him to change the edict he had signed and let the Jews stay in Prague, the place they considered their home. Rudolf was so impressed with Rabbi Loew's wisdom and personality that he promised never to chase the Jewish population away and not to castigate the whole community for sins committed by individuals. Those would have to be punished by a separate tribunal without affecting all of the Jewish population. Rabbi Loew became a regular guest in the palace and his outstanding reputation spread far and wide.

However, all this did not last long. Rudolf spent most of his time dealing with alchemy and studying astrology, and his tutors, who disliked Jews, were able to influence him again against them. About two months after Rabbi Loew's initial visit to the palace, Rudolf authorized another order to banish the Jews from Prague.

That same night the emperor had a strange dream.

He dreamed that he was in his imperial carriage driving through an arid land. There was no shade in sight and it was tremendously hot and humid. Rudolf was thirsty, sweaty, and could hardly breath. His lips were parched and his tongue stuck to the roof of his mouth. He felt he could not handle this discomfort anymore when suddenly a river appeared behind a bend. He gave orders to stop the carriage and in great haste took off all his clothes to immerse himself in the cold stream. He felt refreshed in a short while but, when he returned to the bank of the river, he discovered that his clothes as well as the carriage and all his entourage had disappeared, vanished into thin air.

Depressed and angry, he waited till night fall so that he could, under the cover of darkness, start his long walk home. He marched all night and at dawn he saw Prague from a distance. On his way he encountered a group of woodcutters but they just insulted him and chased him away without giving him a helping hand. Finally a beggar took pity on him and provided him with a few spare rags so that Rudolf could cover his naked body and continue his journey back to the capital. When he reached the gates of the city, a coach pulled out and he recognized it as one of his own. He stopped the driver and demanded to be recognized. It did not work. The reinsman insisted that he had taken the emperor back to his palace the previous evening. He laughed at first and then cursed the beggar for stopping him and threatened to use his whip if he did not move aside.

Rudolf realized what had happened. Somebody he knew well had impersonated him and stolen his throne. He had taken the royal clothes from the river bank and was now enjoying his status as the emperor. Rudolf sat down in the dust and in vain tried to find a solution to his problem. All day long he wandered, crisscrossing Prague and gave in more and more to hopeless despair. Who would believe him that he was the emperor and that there was a false ruler at the castle?

Towards evening with swollen, bleeding feet and a growling belly, he found himself in the Jewish ghetto and stopped in front of the Old-New Synagogue. He suddenly remembered Rabbi Loew and with his last ounce of strength found the way to the rabbi's house. The rabbi greeted him with great respect and compassion. After he washed up, ate, and rested a little, Rudolf turned to the rabbi for help and support. The rabbi nodded his head while the emperor was talking and told him: "Every criminal goes back to the place of transgression. It is going to be very hot tomorrow too and I am sure that your double will go back to the river to the place of the crime where he robbed you of your fortune and title. Your Majesty should return to that place and do to the felon what he has done to you."

With new hope in his heart the emperor promised to reward Rabbi Loew and augment his fortune with precious stones and gold.

The rabbi responded sadly: "If Your Majesty wants to show his gratitude, please help me. Now that you have tasted the bitterness of injustice and misery, you know how the Jewish people feel. This is what we have been going through for centuries. Let me ask Your Majesty, once and for all, to cancel the harsh decree of expulsion and forever promise the Jews will be able to live in this land in peace and tolerance."

The emperor gladly fulfilled the rabbi's request and signed a document the rabbi had prepared for him. Early next morning he returned to the river, hid behind a bush, and waited for things to take their course.

Only a short time elapsed and Rudolf noticed from afar the dust that rose in front of a carriage. Soon he recognized the imperial coach and sure enough in a few minutes his double descended from it and tossing away his clothes jumped into the cool waters of the stream. Rudolf sneaked from behind the bush and took the clothes that the felon had carelessly dropped. Immediately he put them on and, ascending into the carriage, commanded the coachman and his escorts to head home in haste. The horses took off as if they were possessed by some bad spirits and the emperor was shaken harshly despite the soft pillows he was sitting on. He was about to complain to his servant when he suddenly woke up and found himself in bed in his own chambers. He realized that it had been only a dream.

Getting up, Rudolf paced back and forth for a long time. He was deep in thought. At a certain moment he happened to glance at a small golden table adjacent to his bed and stopped short as if he had seen a ghost. On it nicely spread out were the old clothes the beggar had given him, and on top of them the deed that he had signed at Rabbi Loew's house. At the crack of dawn he summoned his advisers and ordered them to cancel the decree against the Jews and grant them a permanent home in his country.

This is how Rabbi Loew succeeded once again in protecting his community and saving the Jews from disaster.

43

The Student

Many years ago a student by the name of Hans came to Prague in search of his fortune. He had studied philosophy at the University of Heidelberg for many months and being very poor had suffered extreme deprivation. His disappointment was also pronounced since his studies did not fulfill his expectations. He had heard about the magic city of Prague and was curious to explore it on his own.

Shortly after his arrival, he visited the house where Faust had succumbed to the devil and stood at the gate for hours wondering how he too could summon the evil one and make a pact with him. He was of no religious affiliation and had no scruples about joining the devil to live a happy and prosperous life. What would happen afterwards was of no concern to Hans. He just lived for the moment and yearned for a nice place to dwell, good food to eat, and not having to worry about tomorrow. After a few days he gave up on finding the devil or Satan finding him and drowned his sorrows in the local pubs. While drinking the excellent Czech beer, he did not seem to be aware that his meager savings were running out and that soon he would be penniless.

An old man, who was a regular customer at the pub Hans drank at, noticed the young man and, being of a curious nature, wanted to find out who he was and why he looked so miserable. When the mysterious stranger approached Hans, he thought at once that he had lucked out and that the burly old man with the luminous eyes and shaking hands was Satan in disguise who finally had come to strike a deal with him.

"At last," he said. "True to your nature, Your Highness, or is it Your Devilness, you take pleasure in making a man wait and suffer. But, never mind, here you are and let's get down to business."

The old man looked behind him since he marveled at Hans' words, but seeing nobody there assumed that Hans was drunk and naturally, under the circumstances, quite confused. He tried to tell him that he was just an old sympathetic drinker, but after a while gave up since Hans would not accept his explanation. When he realized who Hans thought he was, he felt at first insulted but, since he had a sense of humor and was somewhat flattered too, he decided to play along with the young man.

"All right, all right," he said, sipping from another skein of beer he had ordered for himself and the student. "You got me. But you see, my dear fellow, business is not good these days and I am afraid that there is nothing much to offer you. Hell is overcrowded and I am in no need of new souls! Yet since you have searched for me with such zest," he added. "I came to give you some advice and offer an alternative."

Hans initially expressed disbelief but, when the stranger threatened to leave, gave in and thought to himself that it was better to get some new ideas rather than sink into complete despair.

"Have you heard of the Golem of Prague?" asked the old man.

"Yes," said Hans. "That stupid piece of clay that could follow orders, if it is really true! But what does that have to do with me finding a fortune?"

The old drunkard spent a long time telling Hans the story of the mud man and all the marvels he had been able to do. He emphasized mainly the fact that, with such a servant, Hans could live a good life and use him also as a bodyguard in times of trouble. This unusual assistant could fetch him anything he needed at anytime. He could marry a rich girl whose parents would be delighted to have such a formidable aide. Hans could even discover secrets unknown to other human beings, if he was ready to pursue the path that he suggested which was to resuscitate the Golem who was lying lifeless in the attic of the Jewish synagogue.

Hans hesitated, but not for long. The idea began to appeal to him. The more he thought about it the better it sounded. Finally, he turned to the old man and asked for his help. He needed the secret, sacred amulet that Rabbi Loew had used to bring the Golem to life.

"Oh, no, no, dear fellow," said the devil. "I cannot do that. You have to find it yourself. I could not touch that thing unless I were an angel. I will, nevertheless, keep an eye on you wherever you are and if necessary come to your aid later."

For the next few days the young student spent his time studying any material he could find that described the life of the Maharal, the birth of the Golem, and mainly the kabbalah. He stopped at the libraries the old man had suggested and visited the old ghetto of Prague. He was fortunate to find in an old bookseller's shop a small decrepit volume which described the making of the Golem. This important manuscript was written by Rabbi Loew's follower and son-in-law, Yitzchak ben Shimshon Hakohen Katz, who had helped the famous rabbi in the creation of the Golem. Finally, almost at the end of his strength and with a few last pennies in his pocket, Hans found the formula and wrote it down on a small piece of paper.

Waiting for night to fall, the desperate student went to the same pub and spent his last coins on a glass of beer and modest dinner. He figured that once he had the Golem he wouldn't be needing any money and spent all he had left with no concern. He was hoping to meet the old man again but "the devil" was not to be seen.

When the clock struck midnight, Hans left the pub and approached the old synagogue. It was a very dark night. The moon was covered by a blanket of dense clouds, and only a few stars were able to show themselves and faintly glitter here and there in the firmament. Hans proceeded carefully; he could not be caught. There was nobody to be seen in the streets. He was able to get to the entrance of the temple and pick the door lock with ease. He had some previous experience and was very good at it. Inside the air was heavy with a musty smell and the darkness was even thicker than outside. Using a small candle, Hans carefully made his way to the attic. In the same old manuscript he had bought, he had found a plan of the synagogue and memorized it well before embarking on his adventure.

When he reached the attic, he felt like screaming "Eureka!" but told himself that it was still too early to celebrate. He saw a heap of old papers, books, and prayer shawls all piled up in the middle of the attic and started throwing them aside. For awhile he did not find what he was looking for and was getting tired and frustrated when suddenly his hand touched something solid and dry. He froze for a minute and then continued digging with frenzy, knowing that he had almost uncovered the Golem. And there it was, a huge mass of dark soil, hard and cracked in many places, with no shape to it except for the head. There it was, the huge head of the Golem intact, with its eyes closed, lying on a prayer shawl. Hans' heart started pounding. With his knees shaking and almost fainting from a feeling of fear mixed with joy, he inserted the small piece of paper with the formula he had written on it into the open mouth of the mud giant.

Nothing happened for a few minutes but then the cracks in the body of the Golem began closing up and the whole mass began regaining shape. First the legs and then the torso and arms began moving and the Golem sat up. The cracks in the head were also healing but he did not open his eyes. A strange glow was coming from the soil and Hans thought that the Golem emitted a muffled yet painful groan. He knew though that was impossible since the Golem, an incomplete soul, had never been granted the power of speech. Suddenly the Golem began growing. His frightful frame became bigger and bigger by the minute and he expanded like yeast dough. Soon the head of the Golem would be hitting the ceiling of the attic and the whole building could collapse. Hans was petrified to see what was happening, yet he had enough strength left in him to jump up and quickly grab the piece of paper sticking out of the Golem's mouth. Every thing stopped that second and Hans felt a bit of relief as if he had already escaped the danger. Yet he had not. The giant stood for a moment as if frozen in time but then his enormous frame started crumbling. Before Hans realized what was really happening the mountain of mud buried him completely under its weight.

Hans had found the Golem, never to leave him again. He had manufactured an imperfect shem and as such had not been able to revive the Golem but rather, as the Maharal had predicted, led himself to his own destruction. The young man had been one of those students who cannot contain the knowledge they accumulate. All he thought he had learned went through him like a sieve. He could have saved himself if he had realized that the Golem had been summoned to fulfill the sacred task of protecting the Jewish people. He was not meant to serve any one person's selfish needs.

And maybe the devil had been there after all. . . .

III

Laughter and Ridicule

There is no life without laughter.
—Czech proverb

44

Greater Than the Maharal

In a small village in Hungary there lived a rabbi who was very pompous and conceited. After some time he decided that he could do better than just serve a tiny community of simple Jewish souls and notified them that he would be leaving soon for the big city of Budapest.

The congregation took it very hard. Most of the people in the village were extremely poor and they had had difficulty in the past finding a rabbi who was willing to live amidst them and share their troubles and trepidations. A small delegation was sent to the rabbi to plead with him to stay.

As the three men stood in front of the rabbi, they begged him to remain in their village since everybody had such great regard for him and would feel lost if he left. The rabbi felt quite flattered and his sense of self importance rose even higher. Having no intention of staying and not being a very charitable and kind man, he decided to have a little fun at their expense.

"My dear fellows," he said sitting in his arm chair while the others were standing with their heads bowed. "I would love to stay if I could find at least ten people like you in the congregation!"

The citizens liked the reply and felt that there was still some hope left. They hastened to assure the rabbi that they were quite positive that there would be at least ten very decent and intelligent men as themselves among the villagers.

The rabbi looked at them mockingly and, instead of agreeing to stay as they hoped, said laughing with all his might: "That is the trouble, if there were only ten like you I could grin and bear it. The problem is that there are at least hundred that resemble you in body and mind, like kernels in a shrunken pomegranate!"

With those words the rabbi dismissed the delegation who returned home depressed and sad. Later on though, after thinking about it and discussing it among themselves and other members of the congregation, they became furious. Their anger grew the longer they talked about it and they all decided that the rabbi, despite his knowledge, had no right to insult and play jokes on them just because they were simple and ordinary people. After all he himself had two sons who were not very bright and, as such, far below the average inhabitant of the village. They decided to pay the rabbi back with the same coin.

The same trio approached the rabbi once again, although he had told them that he was getting ready to leave the next day and that there was no way on earth he would stay in their dismal little place.

They found him standing in front of his house this time and when he gruffly returned their greeting, said in a tearful voice: "Dear rabbi, the reason we cannot accept your decision easily is that we think of you so highly and cannot bear the idea of losing you. To us you seem greater than the famous Maharal of Prague, blessed be his memory!"

It did not occur to the insolent rabbi that he was being overpraised and he was thrilled by the exaggerated compliment. He had no intention of changing his mind but wanted to hear more of the honeyed words of the villagers since he was ready to believe and accept any praise any time.

"What exactly do you mean by that?" he asked, smiling sweetly at the simple folk standing in front of him.

"Just one thing, dear rabbi," responded one of the men. "The only comparison between you and the great Rabbi Loew is that he had one golem while you have two!"

And with those words they turned their backs to him and walked away.

45

The Worm

The Rambam began studying medicine as a very young lad while serving as an assistant to one of the prominent doctors in Egypt. The Egyptian medic noticed how bright and perceptive the young Rambam was and developed a keen dislike for the boy which originated from his intense fear and apprehension that one day the youngster would become a better doctor than himself. To prevent that from happening, he used any excuse to send the Rambam on different errands and assigned him to tasks that had little to do with medicine. Nevertheless, the young man was still able to absorb an unbelievable amount of medical knowledge and developed a great deal of common sense as the Egyptian doctor found out on a very special occasion.

One day a very sick patient came to see the doctor. He was one of the three most important viziers who served the Sultan of Egypt and the doctor saw him at once, treating him with great respect. The vizier complained of throbbing headaches that prevented him from functioning and disabled him completely from any activity he wanted to participate in. The doctor examined him and prescribed a few drugs he hoped would help. Yet, within a day the man was back complaining of even worse pains. The doctor decided to operate, hoping that when he opened up the vizier's head, he would see what the problem was and be able to treat the sick man.

On the day of the operation the Rambam, who knew what was going to take place in the surgical chamber, ascended to the roof. There, through a small opening, he was able to watch what the surgeon was doing. When the skull was opened up and the brain disclosed, the doctor noticed that a small worm had penetrated inside and was crawling all over the place. The surgeon picked up one of his metallic tools and was going to try to seize the worm and remove it from the man's brain. At that moment he heard a voice from above asking him to stop. When he looked up he saw his young helper peeking through the roof, begging him not to touch the patient's brain unless he wanted him to die. The doctor hesitated. He wanted to disregard the youngster, yet he was terrified what would happen if such a distinguished man were to die under his knife. He motioned to the Rambam to join him at the operating table.

While the doctor was waiting for him, the Rambam quickly went to the kitchen and pealed a large leaf off a cabbage head. He entered the surgical chamber and carefully approached the table where the sick man was lying. Gently he placed the leaf close to the open skull. Within a few seconds, to the doctor's amazement, the worm smelled the familiar food, crawled from the inside of the brain straight onto the cabbage leaf where the Rambam was able to remove him with ease. The man was saved and recovered very quickly from his ordeal.

Thus the young apprentice endeared himself to the great doctor whose reputation he had saved. He had spared not only the life of a man but also that of a worm. He respected and cherished life no matter how insignificant it seemed to be. In time the Rambam became one of the most famous doctors in Egypt who never refused to see a patient regardless of title or fortune.

46

The Shulklopfer

In his prime Ezra had been the best shulklopfer the village had known. He was always up before dawn and thanks to him nobody ever missed services. At first he knocked on each door gently. When he made his second round and still there was no motion inside a house, his knocking became louder and urgent till everybody was awake. Those days were gone though. His bad vision as well as his arthritic legs and arms prevented him from performing his job as he had done in the past. A young shammes took over the task and Ezra spent his days in the synagogue and adjacent shul, listening to the rabbi, and watching the children studying the Talmud.

The old rabbi who ran the shul was a gruff, ill-tempered man. The ten children who attended the school were between the ages of four and ten and very afraid of him. The only time they relaxed was when the rabbi went home for lunch and left them in the charge of Ezra who loved all of them and told them stories while they ate their food. Ezra remembered so many tales, some sad, some funny, and the children liked them all. They looked up to the old man who gave them a great deal of affection and never lacked understanding and patience the way their teacher did. Ezra had lost his wife a few years back and his two sons lived in a large city so that he had nobody left in the village who really cared about him. The children brought him much pleasure. To them he was not just a discarded old man nobody needed but a friend, maybe the best friend they ever had.

One warm spring day after the rabbi left at noon, Ezra asked the children to join him in the shul's small yard. It was a lovely day. The sun shone brightly and one could feel a light breeze. Ezra wanted his little friends to enjoy with him the fresh air and the chirping of the happy birds and the sweet smell of early flowers. The rabbi was always angry when his students left the room but Ezra thought that on such a beautiful day even the rabbi might be less irritable than usual.

Sitting on a bench with the children surrounding him Ezra felt happy. The story he told them that day was about a rabbi who had a big family at home and very little income to support them. Stories of poverty were familiar to the children; all of them knew what it meant. The rabbi in the tale had only one pair of pants which his wife washed and mended every week. In time the material became so thin and frail that the rabbi had no choice but to purchase another pair. A rag merchant happened to pass through the village and the rabbi purchased for a good price a pair of old pants that were in decent condition, but somewhat big for him. He tied the excess material around his waist with a string but had trouble keeping the pants from dragging on the floor and asked his wife to shorten them for him. She was so very busy with her children that day that she told him to ask his mother who lived with them to do the sewing for him. The elderly woman was not willing to do so. Her eyes were blurry and that day she was not feeling well. She sent him to his sister who lived next door, yet she too could not oblige since she was helping a neighbor in need.

The disappointed rabbi returned home and went to sleep, carefully folding his new pants over a chair. His wife was still busy with her household chores and, when she finished and saw the pants on the chair, decided to shorten them and surprise her husband. She finished doing so and, remembering another task that she had left undone, returned to the kitchen. In the meantime the rabbi's mother developed a bad conscience for having refused her son's request and, sneaking into his room, "fixed" the pants for him too. The sister who was a kind-hearted woman did the same! She took the pants from the chair and returned them to her brother's house after fulfilling his wish. When morning came the rabbi was truly surprised to find that his pants had shrunk overnight and they barely covered his knees. He did not say anything though and left for the synagogue as usual. At least, he thought, those pants were in one piece and would not fall apart.

When Ezra finished his story the children looked at each other puzzled. Their own rabbi had a pair of short pants himself. They did cover his knees but the socks and the holes in them were seen and even some of his skin. Ezra was sitting quietly watching the children's reaction. One of the older boys hugged him and asked:

"Were the pants of that rabbi brown?" Ezra nodded his head.

"Were they dark brown and had some threads hanging from the side?" asked another child. Ezra nodded again.

"Was there a round, black stain on the left side?" asked all of them at once. Ezra smiled this time and did not even have to nod.

The rabbi was just coming back from lunch. As he approached he lifted his arms, angrily motioning to the children to get into the shul. When he came even nearer, it became quite obvious who the bearer of the short story pants was. The children giggled and ran into the room. The rabbi gave Ezra a nasty look and followed them. Soon it was very quiet again.

Ezra decided to sit in the sun for a little while longer.

47

The Golem Goes Shopping

Initially when Rabbi Loew created Josef the Golem, he sternly told his wife not to use the Golem's services for any household chores. A few years passed and one day Pearl was busy preparing a big wedding celebration for a poor orphan. Since everyone else was busy and Pearl had no personal help available, she sent the Golem to buy a fish and some apples for the feast. She thought that this was a good deed, and as such would not be considered a private request. She gave Josef a note with instructions for the fish merchant and the produce woman and sent him on his way.

The Golem strolled down the Vltava river where he got a live twenty-pound carp. Since he had been sent off in haste and was not given a shopping bag, he solved the problem by inserting the enormous fish head down under his shirt with a big part of the carp's tail sticking out. On the way home though, the struggling fish's tail hit the Golem in the face with such strength that he almost toppled over. The Golem did not forgive the fish for the slap. Running, he went back to the bank of the river and threw the fish into the water to drown it. He did it so quickly that the fish merchant could not prevent it. Josef reached home empty-handed and when he motioned to explain what he had done and why, everybody had a good laugh, that is everybody except Pearl who was desperate since she still needed the fish for the wedding.

The Golem quickly headed again for the market to get the apples. He handed Pearl's note to the produce woman. She carefully weighed the right amount and was about to drop the apples into a sack when the Golem insisted he wanted to carry the fruits on his shoulder. When the produce woman laughed in his face and mocked him, he became extremely angry. In a flash he grabbed the woman along with her baskets and stand, and placed everything on his shoulders. To the great amazement of all present, he rushed through the marketplace. Frightened to death, the woman screamed with all her might but to no avail. The Golem reached Rabbi Loew's home, placed his load in the courtyard and ran to the kitchen where he summoned Pearl. In the meantime, a crowd gathered to witness what was happening to the produce woman. In the wink of an eye, the Golem set up the stand and the baskets the way they had been in the marketplace and placed the woman in the midst of it all. The woman who had lost her voice out of sheer fright, regained it suddenly and yelled once again as if her life depended on it.

Rabbi Loew heard the commotion and from his window saw the Golem and the gathering of people. He asked Josef to approach him and tell him what had happened. The Golem obliged and described the whole incident in sign language. A smile emerged on the Rabbi's face, he turned to his wife and said, "So, today you had to fix a wedding. But from now on you should heed my words and not use the Golem for household work."

And so it was from then on.

48

Two Jobs Instead of One

A particular small community in Hungary was so very poor that they could not afford a shochet. They had a few meetings to discuss how they could take care of the problem but there seemed to be no solution. A good shochet was just too expensive and that was it. Finally one of the older members of the village had an idea. Since they needed a watchmaker as well, he suggested hiring somebody who could do both jobs. That way they could adjust their budget, keep kosher, and have their clocks repaired when necessary.

The community was very fortunate to find an old man who had been a watchmaker when he was young and also a shochet for a while. He had changed his profession when times were hard and learned a new skill that was always in demand. When he arrived, the new shochet/watchmaker was greeted with great honor and asked to perform his duty as soon as he had rested from his trip.

Things did not go well at all. The problem was that the chicken he slaughtered continued walking and the clocks he repaired stood still.

The community was extremely disappointed. Things really did not go well.

49

Stuck in the Mud

Once there lived a coachman whose days were coming to an end. He summoned his three sons and told them: "Dear sons, I am not able to hold onto the reins anymore and will be leaving this world in a short time. I would like one of you to continue and follow the path of our forefathers by being a carriage man. I am going to test each of you and the one whose answer is the best will inherit the cart and the horses."

The old man addressed the oldest son and asked him: "What would you do if the cart and horses get stuck in deep mud? How would you get them out of there?"

"That is a silly problem, dear father," answered the first born with a smirk, "It is very simple. I will harness two additional horses to the cart and pull it out!"

The coachman turned his nose up. His oldest son's answer did not seem to be to his liking. He asked his second child the same question.

"Father, dear father, all I will do is to unload the cart, pull it out with the horses and then put the load back!" triumphantly responded the second son.

The old man was not impressed by this response either. His gaze fell on the youngest of his offspring.

The young man smiled at his father:

"Father, do you take me for a horse? Do you really think I will get myself into this kind of situation, into the mud so to speak, and break my head later on how to correct it? I will be careful to prevent it from happening in the first place and then I will not find myself in trouble!"

Do we have any doubt who inherited the cart and the horses?

The youngest son did.

50

The Toothache

A young couple who lived in great poverty had just finished their Friday evening meal and retired for the night. Soon after they laid their heads on the pillows, the wife began complaining that she felt a sharp pain in one of her teeth. The husband tried to calm her down and suggested she fall asleep, hoping she would get over it by morning. Yet the pain did not subside. The husband was very upset. There was nothing he could do to help. They were so poor they hardly had a few coins to buy the basics for the Sabbath, not to mention money to pay a doctor.

The young man started chanting a prayer and after a while was relieved to see that his wife had fallen asleep. He also slumbered off only to be awakened by his wife's cries and moans. The ache had returned with a vengeance and once again they were at a loss as to what to do. Suddenly the husband remembered that his mother had told him some time ago that a few drops of palinka applied to the cheek would ease or even get rid of the pain. He got up and desperately searched for the bottle of spirits he knew they had in one of the cupboards. Since it was already Sabbath he could not put on any light and made his way in the dark hoping to find what he was looking for.

He hit himself a few times in different parts of his body and was close to giving up when finally, hurting and sweating, his hand grabbed the neck of a bottle which was stacked in the back of one of the shelves. Feeling calmer, he carefully carried the precious container to his bed and using his handkerchief, applied the liquid thoroughly to his wife's left cheek where the trouble was. He kept asking her every minute whether she was feeling better and sure enough after a short while she admitted she felt remarkable relief. They both fell asleep exhausted and thankful, hoping their ordeal was over.

In the morning, when the sun came out and they woke up, the husband almost fainted. Looking at his wife he saw a disheveled woman whose face was almost as black as tar. She did not realize the way she looked and opening her eyes smiled at her husband. Her white teeth shone and sparkled against the dark background and she had the appearance of a ghost. The husband in his haste and not being able to see in the darkness had mistakenly taken a bottle of ink instead of the spirits and rubbed it on his wife's cheek.

The toothache did not come back.

This treatment, nevertheless, is not recommended.

51

The Rabbi and the Coachman

A famous rabbi, the grandson of a miracle worker, hired a reinsman and his cart to drive him around Hungary. Every Saturday they stayed in a different village where the congregation greeted the rabbi with great respect and honored him for as long as his visit lasted. When he left, the carriage was overloaded with presents and food items to facilitate the next phase of their journey.

The coachman was very jealous of the rabbi and one day, not able to contain his envy, turned to him and said: "Rabbi, you are so lucky! Wherever you go people admire you and bow to you. You stay in the best homes in town with the richest and most important members of the community, and all you do is give the same sermon over and over again. Is that fair? And look at me, in great need, wearing rags, and being always dismissed and ignored! I wish that, at least for one day, I could be you and enjoy the honor and all the bounty you get!"

"If that is really how you feel," answered the rabbi with a smile, "there is no problem. Next Sabbath we shall switch roles. You will be seen as the rabbi by the whole world and I will be the humble coachman that you are."

The suggestion appealed to the cart driver. They exchanged their clothes and, sure enough when they drove into the next village, the rabbi was the coachman and the coachman became the rabbi. All went well as planned, the congregation honored "the rabbi" as expected and he was led into an elegant room where he spent the night in comfort after feasting on a superb dinner.

When the time came to address the community, the carriage driver complained of hoarseness and congestion which prevented him from lecturing. The audience was very understanding and sympathetic, yet they begged him to tackle just one argument which had been discussed for a long time by the learned elders of the synagogue. The fake rabbi listened carefully. His face was solemn for a moment yet, after coughing for a few minutes to illustrate that he was truly making an effort to accommodate them, he grinned broadly and said: "Your question is a very important one but is also very easy to answer. So simple is it that even my coachman, who is not a sage but quite a simple man, can explain it to you."

He pointed to the end of the room where the real rabbi was sitting and asked him to do as told. The fake coachman presented a drasha that kept the whole village in awe and very embarrassed as well.

52

The Waterspirite

In Muglinov near the town of Ostrava in Moravia, there stands an old mill where day and night the local miller used to grind different kinds of flour for his customers. The building still remains there but its days of glory are gone and today it is a dilapidated machinery workshop. Its story would also be forgotten were it not for some old folks who like to talk about it over a mug of good beer.

The mill originally was in a different location. Its bright, red brick walls were sprayed daily by the cold waters of the river Ostravice and the majestic wheel that provided the power for grinding turned slowly and endlessly hour after hour. In those days the miller, a devoted, young Jewish man, made friends with the watersprite who dwelled in the deep waters of the river not far from the mill.

The watersprite, as watermen go, was a dangerous creature. According to the Czech legends he liked to drown people who upset him for one reason or another. He kept their souls nicely stacked in little covered pots in his pantry in the depths of the mighty stream. Occasionally, a soul managed to escape if the cover of the pot was somewhat displaced, and then the watersprite's rage knew no bounds. The waters of Ostravice rose in great anger. The waves inundated the banks and the homes of those who lived nearby, and the wrath of the sprite did not cease till he managed to replace the souls he had lost. The miller was aware of the watersprite's reputation and was afraid of him at the start of their relationship. Nevertheless, doing business with the sprite, he realized that the waterman was as honest as they come and always provided the power he needed for the mill to run. In return, all the watersprite asked was to drink some beer with the miller every evening except for Fridays at the end of a day's work. He turned out to be a very lonely creature who craved company and enjoyed the miller's good spirits and cheerful attitude.

At the time of the Jewish holidays, the waterman stayed away and did not interfere with the habits and observances. Only at Purim was he able to mingle with the numerous guests the miller liked to invite. At such occasions he was very popular and almost always won first prize for his green, damp outfit that people considered very original and unique. He and the miller always exchanged a wink and had a good laugh afterwards when they met and discussed the festivities of the day and the foods the watersprite liked so much. He was fond, in particular, of the hamantaschen and could never have enough of them. He usually overate and had an upset stomach for a few days, but insisted he would not change his habit and that it was worth the pain.

Years went by and the miller's son took over his father's business. The watersprite hardly felt the passage of time when the grandson of his good friend inherited the mill. He mourned the death of the son as he had the father, yet had a good relation with all the members of the family and that was a great consolation to him. He continued helping them with their work. One day the old mill was pronounced unsafe and condemned. The miller at that time had lost most of his fortune, times were changing, and old mills with their antique way of grinding were considered obsolete. He told the watersprite that to survive he would have to relocate to a different place and work for another miller who used modern machinery. The watersprite was despondent. He cared for his old friend and did not want him to become the servant of a wealthy miller. He decided to help, explored the area, and summoned all the watersprites he knew.

They came from near and far away. From the High Tatras of Slovakia and the plains of Bohemia, down rivers and streams, they answered the call of the old watersprite whom they respected and admired. The watersprite found a place that he knew the miller could afford to buy. It was not far from the river, yet real estate in that undeveloped part of the city was dirt cheap. The miller sold all his assets except the building itself, was able to buy the land the watersprite suggested, and still had some money left over.

In the dead of night, the army of watersprites transferred the mill, brick by brick, from the old location to the new one and nobody, nobody except the miller, could ever understand how it had happened. The grateful man threw a beer party for the watersprites and when they left, each back to his river or lake, he promised the watersprite that he always would be considered a treasured member of his family. The watersprite was the happiest of sprites that day since he loved the miller and his family dearly. The miller bought some modern machinery with the money he had saved and prospered from that day on and for many years to come. He used to visit the banks of the river, where the old wheel stood silent and frozen, and meet with his watery friend over a glass of beer. The sprite preferred this arrangement since as a rule he did not like to spend time too far from the banks of his river. Dry environment did not agree with him very well, particularly as he got older, and seldom did he visit the miller at the mill.

Many years have gone by, the last miller that used to own the Muglinov mill passed away a long time ago. The old mill, now a workshop, dusty and run-down, does not resemble at all what it used to be. The old folks, drinking their beer in the pub just across the street, talk about it sometimes. It seems that on dark nights, once in a while, one can see in the dim light the outline of an old, bent watersprite. He walks slowly, sighing heavily while approaching the building. He circles it a few times, sprays himself with a water hose till he is dripping wet, and disappears in the darkness.

53

A Difficult Question

A zealous student of the Torah asked his rabbi the same question every year. The rabbi was as unrelenting as the young scholar and always told him to try to find the answer on his own. One year, however, the pupil received a response. The rabbi was becoming tired of the young man's incessant inquiry and thought that if by then the student had not been able to figure it out by himself, he probably never would. Yet he decided, as was his way, to explain it by means of a parable.

"You pointed out," said the rabbi to the young scholar, "that the Torah was given to the people of Israel during the holiday of Shavuot, on the sixth of the month of Sivan, yet you wonder why we celebrate the event of Simchat Torah at the end of the month of Tishrei?"

The young scholar nodded his head and anxiously awaited the long-desired answer to the question. His eyes were glued to the rabbi's lips and he did not notice the sparks that lit up in the teacher's eyes. Just for a moment they lingered there and in a flicker they were gone. The rabbi went on and said: "Let me tell you a story."

The student turned his eyes upwards in desperation. Another long tale, he thought to himself, and probably again no solution to the problem.

The rabbi went on: "Once a very rich Jew celebrated the wedding of his eldest daughter. It was a very fancy affair and there were many guests and relatives who feasted with delight. The tables were full of the best of food. The wine was flowing while people sang and danced and congratulated the blushing bride and the beaming bridegroom. Yet the father of the bride was all gloom and doom. He stood in a corner, worried and unhappy, and watched all that was happening with a frown. The guests were puzzled at his strange behavior and finally approached him and asked why was he not rejoicing at such a happy personal event. The father looked at them with sadness in his eyes and said, 'Dear friends, how can I be joyful and satisfied at the time of the wedding when I do not know whether the match will work out well? I cannot rejoice now but after a certain amount of time, when I see that the couple is living happily and getting along, only then will my heart be filled with cheer and elation!"

"And so it is with the Torah," jumped in the young scholar not letting the rabbi continue.

"Moses handed the Torah to the people of Israel in the month of Sivan but not being sure how it would evolve he waited a few months. Only when he perceived that all was well and the children of Israel behaved according to the Law and flourished, did he ask them to celebrate Simchat Torah!"

The student was all flushed and ruddy in his face. The fact that he had understood the parable and found the answer to the question made him extremely proud of himself.

The rabbi nodded his head and a faint smile appeared on his lips.

"He got it after all," he thought to himself. "What a relief!"

54

The Keepsake

When Franz Joseph became king of Hungary in 1867, his popularity rose thanks to his liberal policies and the friendship he proclaimed for the Hungarian people. The Jews also benefited from his kindness and their lives improved considerably. Franz Joseph found friends among the Jews and one of his favorites was a rabbi who led the main congregation in Budapest and was considered a man of great wisdom. The king felt a great deal of affection for the old man and very often enjoyed his company and advice. The rabbi was invited to all the festive events at the castle, and the king made sure that his friend was comfortable. He hired a Jewish cook who knew all the rules regarding kosher food and prepared it meticulously so that the rabbi could participate in the banquets without any concern.

Things went well for quite awhile, yet there was trouble brewing in the palace. Franz Joseph's many advisers, even those who had no personal grudge against the rabbi, resented the friendship their ruler showed him. Their dislike became more intense as time went by till they could not control their jealousy and anger anymore. One day they met in their chambers and devised a scheme that would ruin the rabbi's reputation once and for all.

Preparations were under way to celebrate the birthday of Franz Joseph. It fell on a Saturday to the great delight of the conspirators who knew that the rabbi, despite being a liberal man, would not break the main laws of his sacred day no matter what and that was, basically, all they needed to make their plot successful.

The city was embellished with lights and decorations, and thousands of people lined the streets greeting dignitaries that came to offer the king their congratulations. In the Jewish Quarter the rabbi had received his invitation, and he and his community had chosen an unusual golden goblet to present the king as a gift with their best wishes and gratitude. The rabbi was somewhat apprehensive that he had to go to the palace on a Sabbath but knew he could not decline the invitation under any circumstances. He was worried that the king would not understand and feel insulted, and he wanted to avoid that by all means. He prayed with the congregation at the temple and then walked the long stretch to Franz Joseph's castle. A few carriages stopped on the way offering him a ride but the rabbi was well aware of the malice behind the advisers' polite invitations and declined with grace.

The festivities at the palace were in full swing when the rabbi arrived and he saw the pleasure on Franz Joseph's face when he handed him the unique present the Jewish community had chosen for him. The banquet was superb and the rabbi enjoyed the music that filled the halls of the palace and the tasty kosher dishes the Jewish cook had prepared for him.

After dinner the king summoned all his friends to a private parlor where he thanked them for their gifts and offered them special cigars that were his favorite and especially manufactured for him. The advisers accepted the king's present with sly smiles and watched with enmity as the king handed a cigar to the rabbi. The rabbi showed his appreciation and moved to the far end of the hall where he carefully placed the cigar into one of the pockets of his long black coat. The advisers had followed his motions and when they saw what he had done, they lit their cigars and smoked slowly, savoring the taste of the special treat as well as their victory over the rabbi, or so they thought.

When the king was told what the rabbi had done his ruddy face became flushed even more and his eyes flashed with rage. He summoned the rabbi to the adjacent chamber and furiously accused him of disrespect: "How dare you not to smoke the cigar I have given you! You do not seem to be willing to celebrate my birthday full heartedly and show me regard or esteem. I thought you were a friend and it seems to me now that you take no part in the festivities, hiding in corners, and finding no value in my gift to you! Where is your loyalty? Is this how the Jewish people, whom you represent, honor me?"

The rabbi stood patiently in front of the king waiting for him to calm down and then told him: "Your Majesty, please do not judge me without letting me explain what I have really done! I do pay homage to you as a king and man, and my people feel not only veneration and awe toward you but also affection. That is exactly the very reason why I did not smoke the cigar you gave me. Once smoked—as all the others did—there is only a stub left which is thrown away but I still have the whole cigar which I intend to treasure and keep for generations to come. That way the Jews can always show this cigar to their children and grandchildren and be proud of the fact that I was honored to be your friend and lived to tell about your wonderful deeds!"

Franz Joseph and the rabbi remained friends for a very long time. The rabbi did not desecrate the Sabbath, and the advisers never found out why their scheme failed.

55

An Unending Story

Once there lived an emperor who loved stories, particularly long tales without an end. One sunny afternoon, he issued a decree that whoever told him a story that would never end would win a very special prize.

People came from faraway lands and their stories were very, very, very long. Some took days, some weeks and even months, but in the end, even these prolonged, voluble tales had to come to an end. And so they did and nobody ever won the precious reward.

One rainy day an old Jew arrived at the emperor's palace and when he was allowed to see the ruler, he bowed low and told him: "Great emperor, I have a very special story for you! You will not have to listen to it for days, weeks or months, but still it will never end!"

The emperor was thrilled and curious and asked the Jew to begin his tale.

And so he did: "Once upon a time there lived a king who loved to hunt and engaged in this activity continually. He was a loner by nature and spent the days in the woods all by himself. One wintry day he rode his horse in an unknown part of the woods and became stuck with him in deep mud."

The old man stopped telling his story.

"And sooo . . ." asked the emperor impatiently, looking at the silent old man, "what happened?"

"Nothing, Your Majesty," responded the Jew. "When the horse succeeded in freeing his hind legs from the mud, his front legs sank into it."

"And what next?" asked the ruler.

"Nothing. Nothing happened to the king or to his horse in the depths of the woods. When the horse pulled out his front legs, his hind ones sank deep into the mud; if he was able to free his hind ones, the front legs sank back into the sticky, saturated soil."

And so nothing actually did happen. The king and his horse were stuck so very deep in the mud that they could not get out of it. They kept trying. They really did. The old Jew in the meantime got a rich award for his endless tale.

56

The Porridge

Josef the Golem frightened many people despite the fact that all the inhabitants of the ghetto knew that he was meant to be their protector. Yet his huge frame, which was said to be mightier than Samson's and bigger than Goliath's, brought trepidation into people's hearts each time they saw him slowly moving across the ghetto or sitting at the door of the synagogue without any expression on his face. They could not tell whether he was really dumb or whether he had any feelings or needs of his own. They knew from a few incidents that he could be quite human but there were not too many indications of good–natured kindness on his part. Also they had no idea what his powers really were and whether only the rabbi could tell him what to do.

One day they found out.

There was an orphanage in the Jewish ghetto and the children were well cared for, yet they did not get too much attention or love. With no adults to caress them and play with them, they were at times despondent and quite lonely. The Golem, on one of his walks around the ghetto keeping vigil and guarding the gates from intruders, noticed the little ones playing in the yard adjacent to the orphanage. He stood at the fence for quite a while and the children, to whom he was a familiar figure, came closer and closer. They began talking to him and finally invited him to play with them. He did not know how but soon enough the children were climbing all over him, pulling on his clothes, laughing and giggling when he gently took them off his shoulders and placed them back on the ground. From that day on, the Golem visited the orphanage each time he did his rounds and the children loved him. He seemed to have a lot of affection for them too and kept an eye on the little ones, protecting them from falls and any kind of accident that could happen to them.

One day a fire broke out in the orphanage. The children panicked and were unable to get out of the building. One by one the Golem carried them to safety without seeming to be affected by the fierce flames and dense smoke. The fire was finally extinguished with his help and, despite the fact that there was some damage to the building, nobody got hurt.

Yet, a greater disaster was pending.

Emperor Rudolf, influenced once again by his vicious advisers who hated the Jewish population, gave in to the idea of starving the Jews to get rid of them. Supplies of food did not reach the ghetto and they were not allowed to purchase anything outside the gates. Children suffered the most and the Golem seemed to be in pain, not because he was hungry since he did not seem to need food at all, but because his small friends were starving. A little girl was the first to be on the verge of death one day. She was very weak, lying in her narrow cot unable to stand on her feet. The Golem was watching her sorrowfully through the window when the child looked at him and said: "Josef, why don't you make us some porridge in a magic pot, just the way it happened in the story we told you? Then we will all be able to eat as much as we want and nobody will be hungry!"

A gleam lit up in the Golem's brown, muddy eyes and he stepped inside the room. He approached the little girl's bed and looked at her as if trying to tell her something. She whispered a few words and he looked at a big pot that was sitting on the fireplace. Turning his back to the hungry children, Josef approached the stove and stood there for a while moving his hands in a peculiar way. Suddenly they heard a sizzling sound and from the pot rose steam and the smell of a delicious porridge being cooked, almost ready to be eaten. Quickly the Golem supplied the children with plates and spoons, and distributed the tasty porridge to all of them. The keepers of the orphanage came running and soon the whole ghetto knew about the miracle that had taken place. People rushed to the orphanage to fill up and the pot kept cooking and cooking, till nobody was hungry anymore.

When the hunger pangs subsided and the porridge still kept coming, everybody became worried. Nobody knew how to stop the pot from cooking and the Golem was of no help this time. The porridge ran over, sliding, gliding, and covering the floor of the orphanage. Soon it got out into the streets and, continuing to grow and swell, penetrating through the doors and windows of the houses. The Golem was busy again rescuing the children from the orphanage overflowing with hot porridge, and people were running frantically in all directions looking for Rabbi Loew. He was praying at the synagogue and, when he heard what had happened, he rushed to the orphanage making his way with difficulty through the sticky mess that filled almost all the streets of the ghetto. With his arms stretched above his head, he called out to the Golem to stop the pot from cooking. The Golem hesitated, not knowing what to do, but then seemed to remember something. Raising his hands in the same strange way he had done earlier, he turned towards the pot which at that very moment stopped cooking.

The inhabitants of the ghetto had to eat the porridge for many days till their homes and streets were clean again, and many of them never wanted to taste porridge for the rest of their lives. When Rudolf heard about the incident, being of a very superstitious nature and susceptible to mood changes, he reversed his previous ruling and allowed the Jews to acquire their food supplies in a more conventional manner. He developed a dislike for his advisers and the Jews were left alone for awhile.

And Joseph the Golem? He kept an eye on the children for as long as he lived.

57

Either Too Few or Too Many

High, high up in the courts of heaven the angels were having a meeting. They had to decide which souls should be sent down to earth to relive additional lives. Many lost souls were floating around in the heavenly domain waiting for the day they would be told to grow bones, skin, and flesh and descend to earth to fulfill their destiny and redeem themselves.

One such soul was summoned in front of the angels and told that the time had come and he was about to join the human race. When he asked what his task would be among people, he was told that it had been determined that he would become a cantor.

"A cantor? What is that?" asked the innocent, inexperienced spirit. "What will I have to do?"

"A cantor is a man blessed with a very special talent," answered one of the angels. "God has given him the gift of a beautiful voice and he sings to the people of his congregation at all the major holidays and special happy occasions, like weddings, brits, and bar mitzvahs. He is respected and loved by all and wherever he goes people pray with him and treat him with great respect. They will compare you to a nightingale because of your beautiful voice and call out each time they see you: 'Here comes the Hazan, here comes our wonderful cantor!' You will help the people of Israel to lift their souls in song and praise God every single day."

The spirit listened attentively and liked the job description.

"And for how many years will I be doing this?" he asked.

"You are destined to be a Hazan for fifty years," was the answer.

The spirit was disappointed. "No, No!" he said, "That is not enough. Fifty years? Fifty human years. That is a drop in the sea, that is nothing! No way!"

And he refused to descend to earth.

The committee of angels agreed to discuss the matter somewhat further and, in the meantime, they called upon another spirit to appear before them. They laid upon him the task of being a rooster and spending time on earth with other fowl.

The future rooster asked what his assignment would be and was told that he would be "a man" within a gathering of hens and call out every morning to the inhabitants of the village to wake up for service. His work would be very important and he would get much praise and respect from all. On top of that he would be admired and spoiled by the many hens in the group who would serve all his needs with a great deal of affection.

The spirit pondered for awhile and agreed to become a rooster but did not like the idea that he would have to spend twenty-five years doing that and asked to be granted only fifteen years which was enough as far as he was concerned.

The angels promised to consider his request and the spirit continued to float in the heavenly domain waiting for their signal to fly downwards.

The next soul that was called upon found out that he was about to become a dog. Wondering what that was, the simple spirit asked the angels to elaborate.

"A dog is a very important animal," began one of the angels. "He barks and that sound is respected and feared by all, humans as well as other creatures. He guards the homes of the rich and the poor and chases after cats, mice, and any animal that deserves to be reprimanded. He insists on discipline and does not tolerate people who have bad intentions. His senses are very keen, particularly his smell and hearing, and he is pampered by all."

A second angel added: "Delicious bones are given to him and many times humans share their favorite foods with him. He receives gratitude from those he protects and is loyal to, and great esteem from those who fear his mighty voice and strength."

The spirit seemed to be pleased with the description and, as did the others, also asked how many years he was destined to spend in his new form.

"Your lot has been cast for fifteen years!" was the answer.

The spirit was far from rejoicing this time.

"Five years is plenty for me," he begged. "Please accept my plea!"

And they did.

The committee summoned once again the first spirit who was meant to become a cantor and told him that it had been decided to grant him more time on earth. He would live seventy human years as a Hazan. Yet, after the initial fifty years of marvelous singing, he would sound for ten years as a rooster, and bark as a dog for the last ten years of his life.

The spirit descended to earth.

His destination is unknown.

58

Emperor Rudolf in Captivity

In May of 1593, Rabbi Loew was suddenly summoned to Rudolf's court. The emperor greeted the Rabbi with respect and friendliness as usual, but the rabbi had a premonition that there was trouble brewing. Rabbi Loew was right as usual. Rudolf told him apologetically that he had been forced to draw new papers regarding the Jews and that his advisers had explained to him why it was necessary to expel the Jewish population from Prague. The emperor did not offer any explanation, only added that it saddened him to do this to his revered friend the rabbi, but he had no choice. Rabbi Loew knew that there was no point in arguing with the emperor who, at times became rather irrational and moody, and was susceptible to influences coming from different people or groups.

Rudolf asked the rabbi to follow him to the royal gardens and join him for a snack. The rabbi accepted the invitation with a heavy heart and was in a pensive mood. Rudolf was somewhat baffled that the rabbi did not plead with him. Nevertheless, his thoughts wandered and, sitting on the gilded chair, he told the rabbi about his own troubles which were always his primary concern.

There was a certain count, a vassal of the emperor, who had suddenly refused to follow Rudolf's rules and decided to seek his own independence. The emperor was contemplating a proper punishment and thought that he had to go to war with the rebel. While talking, Rudolf began feeling drowsy and decided to take a nap right there among the tall trees and fragrant flowers of his park. He requested the rabbi stay with him while he slept and Rabbi Loew obliged graciously. Rudolf promptly fell into a deep slumber and had a very peculiar dream.

He was at war with the rebel and things were not going well. The two armies clashed on the battlefield and, although Rudolf's army was much bigger and better equipped, he was vanquished, taken prisoner, and thrown into a dungeon. The cell was extremely small and the defeated emperor had only one small, narrow window to gaze at the outside world. That was also the way his captors threw food at him since, strangely enough, the cell did not have a door. The subjugated ruler spent many years in that condition, in utter despair. Then one day he saw Rabbi Loew through the small opening in his cage and called out to his friend to help him and save him from a fate worse than death. Rabbi Loew approached the window and, holding out his hand to Rudolf, asked him whether he would destroy the eviction papers against the Jews if he helped him. The weakened emperor burst into tears and told the rabbi that, after eleven years in captivity, he had no power to do anything anymore.

Calmly, Rabbi Loew asked the emperor to give him the key to the secret drawer where he kept his papers, pointing out that he wanted to see if they were still there and if so he would burn them. With the last glimmer of hope in his heart, Rudolf looked doubtfully at his clothes that were coming apart at the seems and reached into his torn pocket. To his amazement he found a key and handed it to the rabbi.

The rabbi rushed to the palace and to Rudolf's chamber, while the emperor was still fast asleep, and destroyed the fatal document. He returned, as quickly as he could, to the garden and gave the key back to Rudolf. The emperor placed it again in his torn pocket and was dumfounded when the rabbi managed to squeeze him out through the meager opening of the cell, and he found himself in front of the royal castle. The rabbi led him to the magnificent hall where his throne stood and helped him to sit down.

At that very moment the emperor woke up and his face was covered with tears. He was delirious with happiness that his hardship had ended and that he was back in power. When he saw Rabbi

Loew quietly sitting on a chair next to him, he got up and embraced the old man with a lot of affection, thanking him from saving him from captivity and for being such a loyal friend. Till the end of his days Rudolf had no doubt that it was indeed the rabbi who had saved him from his ordeal.

Rabbi Loew wrote down this incident in his secret notebook and only after his death did the Jews find out that he had sent the "angel of sleep" upon Rudolf.

59

The Coin Pouch

Josl the peddler was coming home from his rounds in the villages. It was Friday afternoon and his heart was heavy. He felt sad and bitter after wandering all week from house to house trying to sell his goods and not being able to make but very little. He did not have enough for the Sabbath and he knew, as he approached the pub on the main street, that his good wife Leah would be anxiously waiting for him at the corner, asking for money to celebrate the upcoming Sabbath.

"What can be done," he told himself desperately scratching his head. "I will have to go to the jeweler and sell our very last silver spoon. Shabes has to be honored." He continued shuffling along, feeling the pain in his legs. Suddenly a peasant appeared out of nowhere and asked to see his merchandise. Josl opened his suitcase. The farmer did not bargain. He chose some goods and dropped a few coins into Josl's coin pouch. Josl continued walking happily, praising the God of Israel. He was greatly surprised when he looked back and the peasant was nowhere to be seen. The street was not even a curved one but straight as an arrow.

His wife was waiting for him near the pub and was thrilled when Josl gave her the money for the Sabbath.

The next Friday, Josl was puzzled when his wife did not wait for him at the regular place. As he approached home, his nostrils picked up the divine smell of specially cooked food for the Sabbath. There was a lot of light in the room. A beautiful, golden challah was already on the table and Leah was busy cooking a big fish.

"Did you go to the goldsmith?" he asked in wonder.

"What a silly idea on your part!" she answered laughing cheerfully.

"How did you prepare for the Sabbath?"

"I still have money left over from last week," she replied. "See!" She opened the worn out coin pouch he had left with her and showed him a couple of coins. They looked at each other sharing the same thought, but did not say anything aloud.

The same thing happened the next week. Leah was not waiting for her husband at the street corner and when he reached home everything was ready for the Sabbath. The lights seemed even brighter, the aroma of the food more tantalizing and the whole occurrence more wondrous than before.

Josl knew that when a person experiences a blessing in his home it is perhaps better not to talk about it so as to prevent a mishap. Behind every blessing there lurks a vicious imp or shed who will destroy everything with a venomous puff as soon as something is said.

This went on for years and not just on Sabbath but every single day of the week. Josl's business flourished and he became a respected and wealthy man. In the past, people had looked down on him and dismissed him with a shrug, but now he could contribute money for tzdakah more than others and the rabbi took a real liking to him. Leah who had always sat in the darkest corner of the women's wing in the synagogue, not being able to see a thing, moved to the front row among the most important ladies of the community. Life was good and both husband and wife enjoyed it to the fullest.

When the time came for Josl to leave this world and his friends were standing at his bedside praying with him for the last time, Josl asked them to grant him a few moments with his beloved wife. When Leah approached his bed he said quietly to her: "I am departing from this world, shouldn't I say something?" "It is better if you keep your silence," she answered. "When you get up there, you can thank God by yourself."

Josl followed her advice and did not utter a word but he could not suppress a slight smile. Leah was also smiling and, in this their closest union, they shared the greatest blessing of their lives.

Annotations

The reader will find here sources for all the stories, biographical data on historical personages, as well as comments on selected tales. The bibliography contains all the books mentioned in the following notes.

The most important source for the Czech stories is the collection of Wolf Pascheles, called *Sippurim* (1846). Pascheles' collection influenced many of his contemporaries, writers and poets who drew from the treasury of old tales and presented them in a new form. Among those were Pascheles' own sons, Jacob and Samuel as well as his son-in-law Jakob Brandeis. Other well-known authors of the times who rewrote folktales were Leopold Weisel, Salomon Kohn, Siegfrid Kapper, Leopold Kompert, and the Austrian historian Joseph Freiherr von Hormayr. Some parts of the *Sippurim* were reproduced in 1926 by Siegfried Schmitz and Meir Wiener in Vienna. Another edition of the *Sippurim* was also published in Vienna in 1937 by Heinz Politzer, a poet and linguist, under the name *The Golden Street*. Politzer retold the stories in an effort to keep them simple and close to the natural flow of folktales. Alois Hofman and Renate Heuerová followed the same path and so has the author of this book. In addition, the current collection attempts to preserve and sometimes resurrect the singular Jewish characteristics in the tales which were at times dim or almost completely faded.

IFA stands for Israel Folktale Archives (University of Haifa, Israel). Founded in 1956 by Dov Noy, the Archives store a collection of thousands of stories (each tale has an assigned number), told and recorded by numerous informants. There are also many stories in this book that are drawn from a variety of sources such as individual narratives, remembrances, and anecdotes, some of which I had the privilege to record personally.

LOVE AND TREPIDATION

"The Golden Street" (Czech)

Based on the story "Zlatá Ulice" from *Ze Židovského Ghetta: Pověsti, Legendy a Vyprávění* (Czech), translated from the German by Jana Zoubková. The German authors Alois Hofman and Renate Heuerová drew their sources from Wolf Pascheles *Sippurim* (1846) as well as other anthologies published between 1835–1940.

A similar version of this story can be found in Eduard Petiška's *Golem: Jewish Legends and Fairy Tales From Old Prague*, under the name "The Mysterious Groom." Petiška retold his tale from unknown sources.

Howard Schwartz retells a similar story, "The Underwater Palace," in his book *Lilith's Cave*. A story about a midwife and a cat, "The Clever Midwife" (Morrocan), can be found in *Jewish Stories One Generation Tells Another* by Peninnah Schram, as well as in Peninnah Schram's collection *Chosen Tales: The Midwife's Reward* (Kurdistan) retold by Barbara Rush. There also exists an interesting Hungarian story, "The Midwife and the Frog," in *Strange Things Sometimes Still Happen: Fairy Tales From Around the World*, edited by Angela Carter, as well as a Norse version Angela Carter comments about in the notes to the previously mentioned tale.

Midwives had a very important and vital role in people's lives throughout history. In modern times their popularity faded only to come back once again in recent years. Folklore is full of stories where midwives are either the main protagonists or aid other characters in the tale and their importance is always major. Many of these narratives are full of spirits and creatures from another world as well as different kinds of taboos. The way the midwife deals with these demons or apparitions, the way she solves the problems and knows when to do the right thing, is key to the type of story we are dealing with.

In the Czech tale, the midwife outwits the watersprite with the help of her niece, and because she is reasonable and can fight greed. On the surface she seems to be just a simple woman who knows how to behave and how to overcome difficulties, yet her character is much more complex than that. She is shrewd, compassionate, and capable, but at the same time suffers from human weaknesses and tries to resist them. She follows the watersprite to fulfill her duty despite the fact that she is afraid. She is a gossipper but knows to hold her tongue when necessary. She is also sturdy enough to work under extreme stress and under unusual conditions. She loves animals and considers their welfare just as important as people's. The watersprite is not just another demonic creature who knows only evil. He is a well-educated intellectual and has his principles regarding what is right and wrong. He is an early ecologist, if you will, and does not think much of the human species since, in his eyes, people are mostly corrupt and do not appreciate the gifts of nature.

Maybe the most unique trait is that we are entertained throughout the story, despite its somber tone and tragic events, with a good dose of humor. This is a Czech trademark quite often. There is almost a graphic description of the midwife and her husband which serves as comic relief if we do not want to deal with the despondency of the father and his daughter and the philosophical ideas that plague the watersprite.

For more details about the water spirit, see the story "The Watersprite" in this collection as well as the notes to that tale. See also "The Cat" for another story about a midwife.

It is interesting to point out that the name given to the midwife, Mrs. Shifres, is quite close to the name of the Biblical midwife Shiphrah who, together with her friend Puah, saved the Israelite male babies in Egypt from the wrath of the Pharaoh (Exodus 1:15–22). Shifres, though, is the family name of Hanina's aunt.

A lane by the name Golden Street still exists in Prague, adjacent to the Hradčany Castle where the president resides. Tiny old houses with very low roofs line the narrow street, consisting mostly of one or two rooms. In the Middle Ages and particularly in the sixteenth century during the reign of Rudolph II, alchemists toiled in those little cottages trying to turn various metals into gold. In the more recent past, goldsmiths practiced their trade there, hence another explanation for its name. One of the homes bears a plaque stating that Franz Kafka lived there for a while.

"Rabbi Loew's Bethrothal" (Czech)

Based on the story "Zásnuby rabiho Lowa" from *Ze Židovského Ghetta*, and "The Bethrothal" from *The Golem: Legends of the Ghetto of Prague* by Chaim Bloch.

Rabbi Judah Loew was born on the first Seder night 5273 (1513) in Worms, a German town on the Rhine, to Bezalel Ben Haim, descendant of Rabbi Hai Hagaon whose lineage went all the way back to David King of Israel. The name of the child was based on the verse from Genesis 49:9 : "Judah is a lion's whelp; from the prey, my son, thou art gone up."

Rabbi Loew had the symbol of a Czech lion engraved on the stone gate in front of his house to commemorate the visit of the Emperor Rudolph II. This is not necessarily an explanation of the origin of the name but most probably an enhancement to the story about the good relationship between the rabbi and the ruler. There is no historical proof of a close personal relationship with Rudolph. The rabbi's good friend, the scholar David Gans, recorded in his writings that Rabbi Loew was invited by the emperor to visit him in the palace on February 23, 1592. Gans does not tell us about the contents of the conversation between the rabbi and the emperor since the latter expressed his wish that it remain secret. Thus the nature of the contact between Rabbi Loew and the emperor remained a mystery which many legends magnify.

For a while Rabbi Loew's nickname was "The Bachelor" since he waited for ten years to marry Pearl. According to the sages, young people were supposed to wed at the age of eighteen. After Rabbi Loew became famous he was known exclusively by the name "Der Hohe" (The High or Great One).

Many scholarly works were written about the life of the Maharal of Prague, yet there are numerous gaps in the biographical data. One of the main reasons is that Rabbi Loew said very little about himself in his extensive writings. The most detailed biographical study of his life is the chronicle *Tzemah David*, first published in Prague in 1592 by David Gans, and another genealogy of the family of Rabbi Loew *Megillath Yuhasin* by Meir Pereles, a descendant of the rabbi, published in 1902.

In another version of this story, Pearl does not get the saddle from the horseman but he tosses his cloak to her and she finds the golden coins in the lining (*Golem* by Chaim Bloch).

See also other stories about Rabbi Loew in this book: "They Covered Him With Clothes But Could Not Keep Him Warm," "The Last Tear," "Rabbi Loew's Tomb," "Rabbi Loew and the Rose," "Rabbi Loew—The Guardian Angel," "The Descending Ceiling," "The Golem Goes Shopping," "The Porridge," Emperor Rudolf in Captivity." Related stories: "The Rebirth of the Maharal," "The Student," and "Greater Than the Maharal."

"At the Banks of the Vistula" (Polish)

Based on an experience felt by Michele Anish of New York while visiting Poland in the summer of 1996.

"The Jew in the Attic" (Slovak)

Retold from memory. Passed on to the author by her maternal grandmother who was born in Slovakia and grew up in a small village at the foot of the Tatra Mountains.

There are many legends about Lilith, the first wife of Adam, who left him after he rejected her demands for equality. Since then she has been portrayed as a demon whose sole purpose is to bring misery to humanity, particularly to women in labor, newborns, and little children. The three angels—Sanvi, Sansanvi, and Samangelaf—did not succeed in convincing her to return to Adam but she did promise not to attack humans if they had an amulet with the angels' names inscribed on it. She has kept that promise since then. She is depicted often as a beautiful woman, with long dark hair, seductive ways, and wearing mostly a long skirt to hide her not so sexy hairy legs. Fascinating stories and material about Lilith can be found in Howard Schwartz's book *Lilith's Cave* as well as in the book *Reimagining the Bible* by the same author. In particular, see pp. 59–61 in *Reimagining the Bible* a tale about a wicked midwife who happens to be an ally of Lilith and is able to turn herself into a gigantic, black, vicious cat the rabbi has to fight.

Czech folklore has tales about a woman demon called Polednice —Midday Witch—who is also in search of babies and small children. She does not always kill them. Sometimes she abducts them and at times just returns them after teaching a lesson to a careless mother. She operates mostly at noon (hence her name). Although at times she seems to have educational motivation, this character most probably evolved from the negative depiction of the gypsy women who had the reputation of stealing little children. This demon may have been related also to the Latin *dryad* which was originally a spirit of the woods.

The hamsah is an amulet shaped in the form of a hand, from the Hebrew word *hamesh*—five. One of the most popular talismans, it is meant to protect one from illness and mainly the Evil Eye. They are made of different materials and there are variations in their shapes. The hamsah originated in the Middle East: the Moslems call it the Hand of Fatimah after Mohammed's daughter, and the Christians the Hand of Mary. The influence of the Sephardic customs made the hamsah popular within the Ashkenasi communites as well. The shape of the hand (particularly the right one) has always had deep symbolic connotations. Created in the divine image of God, it is considered a source of power, creativity, as well as protection. To shield oneself, a person has to spread his or her right palm across the chest to chase away the evil spirits or cover the mouth with it while talking or yawning so as prevent the demons from entering the body that way. One can also use a protective hamsah as jewelry in the form of earrings, pins, necklaces, and rings.

"The Storyteller" (Hungarian)

From the recollections of Yacov Talmi, musician and teacher from Moshav Nechalim in Israel.

In addition to Yacov Talmi's story about the Jew from Maad, there are two additional versions. One of them is found in IFA # 6814 as told to Gershon Bribram by Israel Yaacob Schwartz. In this version the protagonist is a rag merchant, other than that the details are the same. In IFA # 12617 the same reteller tells the story from memory and explains the origin of the Hungarian saying: "I got to the same place as the Jew from Maad," implying that one can go around in circles.

This story brings to mind the wandering Hershele from Ostropol who returns home without realizing it. While sleeping on the side of the road, he takes off his shoes pointing them in the direction he is going in search of good fortune. A cart that is driving by happens to hit the shoes and turns them around. In the morning Hershele puts the shoes on and goes straight back home. He is amazed to see familiar scenery, a village just like his own, a house, a wife, and children just like the ones he has . . . and all this in the "new place"! He comes to the same conclusion like the Jew from Maad: all places seem to be the same, and there is nothing new under the sun.

IFA # 7131 has another version of the story about the rabbi and the pig, as recorded by Gershon Bribram, based on a tale by Dr. Josef Kraus who served as a rabbi in Hungary.

"Irenka's Doll" (Polish)

Based on *King Matt the First* by Janusz Korczak (first published in Polish in 1923 under the title *Krol Macius Pierwszy*). Also inspired by Korczak's book *How to Love Children* (in Hebrew: *Keycad Leehov Yeladim*).

King Matt the First is a wonderful book about a child king who tries to rule his kingdom wisely and fairly. It is full of psychological insights about children and philosophical questions which sometimes go unaswered. It is enjoyable reading for youngsters as well as adults.

This story is dedicated to the memory of Henryk Goldszmit, the Polish pediatrist and educator who wrote under the name of Janusz Korczak. Born in 1878 in Warsaw into an assimilated Jewish family, he followed in the footsteps of his grandfather who had also been a doctor. Korczak fought for the rights of children in general and the improvement of the life of orphans and abused youngsters in particular. Korczak never had a family of his own since his grandfather had suffered from mental illness and Korczak was afraid to pass it on to his offspring. As a young man he became the director of an orphanage and worked for his own Jewish institution as well as a Catholic orphanage in Warsaw. His devotion to his work and his love for children made Korczak famous in Poland and he also gained high esteem for his literary achievements. Over the years he wrote more than twenty books. When the Nazis occupied Warsaw, Korczak became the guardian angel of the children and continued protecting them till the day he died. For a while, thanks to his fame and connections, he and the children were able to survive. The regard people held for him seemed to affect the Germans and they did not persecute him for some time. But it did not last for long and the day came when the children were scheduled to be deported to Treblinka. Korczak, despite his influence, was not able to change the edict. He himself would have been able to escape, but, since he could not save his Jewish orphans, he chose to join the children and departed with them to the death camp.

On August 6, 1942, Korczak perished with two hundred children in the ovens of Treblinka, comforting them in their final moments as he did throughout his life. Maybe he did tell them for the last time, just as he had done many times earlier, that they were going toward a superior domain, toward freedom. He believed and fought for a better world for children all his life, one in which honesty, spontaneity, love, lack of greed and vanity would rule, a world that he believed only children could help create.

Bruno Bettelheim, in his introduction to *King Matt the First*, writes: " I understand that the memorial at Treblinka to the more than one million Jews who died there consists of rocks bearing the names of the cities or countries the victims came from. Only one of these rocks is inscribed with an individual's name. The inscription reads: "Janusz Korczak" (*Henryk Goldszmit*) *and the Children*."

"A Simple Wife" (Hungarian)

Based on two stories: IFA # 10280 as told to Abba Birbram by Eliezer Santai and IFA # 6058 recorded by Rivkah Glik, narrated to her by her Hungarian mother.

"They Covered Him with Clothes but He Could Not Keep Warm" (Czech)

Based on material found in *Velký Pražský Rabi Jehuda Löw: Morenu-Ha—Rav a Děvečka Abizag* by František Kafka. Kafka drew inspiration from *Sippurim* by Wolf Pascheles, *Old Czech Legends* by Alois Jirásek, the Old Testament, and some unknown sources.

The title of the story is derived from a biblical quote: "Now King David was old, advanced in age; and they covered him with clothes, but he could not keep warm" (Kings 1, 1–4).

The story was also influenced by the tale about Abishag the Shunammite as narrated in Kings 1, 2–4: "So they searched for a beautiful girl throughout all the territory of Israel, and found Abishag the Shunammite, and brought her to the king. The girl was beautiful; and she became the king's nurse and served him, but the king did not cohabit with her."

Rabbi Loew was different from most of his contemporary rabbis since he preferred the Aggadah (the legends, parables, and teachings of the the Talmud) to the Halachah (the dry legal matter of the Talmud). Yet, he considered them inseparable, the pure wisdom of God combined with the practical action that has to be taken to live in the world according to God's rules. His belief was deep and constant. Rabbi Loew always stressed that the world cannot exist without its creator but God can exist without the world. His philosophy was based mainly on the notion that God created the world in three phases, the creation, the survival—detached from God to a certain extent—and finally the world's return to God. Thus, men live in the second phase, which is connected to the first phase since God continually recreates the world. At the same time the second phase is tied to the third phase. Therefore, a person who has sinned has to feel repentance since it will lead him back to God and he can do that with the help of the Torah. It is the only link with God and surpasses human wisdom since it contains God's knowledge and also His order of the world. It should be studied with great joy since it leads men to freedom and perfection. These ideas of Rabbi Loew are his basic philosophy in a nutshell, yet they appear clearly or at the fringes of the stories that deal with his life and personality.

According to differing sources, Rabbi Loew was born in 1512 or 1513 and died in 1603 or 1609 so that he was not over 100 years old as some of the stories claim.

See also other stories about Rabbi Loew in this book: "Rabbi Loew's Bethrothal," "The Last Tear," "Rabbi Loew and the Rose," "Rabbi Loew's Tomb," "Rabbi Loew—The Guardian Angel," "The Descending Ceiling," "The Golem Goes Shopping," "The Porridge,"

"Emperor Rudolf in Captivity." Related stories: "The Rebirth of the Maharal," "The Student," "Greater Than the Maharal."

"The Blank Face" (Slovak)

Based on the novella "O Smutných Očich Hany Karadžičové" in Ivan Olbracht's book *Zakarpatská Trilogie*. It is the story of a young Jewish girl who was brought up in a very strict Orthodox environment in a remote valley at the foot of the Carpathian Mountains. Struggling to free herself from a restricted life that held her captive, she succeeds in finding her way out and into happiness, but she has to pay a heavy price. She is never truly free nor can she find relief from a devastating feeling of guilt she constantly experiences.

Ivan Olbracht, a Czech writer, was born in 1882 and died in 1952. He has been compared to a certain extent to Shalom Aleichem since he also described a forgotten village in a remote place in Eastern Europe, called Polana. There Orthodox Jews lived and struggled to survive just like Aleichem's protagonists in Anatevka. Olbracht spent the summers between 1931 and 1936 in the Carpathian region and studied not just the way of life of the village inhabitants but also their folklore, superstitions, and legends. He felt affection and compassion for the poor Jews who fought to kept their traditions alive and who suffered under very harsh conditions. He described their strength, their stubbornness, and their will to survive, but he also wrote realistically about their primitive way of life and their fanatic rejection of any change for the better, believing that it was the will of God.

A movie called *Golet in the Valley*, based on another tale by Olbracht dealing with the Jewish life in the Carpathian region of Slovakia, was filmed in the Czech Republic in 1993.

"The Seamstress" (Polish)

In memory of Beckie Shelkowitz, a remarkable woman, the grandmother of Michele Anish who lives in Brooklyn. Based on an interview with Joyce Winfield in December of 1972.

"The Abyss" (Czech)

Based on "Propast Víry" from *Ze Židovského Ghetta* by A. Hofman and R. Heuerová.

Miriam and Rupert are ill-fated lovers who cannot be together since they belong to different religions and status in society. This story is very different from the well-known tale about the Dybbuk (S. Anski's famous play), yet we can hear a faint echo resounding and point out some similarities. Although the gap here is much wider than the one that separated Leah and Hannon in "The Dybbuk," they cannot be torn apart and find themselves in death just as Leah and Hannon did. Like Hannon who took over Leah's body and soul since she belonged to him and the promise had to be kept, so did Rupert come to demand what was his, to take away the daughter that Abraham could not possess as a piece of jewelry. This motif appears in many stories throughout the European continent: the tale of the ghostly lover who comes back to get his promised bride, whether she has changed her mind or not. The famous Scottish version named "Sweet William's Ghost," the Irish version "The Demon Lover," the German "Lenore," the Russian "Svyetlana" and Polish "Ucieczka" are only a few of the ballads that deal with the same popular theme. The nineteenth century Czech poet Karel Jaromír Erben, in his famous book *Kytice* (*The Garland*), tells us a similar story with a different ending in his ballad "Svatební Košile" ("The Wedding Shirt").

The beauty of Miriam is compared to that which is attributed to gemstones. Taking into account that her father was a jeweler and knew the value of precious stones, the maiden's physical, as well as some spiritual qualities, are easily described in those terms.

Onyx is a name applied to a variety of quartz stones used since ancient times for every sort of adornment. Onyx comes in many colors, but when jewelers refer to onyx in general they mean the black stone that has a very special gleam.

The ruby stone comes in many shades of red, but the most highly valued is the stone called *pigeonblood* which resembles the color of the blood of a dove or pigeon and has a touch of purple. This kind of ruby is the one that is worth many times more than a diamond.

There is no way to describe the color of a true emerald; it could be rich grass green or deep transparent green with a high luster. The emerald was considered in ancient time as having beneficial effects, particularly on eye illness, was able to foretell the future, and was used as an antidote for spells.

A genuine pearl can come in many shades. The most common is the white and pink which would explain why the texture, color, and luster of beautiful skin is often compared to that of a pearl. They are very delicate and have to be protected from harsh sunlight, temperature variations, and pollutants in the air. They are since times immemorial a symbol of loyalty, honesty, and purity.

In a way, Miriam reminds us of Dinah, the protagonist in S.Y. Agnon's story "Agunot." This maiden dwells in Jerusalem and is fascinated by a young artisan her father hires to build a Holy Ark. He is also, on the surface, a simple carpenter, yet he has the soul of an artist which becomes very obvious in the story. His strong hands carve delightful designs in wood and the girl cannot take her eyes off them. The air is filled with the sensual attraction these two young people feel for each other similar to the way Miriam and Rupert sense it. Yet Agnon's narrative is far from being just a plain folktale. It is an intricate poetic story where many layers of symbolic meanings cover one another, where the sacred and the profane mingle and separate constantly. Sin and repentance walk hand in hand and the outcome is unexpected.

"The Hunchback" (Hungarian)

Based on two stories: IF A # 4354 recorded by Pinchas Gutterman, as told by Tsvi Friedman, and IFA # 8031 recorded by Gershon Bribram, told by Dr. Josef Kraus.

Rabbi Job has his own very special way of taming a shrew and is very succcessful without having to toil too hard or too harshly.

"The Treasure" (Czech)

Based on details found in *Staré Pověsti České* by Alois Jirásek and *Velký Pražský Rabi Jehuda Löw* by František Kafka.

The search for treasures as well as their discovery are motifs found in hundreds of stories. The fortune turns out to be mostly tangible and at times spiritual, but finding it in most cases, requires the overcoming of many difficulties. The protagonist who gets the prize is usually a brave person who has proven to possess such integrity that he or she deserves to receive the gift. In most cases true happiness does not exclusively depend on it, but it is just an additional bonus to one's future life. The hero often shares his wealth with others who are less fortunate than himself.

In Peninnah Schram's book: *Jewish Stories One Generation Tells Another* we find a similar story "The Iron Chest" (variations of which can be found in Sephardic Jewish folklore as well as in Yiddish and Slavic tales).

"The Treasure," despite its fairytale elements, is solidly based on the events in the life of a man whose influence on the Jewish and Gentile community of Prague during his life and even after his death was phenomenal. If the magical is taken out of the tale, the legend still remains and the truth will be always enhanced by what people want to believe in and save for future generations. See also the story "The Wandering Jew."

"The Gilded Slippers" (Polish)

Retold from a folktale by Y. L. Peretz, called "The Golden Shoes" which is a Hebrew translation by S. Orbach from an old anthology in Yiddish by Jacob Fichman printed in Palestine in 1894.

In Peninnah Schram's book, *Jewish Stories One Generation Tells Another*, we find two Jewish versions of the Cinderella story, as well as a short summary of "The Gilded Slippers" which in her collection bears the name "The Match." Isaac Leib Peretz calls it "The Golden Shoes" and its subtitle reads: "A Tale."

The mysterious woman is a well-known Jewish folk figure—Sara Bat Tovim—who is in charge of matchmaking and, according to tradition, helps out in times of difficulty to bring the right people together.

An unusual Czech take–off on the Cinderella story, a parable in IFA # 1487 recorded by Tsvi Sofer, is worth mentioning. The small size of the shoes has been a major issue in all the Cinderella variants and considered a complimentary attribute. In this tale, however, the size of the footwear, although also crucial, has a rather negative connotation. A very poor Jew is moving to a new location and finds that Poverty, his long–time companion, is not going to be left behind and follows right along with him. The despondent man begs Poverty to move in with a rich person rather than stick with his family. However, Poverty points out that she has no shoes and is ashamed to dwell in a wealthy man's house. The poor man sells the last of his meager possessions and buys a pair of slippers for Poverty in order to get rid of her. Unfortunately, no shoes fit Poverty, any slippers he finds are too small . . . and thus Poverty continues to accompany him barefooted.

"No Miracle" (Hungarian)

In memory of Esther Klein, the mother of Yacob Talmi, musician and teacher from Moshav Nechalim in Israel. Based on his personal narrative.

"Kytička" (Czech)

Based on "Jak Kytička v Plamenech o Život Přišla" in *Ze Židosvkého Ghetta* by A. Hofman and R. Heuerová.

LIGHT AND SHADOW

"Kaddish" (Czech)

Based on "Amen" in *Ze Židovského Ghetta* by A. Hofman and R. Heuerová.

The Angel of Death is usually depicted as a frightening and menacing figure with hardly any compassion. In this story, nevertheless, he appears as a kind and understanding creature who helps the dying woman and fulfills her request.

"The Dancing Maiden" (Czech)

Based on "Tančicí Židovka" from *Praha Plná Străsidel* by Miloslav Švandrlík and by word of mouth. Witnesses claimed that one can get a glimpse of the ghost of the Dancing Maiden after dark in the neighborhood of the former Ozerova Street, in front of the Burial Society Building. It is, nevertheless, not a good idea particularly for men. Some say that the Dancing Maiden did not die but found a new home in a house of ill-repute called "At the Kučeras" that existed on Ozerova Street in the past.

"Ice Candles" (Polish)

Based on IFA # 1951 as told by Efraim Tzoref from memory.

The Baal Shem Tov (Master of the Good Word), born Israel Ben Eliezer in Poland (1700–1760), also known as the Besht, was the leader of the Hasidic Movement. He was self-educated, knew the secrets of the kabbalah, and believed in a divine communion with nature. In time he became a wandering folk healer, aquired the reputation of a saintly man, and had many followers. Legend tells us that he was able to ascend to heaven, meet the Messiah, and create a golem. The Besht taught that people could rectify the evil in the world by living a clean life and worshipping God every day, not just by keeping the commandments. He believed that every man could reach God and preached veneration and love expressed in simple prayer rather than the study of Torah. His teaching appealed to the poor and mostly uneducated Jews whose devotion and admiration the Besht retained even after his death.

See also the story "The Rebirth of the Maharal" and "The Gilgul of the Baal Shem Tov."

"Bella Ella" (Czech)

Based on "Bella Ella" from *Ze Židovského Ghetta* by A. Hofman and R. Heuerová. Original story drawn from W. Pascheles *Sippurim* (1846).

"The Descending Ceiling" (Czech)

Based on "Rabi Loew and Rudolf II" from *Ze Židovského Ghetta* by A. Hofman and R. Heuerová.

This is a mystical tale about Rabbi Loew which offers an insight into Emperor Rudolph's fickle personality. Rabbi Loew was able, thanks to his knowledge of the kabbalah, to oblige the moody ruler so as to prevent him from hurting the Jews and in a way taught the proud Rudolph a lesson on the limitations of men. Since that day, so it was told, the emperor was more respectful to the dead and avoided forbidden areas that were beyond his command.

A similar version appears in *Lilith's Cave* by Howard Schwartz with additional comments and examples of tales that deal with the invocation of the dead and the meaning they convey.

A. Hofman and R. Heuerová in their introduction point out that there is also a possibility that this particular story about Rabbi Loew was influenced by one of the Faust legends popular during the time that Pascheles wrote his book. One of Faust's requests of the devil was to be able to see the dead heroes of ancient Troy who promptly appeared before him.

See also other stories about Rabbi Loew in this book: "Rabbi Loew's Bethrothal," "They Covered Him With Clothes But Could Not Keep Him Warm," "The Last Tear," "Rabbi Loew and the Rose," "Rabbi Loew's Tomb," "Rabbi Loew—The Guardian Angel," "The Golem Goes Shopping," "The Porridge," "Emperor Rudolf in Captivity." Related stories: "The Rebirth of the Maharal," "The Student," and "Greater Than the Maharal."

"The Rebirth of the Maharal" (Polish)

Based on IFA #1946 as told by Ephraim Tzoref from memory.

See also the story "Ice Candles" and "The Gilgul of the Baal Shem Tov."

"The Bartered Song" (Hungarian)

Retold from the story by Yacob Talmi, musician and teacher from Moshav Nechalim in Israel.

There exists another variant of this musical tale in Charles Fenyvesi's book *When the World Was Whole: Three Centuries of Memories*. The melody is the same but the story has two different versions. In one of them the Rabbi of Kallo overheard a shepherd playing a melody on his flute and liked it so much that he asked the shepherd to teach him how to play. After he learned the song, the rabbi returned the flute to its owner but the flute was not able to produce a sound from then on. Never again could it be used as a musical instrument (Did the rabbi play so badly . . . ?). In the second version, the song was composed by a shepherd whom the rabbi invited for Passover. It is about a golden bird that sings a sorrowful, and at the same time joyful, melody and the words suggest that the bird is waiting, constantly waiting. . . . There is only one line in Hebrew that gives an answer to the Hungarian text: "How long will the wait last?" and the Hebrew answer is: "Till the temple is rebuilt . . ."

The Rabbi of Kallo was extremely popular during his lifetime. Jews and Gentiles revered him and sought his advice. After his death the graveyard where he was buried remained closed. The Jewish community decided not to bury anyone else in that sacred place and opened a new cemetery nearby. Charles Fenyvesi points out that the rabbi's tomb is adjacent to a highway and close to the fence, not in a central area of the graveyard as expected, since the rabbi had requested to be buried close to the road he loved to walk on. The crypt is surrounded by pieces of paper, either neatly folded or rolled into balls that are requests and prayers from people who come to visit and leave them around the tomb or toss them over the fence. There are also papers stuck in the crevices and cracks of the mausoleum. The caretakers collect the hundreds of petitions into big grain sacks, tie them neatly, and line them up behind the grave, ready for delivery. But that is not really necessary since the Rabbi of Kallo knows.

Another version of the story, or rather the explanation of two schools of thought on how the niggun came into being, can be found in the "The Singing Tzaddik" in *Niggun: Stories Behind the Chasidic Songs That Inspire Jews* by Mordechai Staiman. It is interesting to point out that in Stainman's version of the story, the rabbi himself starts out as a singing shepherd and is discovered by another rabbi—Rabbi Arye Leib Sarah—who takes him under his wing and instructs him till he becomes a great teacher himself. Later on in life it became a habit for the rabbi to roam along the countryside in a shepherd's outfit and mingle with simple Jews. His purpose was to be their spiritual leader and help them with their afflictions.

"The Headstone of Anna Schmidt" (Czech)

Based on a short note in Josef Svátek's book of Czech legends, *Prazšké Pověsti a Legendy*, reprinted from the year 1883.

"The Eternal Punishment" (Czech)

Based on "Věčný Kajícník na Pražském Bes Almim" from *Ze Židovského Ghetta* by A. Hofman and R. Heuerová.

The tale brings to mind the Greek myth about the river Styx and the boatman Charon at its banks who transfers the souls of the deceased to Hades, the land of the dead. He is, nevertheless, no skeleton, but is described as an old, unkempt man, gruff and dirty, who demands payment for his services. It is mostly a small coin which was placed in the mouth of the dead. Here we have a take-off from the legend where a skeleton is assigned to the dead man for ever after. He not only rows him from one bank of the river to the other and back for free, but takes part in the punishment as well. If the story strikes us as odd, it might be due to the fact that the Czechs inserted here a dose of sardonic humor as comic relief or just because at times they view the world that way.

The sinner in this tale, despite the fact that he truly repents for the transgression he commited, will not be able to find forgiveness since his sin was so terrible. Being buried in a Jewish graveyard does not solve the problem. He will be cursed forever and his soul will never find peace. There is no place for him in the Olam Haba—the afterworld. The concept of the world to come has been used widely to describe the "life" of the soul after death and is somewhat ambiguous. Here though, it is clear that there is no place in the afterworld for the unhappy dead convert who will not be able to find a place even in Hell and thus is doomed to the endless sufferings of Sisyphus.

"The Magic Ring" (Polish)

Based on IFA # 593 recorded by Ephraim Tzoref, source unknown.

"The Wandering Jew (Czech)

Based on "Věčný Žid" from *Ze Židovského Ghetta* by A. Hofman and R. Heuerová.

The legend of the Wandering Jew has its roots in medieval times. It is a Christian legend about the shoemaker Ahasuerus, who laughed at Jesus as he was taken to his crucifixion and refused to acknowledge him. Jesus put a curse on him, to wander eternally and not to die till the day of his return. He would not be allowed to rest except for brief periods to nourish himself. This story gave rise to many anti-Semitic interpretations and served as a reason for riots and evictions. Some Christians believe that just like the biblical Cain, who suffered because of his sin, the Jews are condemned to wander endlessly because of their rejection of Jesus. There are reports of the Wandering Jew being spotted in different places all over the world (e.g., a Mormon met him in Salt Lake City in 1868, as recorded in *The Dictionary of Jewish Lore and Legend* by Alan Unterman, Thames and Hudson, Ltd., London, 1991).

In most stories the Wandering Jew is portrayed as a vicious person who brings tidings of doom wherever he goes. In our story he is different—a benevolent character whose presence is a sign of blessing and whose suffering is human and evokes compassion. David Pinski's Yiddish play "The Eternal Jew," Rudyard Kipling's tale "The Wandering Jew," and a novel by the same name by Stephan Heym are only a few of the literary works based on this legend.

The Hussite Wars took place between 1419 and 1436. Jan Hus was a Czech religious reformer whose teachings preceded the Protestant reformation. He led a movement against the Roman Catholics and was burned at the stake in 1415. A war broke out between Hus' followers and the Roman Catholics and lasted from 1419 until 1436 when the two sides reached a compromise.

The Přemysls were the ancient kings of the Czech Land. They ruled within the Holy Roman Empire, from 900 to around 1100 C.E.

"Dust Is Not Just Dust" (Hungarian)

Based on IFA #12904 as told to Gershon Bribram by Eliezer Hacohen.

Lodz is a Polish town but, when the Russian Emperor ruled over Poland, it was considered a Russian city. Hungarian Jews, searching for better means of survival, reached far places within the Russian Empire.

"The Borrowed Life" (Czech)

Based on "Cizí Život" from *Ze Židovského Ghetta* by A. Hofman and R. Heuerová.

A similar story, named "The Given Years," appears in the book *Stories and Fantasies from the Jewish Past* by Emil Bernhard Cohn.

This is also a tale about a dying rabbi from Dobrze, a little town in Volhynia, Poland, who is given additional years to live. Some of those years were granted by his devoted followers while a young girl offered the rabbi her whole life, just like in the Czech version. Yet, there is a big difference. The maiden does not hand him her life out of sheer admiration and love but rather fear. The rabbi had scolded her for her carefree and cheerful behavior, and she considers herself a sinner and wants to repent. This is an extreme case of Chozeret BeTshuvah, a repentant.

The rabbi spends his years having visions of the young woman's life. He suffers also because of the realization that he has ruined not only her life but also that of her father who dies despondent, and her destined husband who happens to be his disciple. He actually lives a double life, his own as well as the girl's, and the transitions are astounding. His is a life of darkness, suffering, and deprivation; hers of happiness, love, and joy. He learns to appreciate the wonders of the girl's life and sinks deeper into his own abyss. It is as if the girl's soul has become a dybbuk and will not leave him alone. The congregation considers him almost insane because of his erratic behavior. In the end he dies in the arms of the Torah, well over a hundred years of age.

Emil Cohn has also inserted towards the end of the story the figures of the Gaon of Vilna and the Maggid of Meseritz and illustrates skillfully the deep gap between the Mitnagdim and the Hasidim. To a certain extent, the fight between the two occurs within the rabbi as well. He symbolizes the old ways and tradition while the young girl—the image of life and joy—wants to worship God following the footsteps of the Hasidim.

Emil Bernhard Cohn, a prolific German Jewish writer, was also a rabbi in Berlin, the city where he was born in 1881. He wrote novels, poetry, and essays and excelled in retelling legends from the Jewish past. He was highly regarded by such famous people as Thomas Mann and Max Reinhart. He escaped from Nazi Europe in 1939 and continued his literary activity in the United States. He was killed in an accident in California in 1948.

While reading the beautiful rendition of Howard Schwartz's story "The Cottage of Candles" in *Gabriel's Palace*, a thought comes to mind: this is the tale of a man who is looking for justice and finds his own candle of life in a cottage, in the depth of the woods, on the brink of burning out. Very little oil is left. When he secretly tries adding some oil from a different candle he is caught and chased away, his quest ending in failure for obvious reasons. A person cannot add oil to his own candle of life, but clearly one can add one's own oil to that of somebody else. Is it not exactly what the young woman and the others did? This theme is approached from a different angle in another story in the same book by Howard Schwartz, "The Enchanted Inn," where a person enters a cottage full of burning candles, one of which is about to extinguish. He adds oil to that particular one without knowing that it is his own and is rewarded for it instead of being condemned. After all he did not know to whom it belonged and was not acting out of concern for his own fate.

"The Last Tear" (Czech)

Based on *Pohádkové Vandrování po Čechách* by Vladimír Hulpach. A similar version appears in *The Golem* by Chaim Bloch.

It seems that ever since the incident with the pails of water, the people of Prague used to compare any incompetent worker to the Golem of Rabbi Loew. Johann Wolfgang von Goethe uses the motif of the unstoppable water carrier in his story "Tale of the Sorcerer's Apprentice." Walt Disney gave us the fascinating version of his own in *Fantasia*. An interesting variation, "The Magician's Fellow," appears in *The Dark Way, Stories from the Spirit World* told by Virginia Hamilton in which it is the devil himself who, summoned by mistake by the apprentice, keeps bringing the water. The pupil asked for it initially just to water a plant and out of sheer fear. The magician saves the situation by arriving in the nick of time and the apprentice learns his lesson once and for all. Different variants of this tale are popular in world folklore, particularly in Eastern Europe. For more details see Howard Schwartz's book, *Reimagining the Bible*, p. 80.

It is interesting to point out that there is no elaborate description of the Golem in the stories. He was supposed to be big, tall, and awkward. There are hardly ever any details of his facial features. At times we find a depiction of the fear he brought out in people mainly because of his size and bulk (the tallest he has been described is ten feet tall), and at times he seems to be harmless and placid under normal circumstances. Only in a few stories does he appear to be not just docile and meek but also sensitive and capable of feeling sorrow and pain. In Isaac Bashevis Singer's version "The Golem," the Golem longs to be human and seems to have not just the *nefesh*, the spirit, but also the *neshama*, the soul. At that moment he stops being just the "mechanical man" of most tales.

There are many versions of the Golem story. This magical and extraordinary tale has fascinated writers for centuries and the retelling can never be completed. In antiquity we find the story of an artificial human being in *The Midrash* and *The Talmud* (*B. Sanh. 65b; and Gen. Rab. 8:1*); Raphael Patai in his book, *Gates of the Old City*, discusses folktales dealing with miracle-working rabbis; Greek mythology produced artificial women created by the god Hephaestus that were meant to serve as his aids. The classic story of the Golem of Prague can be found in *Jewish Folktales*, selected and retold by Pinhas Sadeh, translated by Hillel Halkin; more analytical material appears in Howard Schwartz's book *Reimagining the Bible*.

Karel Čapek (1890–1938), a Czech writer famous for his symbolic plays and novels, used the idea of the Golem in his well-known play, *R.U.R.—Rossum's Universal Robots*, 1921. There he coined the word *robot* (from the Czech *robotnik* meaning "serf" or *robota* for "drudgery" or " compulsory work"), introducing a mechanical creature without a soul. Čapek expressed his fear of the loss of individuality and the danger he saw lurking in technology. The concern is obvious in his science fiction and the anti-totalitarian beliefs found in his work.

See also other stories about the Golem in this book: "The Student," "The Golem Goes Shopping," and "The Porridge."

"Two Skinny Goats" (Polish)

Based on IFA # 532 as recorded by Dov Noy.

See also the stories "The Cat" and annotations to that story, as well as the tale "A Billy Goat with Human Eyes."

"The Cat" (Czech)

Based on a note in Theodor Herzl's diary, dated March 19, 1897. Herzl was writing about a meeting he had with his colleague

Eduard Bacher from the Neue Frei Presse. They had carried on a conversation about Jewish legends, how the old stories tend to change and transform themselves to keep the tales alive. On that occasion Bacher told Herzl the story about the cat he remembered from his childhood and which finds its roots in the tale "The Golden Street." Recorded in *Ze Židovského Ghetta* by A. Hofman and R. Heuerová.

In many stories the journey to the Holy Land is completed by miraculous means. It is as if the devoted person has been "travelling" all his life and while praying is coming closer and closer to the Land of Israel. He reaches it at the end, magically in the last period of life, since it is the place where he wants to die. Usually it is a narrow, dark tunnel or cave that brings the person to the sacred destination, or even a path through a delightful orchard, and most often it is a goat, not a cat, that leads the way. Agnon's story "Fable of a Goat" is also based on this folktale where a goat leads the person through a cave into the land of milk and honey. There are many variants of this tale collected in the IFA in Haifa (e.g., see IFA # 532: "Two Skinny Goats"). Also see more about this motif in *Reimagining the Bible* by Howard Schwartz, pp. 179–182.

There is an interesting American Indian myth where a tunnel also provides the path through which people travel and emerge, but in this case it is not out of the world but into it. "You know, everything had to begin, and this is how it was: the Kiowas came one by one into the world through a hollow log. They were many more than now, but not all of them got out. There was a woman whose body was swollen up with child, and she got stuck in the log. After that, no one could get through, and that is why the Kiowas are a small tribe. They looked all around and saw the world. It made them glad to see so many things. They called themselves Kwuda, 'coming out'" (N. Scott Momaday, *The Way to Rainy Mountain*, New York: Ballantine Books, 1970, p. 17)."

"A Billy Goat with Human Eyes" (Polish)

Based on a story in *Osm Světel* (Czech) by Leo Pavlát; retold tales from unknown sources.

See also the tales "Two Skinny Goats" and "The Cat."

"A Healthy Patient" (Hungarian)

Based on IFA # 5269, recorded by Sariah Epstein from an unknown Hungarian source and the story "Nejlepší Lékař (Czech) in *Osm Světel* by Leo Pavlát.

There are many tales about Maimonides (Moses ben Maimon), the Rambam. This particular story has a Polish variant IFA # 1717 recorded by H. D. Armon which is somewhat different but essentially the narrative is the same. In the Polish version it is only one Egyptian vizir who hates the Rambam and decides to ruin him all by himself without accomplices. He fasts for a week, does not wash, or take care of his personal appearance and approaches the Rambam for treatment. It was the Rambam's practice, the story goes on, to treat each patient by looking into his eyes and then an assistant would provide the necessary medicine. The Rambam prescribed for the "sick" vizir two loaves of bread and told him to clean up and take care of his hygiene, pointing out that he was starved and needed care. He also sent him a message through his aide telling him that, while looking into his eyes, he had detected a terminal disease gnawing inside him and that he would be dead within three months. And so it happened.

See also the story "The Worm."

"The Postmortem Bath" (Czech)

Based on *Ze Židovského Ghetta* by A. Hofman and R. Heuerová.

"Rabbi Loew and the Rose" (Czech)

Based on *Ze Židovského Ghetta* by A. Hofman and R. Heuerová.

See also Howard Schwartz's "Rabbi Loew and the Angel of Death"—tale and commentary—in *Lilith's Cave.*

The famous Rabbi Loew deserved to live a long and fulfilling life and so he did. Yet, he did not live a hundred years as the legend tells us and he might not have died because of a rose or despite it. His life was never a bed of roses nor was his death.

According to another version of the legend of his death (*The Golem* by Chaim Bloch), Rabbi Loew did not succeed in tearing out the whole list from the hands of the Angel of Death. A little piece of the fatal scroll remained in the claws of the dark messenger and it was on this tiny scrap of torn paper that Rabbi Loew's name was written. Thus the Angel of Death could pursue the rabbi as long as it took. It never occurred to Rabbi Loew that his was the name on the torn piece of scroll and, typical of his unselfish reputation, he did not worry about it. If that was the case why was he so concerned about his demise? Why was he so afraid of death? Why did he toil and manufacture a device that would warn him of the upcoming danger? Was he especially scared of the wrath of the Angel of Death since he had dared to cross his path?

Another version of the rose legend, as told by Efrayim Sechter from the former Czechoslovakia (Folklore Research Center, Institute for Jewish Studies, The Hebrew University, 1991, Arch. No. 3170a), relates the belief that as long as the rabbi studied the Torah and the Talmud, Death could not approach him. He did so day and night and the Angel of Death could never accomplish his task. But then one day, knowing how much the rabbi loved children, the Dark Angel disguised himself as a little boy and, holding on to a lovely rose, succeeded in distracting the saintly man from his studies and thus was able to take away his life.

Based on other legends, Rabbi Loew was very much aware of the shortness of human life and believed full-heartedly that what really mattered was what came next. Being the man he was, he had no reason to be apprehensive of the afterlife. He died on 18 Elul 5369 following a long illness due to a debilitating cold. Yet even after death, the legend tells us, he continued to serve his beloved community. See the story: "Rabbi Loew's Tomb."

There exist many stories where even simple folk try to cheat the Angel of Death, not just those who have the knowledge and ability to use supernatural powers such as rabbis and learned men. Many times it is sheer shrewdness that saves them for a while and at other times the Angel of Death is depicted as not being very bright. Thus there comes to mind the gypsy story that I recall from childhood about an old woman who tries to hide in a barrel of honey. She later changes her mind and fearfully crawls into her torn down cover. When the emissary of death appears, he is so scared by the sticky "apparition" that he swears never to come back. Another interesting story of the same type is by Karel Jaromír Erben, the Czech poet and folklorist, whose tale *Shoemaker and Death* is an old-time favorite. A shoemaker owns a magic bench, whoever sits on it cannot get up and only the shoemaker knows how to break the spell. When his hour of death arrives, the Angel of Death appears sickle and all, and the shoemaker politely asks him to sit down and relax while he packs his suitcase. Death cannot get up and thus nobody can die. For a long time all creatures rejoice till they realize the chaos and havoc eternal life can create. And thus in the end the shoemaker releases the Angel of Death and humbly follows him to his last place of rest.

"The Gilgul of the Baal Shem Tov" (Polish)

Based on IFA # 2054, recorded by Dov Noy as told by Menashe Ungar.

See also the story "Ice Candles" and "The Rebirth of the Maharal."

"Rabbi Rashi" (Czech)

Based on *Ze Židovského Ghetta* by A. Hofman and R. Heuerová.

The ending of this story leans heavily on a Czech folktale which has always been popular. The well-known poet Karel Jaromír Erben used it in the opening poem of his book of ballads *The Garland*. It is the tale of despondent orphans who cannot accept the fact that their mother has died. Day after day they visit her grave and mourn. The mother feels sorry for her unhappy children, and her soul comes back in the form of a lovely yet small and simple field flower, the wild thyme. In Czech it is called *materidouška* meaning "mother's soul." Thus, the orphans find consolation while gazing at the tiny flower and inhaling its sweet fragrance. Every spring the blossoms reappear without fail.

"Rabbi Loew's Tomb" (Czech)

Based on *Ze Židovského Ghetta* by A. Hofman and R. Heuerová and IFA # 6556 recorded by Pinchas Gutterman as told by Efrayim Shechter.

Before it became common to erect headstones to mark graves, in ancient times people used to pile a mound of stones to commemorate the consecrated grounds assigned to the dead. Later on it became customary for visitors to place small pebbles or stones on graves as their "signature" and sign of respect.

See also other stories about Rabbi Loew in this book: "Rabbi Loew's Betrothal," "They Covered Him With Clothes But Could Not Keep Him Warm," "The Last Tear," "Rabbi Loew and the Rose," "Rabbi Loew—The Guardian Angel," "The Descending Ceiling," "The Golem Goes Shopping," "The Porridge," "Emperor Rudolf in Captivity." Related stories: "The Rebirth of the Maharal," "The Student," "Greater Than the Maharal."

"The Unblessed Child" (Czech)

Based on *Ze Židovského Ghetta* by A. Hofman and R. Heuerová.

"The Spilled Soup" (Polish)

Based on Osm Světel (Czech) by Leo Pavlát; source unknown.

"Rabbi Loew—The Guardian Angel" (Czech)

Based on *Ze Židovského Ghetta* by A. Hofman and R. Heuerová.

See also other stories about Rabbi Loew in this book: "Rabbi Loew's Betrothal," "They Covered Him With Clothes But Could Not Keep Him Warm," "The Last Tear," "Rabbi Loew and the Rose," "Rabbi Loew's Tomb," "The Descending Ceiling," "The Golem Goes Shopping," "The Porridge," "Emperor Rudolf in Captivity." Related stories: "The Rebirth of the Maharal," "The Student," "Greater Than the Maharal."

"The Student" (Czech)

Based on *Golem* by Eduard Petiška and the legend of Faust.

See also the story "The Last Tear."

LAUGHTER AND RIDICULE

"Greater Than the Maharal" (Hungarian)

Based on IFA # 7381, recorded by Gershon Bribram as told by Eliezer Bratfeld.

The revenge is not in proportion to the insult, yet the people of the little town, being naïve and basically kind-hearted, did the "worst" they could. The conceited rabbi, on the other hand, must have been very shocked to hear the unexpected declaration the simple folk made and felt humiliated which indeed was an appropriate punishment. The question is: did he regret his behavior and change? Most probably not.

"The Worm" (Polish)

Based on IFA # 2940 recorded by Mania Seider as told by Fishl Seider.

There is another version of this tale in Howard Schwartz's book *Lilith's Cave,* included in the narrative "The Humunculus of Maimonides."

See also an additional story about the Rambam in this book: "The Healthy Patient."

"The Shulklopfer" (Hungarian)

Based on IFA # 8627, recorded by Aharon Yaffe as told by Josef Polchick.

"The Golem Goes Shopping" (Czech)

Based on *Ze Židovského Ghetta* by A. Hofman and R. Heuerová.

Ever since the incident with the fish and apples, any time a customer got into an argument with a vendor, the angry merchant would comment that maybe he or she were the Golem of Rabbi Loew. In a somewhat different version of the story, the Golem, while purchasing the apples, does not accept the bag from the vendor and keeps standing there just as a golem does. When the stallholder mocks the Golem and asks him whether he has not had enough, whether he would like perhaps the whole apple stand, the Golem, who initially seemed to be perplexed, likes the idea and picks up the whole stall along with the vendor. He marches straight to the rabbi's home with the stand on his shoulder and the merchant desperately clinging onto it, while people follow him laughing and picking up the apples that are falling off. This story seems to make more sense yet it is hard to know what a golem, particularly the Golem, would really do and maybe the most ridiculous tale is the "true" one. This version of the story appears in *Angels, Prophets, Rabbis and Kings from the Stories of the Jewish People* by Jose Patterson.

Only once did Rabbi Loew use the Golem's services for reasons other than the safety of his congregation since he was sure it was justified. One year just before Rosh Hashana, the weather was so stormy that no fisherman dared go out and fish. The holiday was fast approaching and the rabbi knew that the Golem was the only one not affected by the storm and as such could fish and provide the Jewish community with the necessary food for the holiday. The Golem was given instructions and left for the river to do as told. In the meantime a friendly fisherman brought the rabbi a supply of fish and the rabbi was relieved that the Golem's unusual service would not be necessary. The shammes was sent to summon the Golem from the river and the Golem returned to the synagogue, but not before promptly emptying his full basket of fish into the stream. A version of this story appears in *The Golem* by Chaim Bloch.

In *Yiddish Folktales* edited by Beatrice Silverman Weinreich, translated by Leonard Wolf, there is a story about a different Golem, "The Golem of Vilna," in which the Gaon of Vilna creates a golem which is capable of an unbelievable number of unusual tasks. The Gaon brought him to life by inserting the shem into his ear. The Golem is a wonderful fisherman. All he needs to do is to use the language of the fish which he knows well (according to most golem stories the Golem was not able to produce a sound and fish after all are mute) to call them, and the whole congregation is provided plentifully. In addition to being invisible when the rabbi so decides, the Golem can fly from roof to roof and has uncontrollable strength which he uses, as in all other golem stories, to protect the Jews.

"Two Jobs Instead of One" (Hungarian)

Based on IFA # 8207 recorded by Gershon Bribram as told by Emanuel Frieder.

"Stuck in the Mud" (Polish)

Based on IFA # 2844 recorded by Yaacob Raver from memory.

"The Toothache" (Hungarian)

Based on IFA # 10870 recorded by Gershon Bribram as told by Eliezer Shantai.

"The Rabbi and the Coachman" (Hungarian)

Based on IFA # 7496 recorded by Gershon Bribram as told by Dr. Josef Kraus.

"The Watersprite" (Czech)

Based on a story told to the author by her grandmother who owned the very same mill that still stands in its place.

Water creatures and deities are popular in many cultures. They dwell in rivers, ponds, streams, wells, lakes, seas, and oceans and have been a source of inspiration for storytellers since ancient times. One of the water creatures that abides in Slavic folklore and is widespread is the *vodnik* or *hastrman* in Czech and Slovak folklore. The same appears under the name *dedushka vodyanoi* in Russian stories. The Slovenes call him *vodeni moz* and the Poles *topielec* (drowner). The German, Danish, and Norse are also familiar with him and call him *waserman* and in Scottish and English tales he is the *watersprite* or *waterman*.

The Czech and Slovak sprite is a small, greenish man who likes to wear fancy clothes and makes his own shoes at night while sitting at the banks of a river, singing a merry song to the moon. Although green suits him best, he loves red and all his shoes come in that color. He is forced to make his own footwear since he cannot afford to buy it and also has trouble finding a proper fit. In the past he was of great help to some friendly millers who ran their mills using huge wheels powered by the force of the river stream. He can give a great deal of professional advice regarding the tides and underwater currents as well as horsepower. In some stories he uses his own underwater horses to supply literally the horse power to run a mill! The watersprite will do anything for a mug of beer and at times, when lonely, seeks the company of men. Love is a sensitive subject for him because he is quite unlucky and human maidens do not respond to his courting. It is easy to detect a watersprite since, although dressed as a person, he always drips water from his left pocket and leaves a wet surface on the chair he happens to sit on.

Being a common figure in Czech tales, the watersprite is humanized in many ways. He is usually depicted as a short, chubby, and puffy creature. Sometimes a finger is missing from his left hand. The watersprite likes to sleep during the day and at night sits at the river bend, whistling and clapping his hands. He is also very fond of music, loves to joke, tease, and have fun. Despite his mostly friendly temperament, in some stories he depicts the demonic force of water and its cruelty. When enraged, he drowns people and keeps their souls neatly stacked in small covered mugs in his pantry. When a cover is somewhat displaced and a soul manages to escape, the surface of the streams and ponds becomes bubbly. At such times the wrath of the watersprite does not know limits till he manages to replace the lost souls. Czech literature and music abound with watersprite figures which are very versatile. Antonin Dvořák, for example, in his opera *Rusalka*, introduces the unforgettable character of an old, despondent watersprite who is the water nymph's father. He is a tragic figure and sings his heart out expressing his suffering with the help of Dvořák's magnificent melodies.

"A Difficult Question" (Polish)

Based on IFA #1647, recorded by Chaim Schwarzbaum from memory.

"The Keepsake" (Hungarian)

Based on IFA # 4902, recorded by Zalman Baharav as told by Leowald Levi.

"An Unending Story" (Polish)

Based on IFA # 2969, recorded by Berl Rabach from memory.

"The Porridge" (Czech)

As told to the author by her grandmother when she was a small child.

It is not very often that the Golem is made fun of but, just as in the story about the apples and the fish, people sometimes like to amuse themselves in a good-natured way at the expense of a weakness they find in a menacing figure such as the Golem. Despite being the protector of the Jews, he evoked fear and apprehension. Indications that the Golem was a good-hearted creature and loved childen—orphans in particular—are found in some of Pascheles stories as well as in Chaim Bloch's *Golem*. At times foreign elements found their way into the story and eased the feeling of fright that the strange creature commanded. Such is the story, "The Porridge," that the author's grandmother told her when she was very young and fearful after being told the original tale of the Golem of Prague. It is based on the Czech folktale "Hrnečku Vař" ("Cook, Little Pot, Cook") which is most popular and known to every child in the country. It is the tale of a magic pot that makes porridge and what happens when it cannot stop cooking. The same idea was used in a somewhat different way in the book by Peter Sis *The Three Golden Keys*. An Italian pasta version is found in the book *Strega Nona* by Tomie de Paola. Many stories that deal with magic objects use incantations for the spell to work but the Golem was mute and had to resort to wonder–working motions instead.

See also other stories about the Golem in this book: "The Last Tear," "The Student," and "The Golem Goes Shopping."

"Either Too Few or Too Many" (Polish)

Based on IFA # 1823, recorded by Nehama Tsion as told by Nehama Newtsits.

"Emperor Rudolf in Captivity" (Czech)

Based on *Ze Židovského Ghetta* by A. Hofman and R. Heuerová. Also found in Chaim Bloch's *Golem*.

See also other stories about Rabbi Loew in this book: "Rabbi Loew's Betrothal," "They Covered Him With Clothes But Could Not

Keep Him Warm," "The Last Tear," "Rabbi Loew and the Rose," "Rabbi Loew's Tomb," "The Descending Ceiling," "Rabbi Loew—The Guardian Angel," "The Golem Goes Shopping," "The Porridge," "Emperor Rudolf in Captivity." Related stories: "The Rebirth of the Maharal," "The Student," "Greater Than the Maharal."

"The Coin Pouch" (Czech)

Based on *Ze Židovského Ghetta* by A. Hofman and R. Heuerová.

Glossary

All of the expressions are in Hebrew unless otherwise noted.

Aggadah — Aramaic for "story." Rabbinic lore dealing with ethics, theology, history, and folklore. Has to be distinguished from Halachah that deals with ritual and legal matters.

Am Israel — The people of Israel.

Ashmadai — Asmodeus. Vicious demon king with whom King Solomon had a battle of wits. Well known in Jewish folklore.

Azazel — Name of the location where the scapegoat, which carried the sins of Israel on Yom Kippur, was sent and cast over a cliff. There were two goats offered as sacrifices, one to God and the other one to Azazel. Azazel is also the name of a fallen angel related in one of the legends about King Solomon.

Baal Shem Tov — Israel ben Eliezer (1700–1760). Founder of the Hasidic movement, commonly known as Besht. Folk healer and influential mystic leader. Born in Poland, lived in the Carpathian Mountains.

Bar Mitzvah — At thirteen a Jewish boy is considered a man, a Son of the Commandment, and the event is celebrated with great joy.

Bes Almin — Yiddish for the Hebrew, *bet almin* cemetery.

Brit — Circumcision. The ceremony performed on every Jewish male child, eight days after his birth.

Challah — Plaited loaves of bread eaten on Sabbath and festivals. At each meal there are two loaves on the table to remember the double portion of manna which fell on Fridays and the festivals. The manna that fell in the desert was covered with layers of white dew from above and below. Since the challahs symbolize the manna, they are placed on a white tablecloth and covered with a white cloth.

Chupe — Yiddish from the Hebrew *chupah*; canopy under which a wedding ceremony takes place. It symbolizes the future home of the couple.

Dagon — The main god of the Philistines and the Phoenicians, depicted as half man and half fish. A god that ruled over water, rivers, and streams. Appears also in Slavic mythology.

Drasha — A sermon.

Edom — Ancient tribe of Semitic origin. Considered descendants of Esau and enemies of Israel.

Elohim — One of the Hebrew names of God.

Faust — Also called Faustus or Doctor Faust. Hero of the famous legend about a German necromancer who sells his soul to the devil in exchange for knowledge and power. The first anonymous collection of stories about Faust called *Faustbuch* appeared in 1587.

Franz Joseph — (1830–1916) The popular ruler of the dual monarchy of Austria—Hungary who ruled for sixty-eight years. The assassination of his heir and nephew Archduke Francis Ferdinand in 1914 led to World War I.

Gilgul — The migration of a soul from one body to another after death. Popular theme in hasidic stories.

Golem — Artificial human being created with the help of magic or the use of holy names. There are stories about golems in the Talmud and in Jewish literature from the twelfth century on. Derogatory, implying lack of intelligence, stupidity, awkwardness.

Hachsharah — Intellectual and physical preparation and training for future life in the settlements in Palestine.

Haftarah — A portion from the Neviim – Prophets – comes after the reading from the Torah, on the Sabbath or holidays.

Halachah — (lit. for "walking") The Oral Law, the body of law comprising the rules and ordinances of Jewish religion and civil practice. Contrasted with Aggadah.

Halutzim — Pioneers. Word used in particular for Jewish settlers in Palestine before the establishment of the State of Israel.

Hamantaschen — Favorite three-cornered Purim pastry intended to represent the wicked Haman's ears. Haman is the villain in the book of Esther who tried unsuccessfully to destroy the Jews of Persia.

Hamsah — An amulet in the shape of a hand intended to guard from evil.

Hasid — A person who belongs to a Hasidic group.

Hazan — Cantor.

Herzl, Theodor Zeev — (1869–1904). Austrian writer, journalist, and founder of Zionism. For a few years he was the Paris correspondent for the influential *Vienna Neue Freie Presse*. The First Zionist Congress he organized in Basel in 1897 led to the establishment of the Jewish State in Israel. In his novel *Old-New Land* (1902), he coined his famous statement: "If you will it, it is no dream."

Kabbalah — A general term for the mystical tradition that emerged in the thirteenth century in Spain and France. It has its roots, nevertheless, in the belief (by kabbalists) that it had been given originally to Moses on Mount Sinai with the Torah.

Kaddish — The prayer for the dead. Also a prayer recited by the cantor at the end of a section of the liturgy.

Kippah — Head covering. A small skull-cap worn by all Jewish men during prayers and at all times by Orthodox Jews to remind them of God's presence. Also known as yarmulke or kappel.

Křivoklat — An ancient castle in Bohemia and the wooded area adjacent to it. Used by kings and rulers as a favorite hunting place.

Lilith — The first wife of Adam who deserted him and became a female demon.

Maimonides — Moses ben Maimon, known as Rambam (Rabbi Moses ben Maimon, 1135–1204). Famous philosopher, halachist, and doctor. Born in Spain, fled the Islamic persecution and settled down with his family in Egypt. Best known for his philosophical work *The Guide to the Perplexed* in Arabic. The saying goes: "From Moses to Moses there was none like Moses."

Maskilim — plural of Maskil – lit. learned. The Maskilim were the Reform Jews who objected to the Orthodox ways of Judaism.

Messiah — Meaning in the Bible "the anointed one" term applied to priests and other individuals who had a sacred mission. Later on, after the exile, the Messiah became the divine unknown guide who would lead the Jews back to their homeland when the right time came.

Mezuzah — Doorpost – Parchment scroll placed in a container and attached to the doorposts in a Jewish home. The scroll contains verses from Deuteronomy (6:4–9 and 11:13–21), as prescribed in that particular book of the Bible: 11:20: "You shall write (these words) upon the doorposts of your house and upon your gates."

Mikveh — Ritual bath. The waters in the mikveh must come from a natural spring or river.

Misloach Manot — Food gifts sent on Purim to friends and relatives.

Mitnagdim — Lit. the opposing ones, the Orthodox Jews who objected to the new ways of the Maskilim or the Reform Jews.

Mitzvah — A good deed, originally used to describe the divine commands in the Bible.

Naftali — Sixth son of Jacob and Rachel's maid Bilha. The founder of the tribe of Naftali (Genesis 30:7).

Niggun — A melody, a song popular in particular with the Hasidim.

Olam Haba — The World to Come.

Old-New Synagogue — AltNeuschul. The oldest synagogue in Europe, the most famous in the Old City of Prague.

Palinka — The favorite alcoholic drink of the Hungarians. It is made from ripe apricots or other fruits.

Pilpul — Discourse.

Rashi — Rabbi Solomon ben Isaac (1040–1105). Famous French scholar who wrote commentaries on major texts and established a school in Troyes. A man of saintly character, many legends were attributed to him.

Rosh Hodesh — Lit. the head of the month. Special observances take place at the appearance of the new moon which marks the beginning of the month.

Rudolph II — (1552–1612), succeeded to the Czech throne in 1576 and ruled until 1611. It is mainly thanks to this melancholy, moody, and art-loving ruler that Prague has been considered since his days a city of fantasy and mystery. He was mentally ill and, since he had no children of his own, he abdicated the throne in his brother Matthias' favor.

Shabes — (Yiddish) Sabbath.

Shammes — The caretaker of a synagogue. Yiddish, from the Hebrew *leshamesh*, to serve.

Shavuot — One of the three pilgrim festivals, observed on the sixth and seventh of Sivan. Commemorates the giving of the law on Mount Sinai. It is also called Pentecost since it begins on the fiftieth day after the completion of the seven-week period of the Counting of the Omer.

Shed — Demon, evil spirit.

Shem; shem-ha-meforash — The Tetragrammaton, the four-letter name of God which is never enunciated. Adonai—my Lord—is used instead.

God revealed the name to Moses in the desert. It has been considered by kabbalists as a healing and magical power if used properly by certain pious people, otherwise it brings disaster and destruction.

Shochet — A trained slaughterer accredited by a rabbi.

Shoulet — A thick stew consisting mainly of beans and meat.

Shtetl — (Yiddish) Any small Jewish town in Eastern Europe.

Shul — Yiddish for school. Term used among the Ashkenazi Jews for the synagogue. Originally used to describe a bet-ha-midrash which was used both for studying and praying, hence the connection to the name school. The synagogue was not just a place of prayer but also a meeting place of the community (true to the original Greek meaning of the word: a place where people go together).

Shulklopfer — Also spelled shulklapper (Yiddish). A task given in many places to the shammes or another member of the congregation, to knock on the doors of the houses and wake up people for the early morning services in the shul—synagogue. In Eastern Europe the shulklopfer used a special stick or hammer to knock on the doors.

Simchat Torah — A holiday when the annual completion of the reading of the Torah is celebrated. Rejoicing the Torah.

Sisyphus — Ancient King of Corinth, punished for a variety of sins. Compelled to roll a giant stone up a hill where it rolled down again. Thus Sisyphus's labor never ended and became symbolic of an endless, fruitless task that must be repeated over and over again.

Sivan — A month in the Hebrew calendar.

Tachrichim — Shroud.

Tallit — Four-cornered prayer shawl worn by men during morning prayers.

Talmud — The most important work of the Oral Torah in the form of a long Aramaic commentary of the Mishnah. Also known by its Aramaic name – Gemara. The Mishnah is the earliest surviving work of Rabbinic literature (completed in the third century C.E.).

Tefillin — Prayer tools—ornaments in Aramaic—two small leather boxes worn by adult males during particular prayers. They contain biblical passages. Described in English as "amulets," phylacteries. Although they are not considered magic objects, it is believed that they protect the bearer from evil.

Tikkun Hazot — Midnight service. Prayers and lamentation recited at midnight in memory of the destruction of the Temple.

Tishrei — A month in the Hebrew calendar.

Torah — The Pentateuch, the five first books of the Old Testament.

Tzaddik — A pious almost saintly person.

Tzdakah — Charity.

Tzimmes — A sweet side dish made mostly of carrots with some added fruits.

Vltava — Czech word, one of the main rivers in the Czech Republic known better by its German name the Moldau. The Czech composer Bedřich Smetana made its name well known in his famous composition.

Vyšehrad — (Czech) A famous castle in Prague, sitting on a rock high above the banks of the river Vltava. It was the ancient home of the Přemysl dynasty.

Yeshiva — From the Hebrew "to sit" a seminary where young unmarried men study the Talmud.

Zionists — Members of a Jewish national movement eager to establish a secular home in the Holy Land who were influenced by nineteenth century nationalism in Europe. Theodor Herzl turned Zionism into a political movement.

Bibliography

Anstruther, F. C. *Old Polish Legends*. Retold. New York: Hippocrene Books, Inc., 1991.

Ausubel, Nathan, ed. *A Treasury of Jewish Folklore.* New York: Crown Publishers, 1948.

Bergmann, Judah. *Die Legenden der Juden* (German). Berlin: C. A. Schwetschke & Sohn, 1919.

Biro, Val. *Hungarian Folktales.* Retold. Oxford: Oxford University Press, 1992.

Bloch, Chayim. *The Golem: Legends of the Ghetto of Prague.* Translated from the German by Harry Schneiderman. New York: Rudolf Steiner Publications, 1972.

Bloch, Joseph S. "Golem Legenden" (German). *Oesterreichischen Wochenschrift.* Vienna: 1917.

Bokser, Ben Zion. *The Maharal.* New Jersey: Jason Aronson Inc., 1994.

Buber, Martin. *The Legend of the Baal-Shem.* Princeton: Princeton University Press, 1995.

Carter, Angela. *Strange Things Sometimes Still Happen: Fairy Tales from Around the World.* Winchester, MA: Faber and Faber, Inc., 1962.

Cohn, Emil Bernhard. *Stories and Fantasies from the Jewish Past.* Philadelphia: The Jewish Publication Society of America, 1961.

Cohn-Sherbok , Dan. *The Blackwell Dictionary of Judaica.* Oxford: Blackwell Publishers, 1992.

Domanska, Janina. *King Krakus and the Dragon.* New York: Greenwillow Books, 1979.

Dorson, Richard M. *Folktales Told Around the World.* Chicago: University of Chicago Press, 1975.

Dundes, Alan, ed. *Cinderella: A Casebook.* Madison, Wisconsin: The University of Wisconsin Press, 1982.

Ehl, Peter, Arno Parik, and Jiři Fiedler. *Old Bohemian and Moravian Jewish Cemeteries.* Prague: Paseka, 1991.

Fenyvesi, Charles. *When the World Was Whole: Three Centuries of Memories.* New York: Penguin Books, 1990.

Fichman, Jacob. *Lashon Ve Sepher* (Hebrew). Tel-Aviv: Moledet Publishing Co., 1894.

Frank, Helena, trans. *Yiddish Tales.* Philadelphia: The Jewish Publication Society of America, 1912.

Frankel, Ellen, ed. *The Jewish Spirit: A Celebration in Stories and Art.* New York: Stewart, Tabori and Chang, 1997.

Gaster, Moses. *Ma'aseh Book: Book of Jewish Tales and Legends.* Translated from the Judeo-German. Philadelphia: The Jewish Publication Society of America, 1934.

Ginzberg, Louis. *The Legends of the Jews.* Philadelphia: The Jewish Publication Society of America, 1939.

Hamilton, Virginia. *The Dark Way: Stories from the Spirit World.* New York: Harcourt Brace Jovanovich, 1990.

Hampl, Patricia. *A Romantic Education.* New York: Houghton Mifflin Co., 1992.

Heetz, Aleksander. *The Jews in Polish Culture.* Translated by Richard Lourie. Evanston, IL: Northwestern University Press, 1988.

Hofman, Alois, and Renate Heuerová. *Ze Židovského Ghetta: Pověsti Legendy a Vyprávění* (Czech). Praha: Volvox Globator, 1996.

Hostovsky, Egon. "The Czech-Jewish Movement." *The Jews of Czechoslovakia: Historical Studies and Surveys.* II Philadelphia: The Jewish Publication Society of America, 1971.

Hulpach, Vladimír. *Pohádkové Vandrování po Čechách* (Czech). Praha: Albatros, 1992.

Iggers, Wilma Abeles, ed. *The Jews of Bohemia and Moravia: A Historical Reader.* Detroit: Wayne University Press, 1992.

Jirásek, Alois. *Staré Pověsti Ceské* (Czech). Praha: Státni Nakladatelství Děstské Knihy, 1954.

Jura, R. F. *Staré Povèstí Slezské* (Czech). Plžen: Karel Veselý, 1993 (Reprint from the edition of 1934).

Kafka, František. *Velký Pražský Rabi Jehuda Löw; Nová Vyprávěni z Doby Renesance* (Czech). Praha: Kalich, 1994.

Kalláb, Karel. *Pověsti Hradů Moravskýh a Slezských* (Czech). Praha: Melandrich, 1996.

Kischkin, L.C. *Výbor z Literatury České* (Czech and Russian). Moscow: Idatelstvo Literatury, 1958.

Komorowska, Teresa, and Viera Gasparikowa. *Zbojnicki Dar* (Polish). Warsaw: Ludowa Spoldzielnia Wydawnicza, 1976.

Korszak, Janusz. *How to Love Children*; Keycad Leehov Yeladim. Translated into Hebrew from the Polish by Yaacob Tzuk. Tel Aviv: Hakibbutz Hameuchad Publishing House Ltd., 1963.

——— *King Matt the First*. New York: Farrar, Strauss and Giroux, Inc., 1986.

Kuniczak, W. S. *The Glass Mountain: Twenty-Eight Ancient Polish Folktales and Fables*. New York: Hippocrene Books, Inc., 1997.

Kunz, George Frederick. *The Curious Lore of Precious Stones*. New York: Bell Publishing Company, 1989.

Leivick, Halper. *The Dybbuk and Other Great Yiddish Plays; The Golem*. Translated by Joseph C. Landis. New York: Bantam Books, Inc., 1966.

Meyrink, Gustav. *The Golem*. New York: Dover Publications, Inc., 1976.

Momaday, N. Scott. *The Way to Rainy Mountain*. New York: Ballantine Books, 1974.

Mullen, Patrick B. *Listening to Old Voices: Folklore, Life Stories, and the Elderly*. Chicago: University of Illinois Press, 1992.

Nahmias, Benny. *Hamsah* (Hebrew). Tel Aviv: Modan Publishing House, 1996.

Neugroschel, Joachim. *Great Works of Jewish Occult and Fantasy*. New York: Wing Books/Outlet Books Co., 1991.

Olbracht, Ivan. *Zakarpatská Trilogie* (Czech). Praha: Svoboda, 1972.

Ortutay, Gyula. *Hungarian Folklore*. Budapest: Akademiai Kiado, 1972.

Paola, de Tomie. *Strega Nona*. New York: Simon and Schuster Books for Young Readers, 1975.

Papp Severo de, Emoke. *Hungarian and Transilvanian Folktales*. Ottawa: Borealis Press, 1997.

Patai, Raphael. *Gates of the Old City*. Detroit: Wayne State University Press, 1981.

Patterson, Jose. *Angels, Prophets, Rabbis and Kings from the Stories of the Jewish People*. New York: Peter Bedrick Books, 1991.

Pavel, Josef. *Pověsti Českých Hradů a Zámků* (Czech). Praha: Melandrich, 1995.

Pavlát, Leo. *Osm Světel; Židovské Příbehy* (Czech). Praha: Artia, 1986.

Petiška, Eduard. *Golem: a Jiné Židovské Pověsti a Pohádky ze Staré Prahy* (Czech). Praha: Martin, 1992.

Piercy, Marge. *He, She, and It*. New York: Knopf, 1997.

Podwal, Mark. *A Giant Made of Mud*. New York: Greenwillow, 1995.

Pressburger, Giorgio and Nicola. *The Green Elephant*. Translated by Spence Pierce. London: Quartet Books, 1994.

Ripellino, Angelo Maria. *Magic Prague*. Translated by Marinelli David Newton. Berkeley: University of California Press, 1994.

Rogansky, Barbara. *The Golem*. New York: Holiday House, 1996.

Runes, Dagobert D. *Lost Legends of Israel*. New York: Philosophical Library, Inc., 1961.

Sadeh, Pinchas. *Sefer Hadimyonot Shel Hayehudim* (Hebrew). Tel-Aviv: Schoken Publishing House Ltd., 1983.

Sadeh, Pinhas. *Jewish Folktales*. Translated by Hillel Halkin. New York: Anchor Books, 1989.

Sadek, Vladimir. "The Spiritual World of Rabbi Judah Loew Ben Bezalel." *Review of the Society for the History of Czechoslovak Jews* Vol. 4 (1991–92), 101–119.

Scholem, Gershom. *On the Kabbalah and its Symbolism*. Translated by Ralph Manheim. New York: Schoken Books, 1965.

Schram, Peninnah, ed. *Jewish Stories One Generation Tells Another*. New Jersey: Jason Aronson Inc., 1987.

——— *Chosen Tales: Stories Told by Jewish Storytellers*. New Jersey: Jason Aronson Inc., 1995.

Schwartz, Howard, ed. *Miriam's Tambourine: Jewish Folktales from Around the World*. New York: Seth Press, 1986.

——— *Lilith's Cave*. San Francisco: Harper & Row, 1987.

——— *Gabriel's Place: Jewish Mystical Tales*. New York: Oxford University Press, Inc., 1993.

——— *Reimagining the Bible: The Storytelling of the Rabbis*. Oxford: Oxford University Press, Inc., 1998.

Serwer, Luria Blanche. *Let's Steal the Moon: Jewish Tales Ancient and Recent*. Boston: Little Brown & Company, 1970.

Shahrukh, Husain. *Demons, Gods, and Holy Men.* New York: Schoken Books, 1987.

Shenhar, Aliza. *Hasipur Haamami Shel Edot Israel* (Hebrew). Tel-Aviv: Tsherikover Publishing House, Ltd., 1982.

Singer, Isaac Bashevis. *The Golem.* New York: Farrar Strauss Giroux, 1982.

Sis, Peter. *The Three Golden Keys.* New York: Doubleday, 1994.

Stainman, Mordechai. *Niggun: Stories Behind the Chasidic Songs That Inspire Jews.* New Jersey: Jason Aronson Inc., 1994.

Švandrlík, Miroslav. *Praha Plná Strašidel* (Czech). Praha: Road Praha, 1993.

Svátek, Josef. *Prăzské Povĕsti a Legendy (Czech)* Praha: Paseka, reprint from 1883.

Unterman, Alan. *Dictionary of Jewish Lore and Legend.* London: Thames and Hudson, 1991.

Weinreich Silverman, Beatrice. *Yiddish Folktales.* Translated by Leonard Wolf. New York: Pantheon Fairytale and Folklore Library, 1988.

Weltsch, Felix. "Realism and Romanticism: Observations on the Jewish Intelligensia of Bohemia and Moravia." *The Jews of Czechoslovakia: Historical Studies and Surveys.* II (1971):441–454.

Wenig, Adolf. *České Povĕsti* (Czech). Plzeň: Karel Veselý, 1992.

Wineman, Aryeh. *Mystic Tales from the Zohar.* Philadelphia: Jewish Publication Society, 1997.

Winkler, Gershon. *The Golem of Prague.* New York: The Judaica Press, 1994.

Wisniewski, David. *Golem.* New York: Clarion, 1996.

ABOUT THE AUTHOR

Nadia Grosser Nagarajan was born in Ostrava, a coal-mining town in Northern Moravia, in the former Czechoslovakia. She was educated in Israel and the United States and received her Ph.D. in comparative literature from the University of California at Berkeley. An educator since 1968, she has published children's stories in Israel as well as travel features and miscellaneous articles on literature and folklore in the United States. Nadia Grosser Nagarajan has lectured at several conferences on Jewish education and culture as well as nineteenth century European literature. She has two sons and lives in California with her husband.